A
Certain
Slant
of
Light

Other Graphia Titles

A
Certain
Slant
of
Light

by

Laura Whitcomb

AN IMPRINT OF HOUGHTON MIFFLIN COMPANY
BOSTON 2005

For information about permission to reproduce selections from this book, write to
Permissions, Houghton Mifflin Company, 215 Park Avenue South,
New York, New York 10003.

www.houghtonmifflinbooks.com

The text of this book is set in Walbaum MT.

Library of Congress Cataloging-in-Publication Data

Whitcomb, Laura.
  A certain slant of light / by Laura Whitcomb.
    p. cm.
  Summary: After benignly haunting a series of people for 130 years, Helen meets
a teenage boy who can see her and together they unlock the mysteries of their
pasts.
  ISBN 0-618-58532-X (pbk. : alk. paper)
  [1. Ghosts—Fiction. 2. Future life—Fiction. 3. Forgiveness—Fiction.] I. Title.
  PZ7.W5785Ce 2005
  [Fic]—dc22

                                                                    2004027208

ISBN-13: 978-0618-58532-8

Manufactured in the United States of America
QUM 10 9 8 7 6 5 4 3 2

Dedication

For my mother, who was both Quick and Light—
my first protector, my model of clarity and forgiveness.

Acknowledgments

Thanks to my family—my wonderful parents, the dear Jon Whitcombs, the darling Marshes, my own Nick and Molly, and beloved Cynthia, who mentored me from my teen scribblings. My writers' support group (Kristi, Linda, Leona, Jackie, and Cheri), my star sisters (Hilary, Ruth, and Sat-Kaur), and my Chez Day buddies (Pam and Susan). Denise (my spirit sister), Michael Scott (my biggest fan), and Peter (my pirate in paradise). Compo, my first writing teacher. Ted Gideonse, for all his help and encouragement. Eden Edwards, my editor, for her brilliant guidance. And a special thanks to my agent, Ann Rittenberg, for being spectacular.

One

SOMEONE WAS LOOKING AT ME, a disturbing sensation if you're
dead. I was with my teacher, Mr. Brown. As usual, we were in our
classroom, that safe and wooden-walled box—the windows opening onto the grassy field to the west, the fading flag standing in
the chalk dust corner, the television mounted above the bulletin
board like a sleeping eye, and Mr. Brown's princely table keeping
watch over a regiment of student desks. At that moment I was
scribbling invisible comments in the margins of a paper left in
Mr. Brown's tray, though my words were never read by the students. Sometimes Mr. Brown quoted me, all the same, while writing his own comments. Perhaps I couldn't tickle the inside of his
ear, but I could reach the mysterious curves of his mind.

Although I could not feel paper between my fingers, smell ink,
or taste the tip of a pencil, I could see and hear the world with all
the clarity of the Living. They, on the other hand, did not see me
as a shadow or a floating vapor. To the Quick, I was empty air.

Or so I thought. As an apathetic girl read aloud from *Nicholas Nickleby*, as Mr. Brown began to daydream about how he had kept his wife awake the night before, as my spectral pen hovered over a misspelled word, I felt someone watching me. Not even my beloved Mr. Brown could see me with his eyes. I had been dead so long, hovering at the side of my hosts, seeing and hearing the world but never being heard by anyone and never, in all these long years, never being seen by human eyes. I held stone still while the room folded in around me like a closing hand. When I looked up, it was not in fear but in wonder. My vision telescoped so that there was only a small hole in the darkness to see through. And that's where I found it, the face that was turned up to me.

Like a child playing at hide-and-seek, I did not move, in case I had been mistaken about being spotted. And childishly I felt both the desire to stay hidden and a thrill of anticipation about being caught. For this face, turned squarely to me, had eyes set directly on mine.

I was standing in front of the blackboard. That must be it, I thought. He's reading something Mr. Brown wrote there—the chapter he's to study at home that night or the date of the next quiz.

The eyes belonged to an unremarkable young man, like most of the others at this school. Since this group of students was in the eleventh grade, he could be no more than seventeen. I'd seen him before and thought nothing of him. He had always been vacant, pale, and dull. If anyone were to somehow manage to see me with his eyes, it would not be this sort of lad—this mere ashes-on-the-inside kind. To really see me, someone would have to be extraordinary. I moved slowly, crossing behind Mr. Brown's chair, to stand in the corner of the classroom beside the flag stand. The eyes did not follow me. The lids blinked slowly.

But the next moment, the eyes flicked to mine again, and a shock went through me. I gasped and the flag behind me stirred. Yet this boy's expression never changed, and next moment, he was staring at the blackboard again. His features were so blank, I decided I had imagined it. He had looked to the corner because I had disturbed the flag a little.

This happened frequently. If I were to move too quickly too near an object, it might tremble or rock, but not much, and never when I wanted it to. When you are Light, it is not the breeze of your rushing past a flower that makes it tremble. Nor is it the brush of your skirts that starts a drape fluttering. When you are Light, it is only your emotions that can send a ripple into the tangible world. A flash of frustration when your host closes a novel he is reading too soon might stir his hair and cause him to check the window for a draft. A sigh of mourning at the beauty of a rose you cannot smell might startle a bee away. Or a silent laugh at a misused word might cause a student's arm to prickle with an inexplicable chill.

The bell rang, and every student, including this pale young man, slapped books closed and stood, with a scrape of chair feet, shuffling toward the door. Mr. Brown snapped immediately from his bed dream.

"I'll bring a video tomorrow," he said. "And don't fall asleep during it, or I'll make you act it out yourselves." Two or three of his students groaned at this threat, but most were already gone, mentally if not physically.

So this was how it began. When you are Light, day and night

have less meaning. The night is not needed for rest—it's merely an annoying darkness for several hours. But a chain of days and nights is the way in which the Quick measure their journeys. This is the story of my journey back through the Quick. I would climb into flesh again for a chain of six days.

I stayed shamefully close to my Mr. Brown for the rest of the day. When you cleave to a host, it is not necessary to shadow the person from room to room. I would never follow a male host into the bath, for instance, or into the marriage bed, man or woman. I learned from the beginning how to survive. From the moment I found my first host, I had been devoted to the rules that kept my punishment at bay.

I remembered all my hauntings clearly, but only a few images stayed with me from the time before I was Light. I remembered a man's head on the pillow beside me. He had straw-colored hair, and when he opened his eyes, he was looking not at me but toward the window, where wind was rattling the pane. A handsome face that brought no comfort. I remembered catching a glimpse of my own eyes in the window reflection as I watched this man ride away on a black horse through the farm gate, the horizon heavy with clouds. And I remembered seeing a pair of frightened eyes looking up at me, full of tears. I could remember my name, my age, that I was a woman, but death swallowed the rest.

The pain, once I was dead, was very memorable. I was deep inside the cold, smothering belly of a grave when my first haunting began. I heard her voice in the darkness reading Keats, "Ode to a Nightingale." Icy water was burning down my throat, splintering my ribs, and my ears were filled with a sound like a demon howling, but I could hear her voice and reached for her. One desperate hand burst from the flood and caught the hem of her gown. I dragged myself, hand over hand, out of the earth and quaked at her feet, clutching her skirts, weeping muddy tears. All I knew was that I had been tortured in the blackness, and then I had escaped. Perhaps I hadn't reached the brightness of heaven, but at least I was here, in her lamplight, safe.

It took me a long time to realize that she was not reading to me; nor were her shoes spotted with mud. I held her, yet my arms did not wrinkle the folds of her dress. I cried at her feet like a wretch about to be stoned, kissing the hem of Christ's garment, but she didn't see me, couldn't hear my sobs. I looked at her—a fragile face, pale but rosy at the cheeks and nose as if it were always winter around her. She had gray duck-down hair piled on her head like a bird's nest and sharp green eyes, clever as a cat's. She was solid and warm with a fluttering pulse. She wore a black dress with mismatched buttons, the elbows worn thin. Tiny spots of ink dotted her butter-colored shawl. The cover of the little book in her hands was embossed with the figure of a running stag. It was all real and blazing with detail. But I was shadow, light as mist, mute as the wallpaper.

"Please help me," I said to her. But deaf to me, she turned the page.

"Thou wast not born for death, immortal Bird . . ." As she read aloud the familiar words, I knew what I was. I stayed by her side for hours, afraid that if I looked away from her or tried to remember too hard how I had come to be in hell, I would be thrown back there.

After a score of pages, my host closed her book. I was frightened by the idea that she might put out the light when she went to her bed, and this panic made me fall on her again. I threw my head into her lap like a heartbroken child. The book fell from her hands and dropped through me onto the floor. I was startled at the painless flick of sensation. My host bent to retrieve the book of poems, and as her body passed through me, I felt myself dropping down and then soaring up again as if I were on a child's swing. A most peculiar expression came over her face. She placed the volume carefully under the lamp on the desk beside her and took up pen and paper. She dipped at the ink and began to write:

> *A suitor bent upon one knee*
> *Death asked me for my hand*

I could tell by the black stains on her fingertips that, most likely, these were not the first lines she had ever written. I couldn't tell whether I had inspired her, but I prayed that I had. If I could do some scrap of good, perhaps I would be granted entrance into heaven. All I knew was that this saint was my salvation from pain and that I would be hers until the day she died. And that's what I called her, my Saint. She was as poised as a queen and as kind as an angel.

I was confined to her world but was not her equal. I could fantasize that we were sisters or the best of friends, but I was still only her visiting ghost. I was a prisoner on leave from the dungeon—I knew nothing of my crime or the length of my sentence, but I knew I would do whatever I could to avoid being tortured. Alone in the lilac air of her country garden, I glided 'round her while she wrote hundreds of poems, her hair and her eyes slowly growing white.

One evening, when I had been moving with her along the road to the woods and back, we stopped to observe a fly struggling in a web while a spider waited on a leaf and watched. I could feel my Saint devising a poem about the possibility of spider amnesty, but what I didn't realize was that she had stopped watching them and had marched home and was already dipping in ink before I turned to find her gone.

At first I thought she must be just a few yards ahead, hidden by the hedges at the curve of the road. I rushed toward our home, but it was too late. The old pain returned, first to my feet, like ice slippers, then up my legs, slowing me to a crawl. I could still see the road in front of me, but as I fell forward, I heard a splash and cold rods shot up my arms and into my heart. I called to her until my mouth was full of water. The evening had gone black as my grave. I was back in the hell I'd known before I'd found her. I tried to do what I had done the first time I'd heard her voice. I thrust out my hands, feeling blindly for her skirts, but I felt only wet wooden boards. Clawing at them, I felt a corner and then a flat shelf, then another shelf. I dug into the boards and pulled myself up. When I reached out this time, I felt a shoe. The darkness swam into warm light. I looked up to see my Saint standing on the wooden steps of her pantry, a pen in one hand and a half-written poem in the other. She gazed out at the dusk garden as if she'd heard an intruder in her rose bushes. I was lying on her steps, one hand gripping her shoe, thanking God for letting me come back to her. After that I was ever so careful about staying close to my hosts.

On my Saint's final day, I hoped so passionately that she would take me with her into heaven that I lay in bed beside her, listening to her breathe. She had no nurse, no housekeeper. We were completely alone. I didn't understand how much I would miss her until she lay still as the earth under my head. My Saint. My only voice on the air, singing or testing a metered line aloud. My only companion on autumn walks. My page-turner by the fireside. I prayed for God to let me go with her.

I couldn't recall my past sin, that deed I had done before my death that had banished me from heaven, but I prayed now for God to let me work off my debt beside my Saint. *Remember how I had tried to comfort her when she was lonely*, I prayed, *and how I inspired her when her pen began to scratch out line after line of verse.*

But God neither answered my prayer nor explained Himself. There was not even a moment when her green eyes turned to me in recognition. My friend, my Saint, had simply gone. The familiar cold began to tug at my feet, blistering up my legs, twisting ice into me. I was saved only by the insistent knocking at the door below. I swam down the air, through the bedroom floor, the hall ceiling, the wooden door, and, desperate not to be thrown to the darkness again, embraced the body that stood there. A young man who had been corresponding with her for a year, praising her verse, had chosen that day to call on her for the first time. He stood with a bouquet of violets in one hand, looking up at her curtained windows with disappointment. I shut my eyes, pressed my face upon his hand, and prayed to God to let me have him.

Eventually my prayers were rattled by the sound of horses' hooves. I found myself sitting in the safety of his carriage at my new host's feet beside the violets he had discarded.

And so I was delivered again by a rescuer unaware. I called him my Knight because he had come to my aid when I was in distress. He was a writer, widowed and childless. He wrote stories of knights and princesses, monsters and spells, tales he would have told his dear ones at bedtime. His publishers would print only his books on Scripture, not these enchanting stories. This made him angry and caused him to walk about stiffly, like one who can never take off his armor. I tried to be his friend, and I believe I softened his words more than once so that his books would be accepted and keep his cupboards in bread.

I had another close call with hell while at the theater with my Knight. He had gone with two friends to see a production of *Much Ado About Nothing*. As I stood in the box beside his chair, I fell in love with the costumes and fun of the players. I was as close to my Knight as two posts on the same fence, yet in the moment when I made a wish, I broke a mysterious rule of haunting. I watched the lovers in the pool of light below and wished one of them were my host. A chill beat through my heart. I slid down through the floor and half into my old grave before I could stop myself. I gripped my Knight's hand and dangled there.

"I take it back," I prayed. "I want my Knight." I struggled halfway in and out the window of hell for the rest of the act. An icy pain pulled at me from below as if I were standing on the floundering ship of my own floating coffin, the winter sea up to my hips. "*Please let me have him,*" I begged. Finally, as the curtain fell, I was washed up onto the warm, dry carpet beside my Knight's feet.

After that I was careful what I wished for.

At the end, as my Knight slipped away in a dim corner of a hospital room, I found that again I was losing my only friend. I prayed again to God to let me go with my host, but no answer came. What saved me this time was quite a different voice from those of my first hosts.

A playwright who had broken his arm was laughing with a comrade in the next hospital room, repeating the adventure that had caused his injury. I left my Knight's bedside, pulled out of the coldness that was already sucking at me, and tilted through the adjoining wall, folding my arms around this silly youth. I held him hard until I knew I was with him.

This lad, my Playwright, was nothing like my first two hosts. He had parties in his rooms almost every night until dawn, slept until noon, wrote in bed until four, dressed and went to the theater to work, then dined out and started the whole celebration again. I don't think he was at all aware of me. He and his friends seemed to do little else than make light of their talents. His plays made people laugh, but the only time I seemed to be influential was on certain dark mornings when he would wake after only an hour's sleep, frightened by a nightmare. I would sit at the foot of his bed and recite poems written by my Saint until he fell back into dreams. He drank too much, ate too little, and died too young and quite suddenly at one of his own parties.

A sweet gentleman poet, who was a guest at the event, caught my Playwright as he fell, like Horatio cupping Hamlet's head in his large hand. I chose him instantly. My new host—I called him my Poet—was more susceptible to my whisperings than the previous one. When his mind would dry before a poem was complete, I would take great pleasure in speaking ideas into his sleeping ear. Like Coleridge with his vision of paradise restored, he would wake the next morning and turn my straw ideas into golden lines. He fell in love unrequitedly with several other gentlemen, some inclined toward men and some not, but he never found a mate. My Poet became a lecturer in his later years and mentored a seventeen-year-old named Brown.

My Mr. Brown was a devoted student and wrote such passionate stories and listened so purely to all advice, I chose him in advance. I could tell months beforehand that my host was going to heaven without me. I cleaved to Mr. Brown when he came to say goodbye to my Poet. Mr. Brown was moving west to enter a university three thousand miles away. I chose him partly because he loved literature so very much, but I also chose him because he had a kind heart, an honest tongue, and a clear honor and yet seemed totally unaware of the fact that he was virtuous. This made him especially appealing. I had a half memory of being fooled by a handsome smile, but Mr. Brown's face seemed a true mirror of his spirit. I felt even more attached to him than I had to the others. Perhaps that's why I called him by his name.

I had learned the rules of my survival well during those decades—stay close to your host or risk returning to the dungeon, take what small pleasure you can from a vicarious existence, and try to be helpful. And I do believe that I was helpful to Mr. Brown when he was writing his novel.

From the time he was eighteen, he would spend at least an hour a day working on his book. He kept it in a box that once held blank paper. He would sit in a park or at a table in the library, composing one paragraph each day. He had more than two hundred carefully handwritten pages but was still on chapter five. I would sit beside him or pace around him, watching him think. Each page was as precious as a poem. When doubts or thoughts of mundane life stayed his hand, I would try grasping his pen to urge him on, but my fingers would only pass through. I discovered that the best way I could help him become unstuck in his writing was to place my finger on the last word he had written. This always brought his pen back to paper and a smile back to his lips. It was a tale of brothers fighting for opposing kings in a medieval setting as rich and mysterious as Xanadu.

I longed so to talk to him about this character's name or that character's motives, about a phrase here that described a river and a word there that described a dying man's eyes. I would fantasize, as he slept, long conversations we would have if he could see and hear me—the two of us sipping tea or walking in the country, laughing together over brilliant ideas. But that would never happen, of course. And so it went, my favorite hour of each day spent with him and his book, until the writing stopped the day he met his bride.

They saw each other across a lecture hall and met in the doorway as they left. There was an uncomfortable familiarity about it all. The way she smiled at him, the way he was thrilled when she laughed at his joke, the little excuses each had for touching the other. Her hand on his arm as she asked a question, his knee touching hers as they drank coffee at a tiny table in a pub so noisy they left to take a walk. None of my hosts had lived with a lover. And I'm ashamed to say I felt jealous when this girl moved into his life. At first I pretended I disapproved because he'd stopped working on his novel, but I knew that wasn't the only reason. An instability clutched me, and I found myself afraid of shadows and loud noises. I wanted to stop him, but although she had inadvertently halted his writing, she was undoubtedly making him happy. I wanted to warn her that a man might seem ideal and then turn cold and distant with no cause, but after all, it was Mr. Brown she was falling in love with. It would be a lie to argue that he wasn't worth the risk.

And so because I loved him, I let her be, and because I feared pain, I learned to follow at a distance when they were together. I felt lonelier than I had ever been with any host, but I tried to love her as if she were my daughter. She had no quality I could easily complain about. It would be a sin to whisper discouragement in his ear. And so they were wed when he was twenty-three and she twenty-one. I taught myself to ignore the pangs I felt when he would tickle her while driving in the car or when she would rest her feet in his lap during breakfast. The intimacy hurt because it wasn't for me. I was Mr. Brown's and he was mine, but not the way she was his. Not the way he was hers.

I taught myself the new rules to survive. Move out of the room when they kiss, enter the bedroom only when it is silent, cherish my time with Mr. Brown when he is at work. I obeyed these rules, and one day I was rewarded. Mr. Brown brought out his old tattered box, put it in his briefcase, and drove us to work an hour early. For more than a year now, Mr. Brown had been spending an hour each day, before his first students arrived, working on his novel with me beside him. Feeling inspired by this gift, I had tried to warm myself to his bride by whispering recipes in her ear while she was baking cookies or a cake. I thought I was being as gracious as her own mother might be, until a package arrived from her grandfather, an album of photographs of Mrs. Brown as a baby. The cub-ear curls of her hair and the dimpled backs of her tender hands bit at me like sleet. I couldn't look at them, coward that I was. I wasn't her mother. I had chosen Mr. Brown. And he had chosen her.

Now I was afraid that the rules of my world were changing again. I had been seen by a human. Sitting on the sloped roof of Mr. Brown's small house while he and his wife slept and dreamed below, I studied a crescent moon hung crooked in a plum purple sky and thought about what it would be like to truly be seen. I imagined standing before the young man who seemed to see me and letting him look as long as he wished. How was he doing this? Had he somehow chosen me? I had two strong and seemingly contradictory sensations. One was a fear of being seen by a mortal—as if beheld naked when you know you are clothed. The other was an almost indescribable sensation of attraction—the vine curling toward the sun's light in slow but single-minded longing. I wanted to see him again, to see whether he really was that rare human who saw what others could not. Nothing was more disturbing to me, and yet nothing compelled me more.

By the next school day, when the same group of students entered Mr. Brown's classroom, I deliberately stood in the back corner of the room. I wanted to know whether the boy could see me and not have to wonder whether he was looking through me at a map of the world or a grammar lesson. I stood still as marble in the far corner between the window frame and the cupboard door. I remained calm so that nothing, not even a speck of dust on the floor, would shift from my presence. And I watched the students enter, one by one, dragging their feet, pushing each other and laughing, listening to private music with wires in their ears, and then, finally, the boy with the pale face, moving, almost gliding to the desk he always sat in, near the back, in the middle.

I moved not an inch and waited. The shuffling died down, the murmurs ceased as Mr. Brown began to speak. The boy sat leaning back, his long legs in denim stuck out in the aisle, his white shirt rolled up at the sleeves, shirttail out, his dark green bag of books lying under the chair. I waited.

And then he moved. He let the paper that had just been passed back to him slip off the desktop on purpose; I was sure it was on purpose. And when he sat up and bent to retrieve it from the floor, he turned his head and looked back into the corner of the room where I stood. His eyes met mine for one moment, and he smiled. I was shocked, shocked again though I had longed for it. He sat back up and pretended to read the page, just as the others were doing.

How is this happening? I thought. He couldn't be as I was, Light. I had never seen another like myself. I felt that it was impossible—an instinct told me so. I had never truly believed in mediums, but perhaps this strange boy was some sort of seer. He seemed to have no interest at all in sharing his knowledge of my presence with his fellow classmates or Mr. Brown. It made no sense, and although I was still nervous and full of longing about him, now I was also angry. How dare this chimney sweep of a boy shatter my privacy so matter-of-factly and so completely? What made it worse was that in that moment when he smiled at me, his face flushed. He looked alive and healthy for the first time. It was as if he'd stolen something from me. I felt humiliated, for some reason, and I stormed straight out of the room, without looking back, making a flock of papers flutter off the front row of desks.

Two

—

I wanted to be far away from everything, but that was a lie. It was only that I felt confused. I had taught myself so carefully how to be the contented voyeur, and now there was this person watching me.

I stayed close to the classroom, by the trunk of the pepper tree not five yards from the door, waiting. When, and it seemed like a year, the door opened at last, and disheveled boys and girls crowded out of the classroom and away down the path toward other buildings, I hid behind the trunk. Finally he appeared, his bag over one shoulder, his hair falling over his brow on one side. My core jittered with inexplicable excitement. The young man walked alone, head down, toward my tree. He stopped when he was as close to the trunk as the path would allow, but five feet from me. He didn't look. He smiled, eyes still on the ground, and after one blushing moment, he began to walk again. I had no power to stop myself—I followed.

As I did, I could feel Mr. Brown behind us, walking, as he of-

—

ten did at this time of day, to the administration building. I felt an unpleasant tug. A thread snapped, the threat of a tear in my universe. It was my Familiar pulling at me from one side and my Mystery from the other. The path forked between school buildings, and I let Mr. Brown go his way alone. The boy annoyed me by ducking between the cafeteria and the gymnasium where a small space was set aside for bins of cans and bottles that would be recycled. I followed, but I was not happy about it. I halted as he made to walk directly into the dead end. I was filled with wonder at the idea that perhaps he was going to walk *through* the wall, but he didn't—he stopped, three feet short of it, and just stood there.

To my own amazement, I marched right up behind him and spoke. "Can you hear me?"

"I have ears, don't I?"

I started. What had I expected? "And you see me?" I said.

He kept his head low, turning slowly at the shoulders, peering at me from under a lock of brown hair. He smiled. "Of course."

I backed away a step. "What are you?"

"Don't you mean, who am I?" He carefully pivoted his body toward me. An icicle of fear slid down my throat.

"Why do you see me?" I hissed. I couldn't help myself. Any semblance of manners had dissolved in my alarm.

"Don't be afraid." He wasn't smiling anymore. He looked quite concerned.

"No!" I felt like scolding him, reminding him that we hadn't been properly introduced. My middle was tingling, as if my Mr. Brown were traveling out of range. A deep bone pain began to form in my joints.

"Don't speak to me." I looked around me, somehow certain that every mortal could see me now, but no one else was there. When I turned back, the boy's eyes held such empathy, I couldn't bear it. I pushed through the cold and ran from him like a child spooked by an owl in the night.

I'm ashamed to tell the tale now, of how frightened I was at being spoken to—seemingly pitied. I could hear Hamlet moan, "Poor ghost." I stayed right by Mr. Brown's side the next day, except when he was in the bed or bath. But when he was teaching *that* class I stayed in the tiny school library, reading over the shoulders of students, counting the minutes.

The next morning, when Mr. Brown had risen early to go running, he returned to find his wife in the kitchen making coffee and wearing nothing but one of his ragged T-shirts. He discovered that he had a little extra time to spend with her in one of the armless kitchen chairs, so I chose to pass into the garden. On any other day, I would have been annoyed that we might not have a full hour's writing time before the first class of the day. But today, as I stood staring into the empty birdbath in their tiny back yard, I wondered what the one who had spoken to me was doing at that moment. I didn't mean to, but I imagined him with a girl, evoking the same sounds from her that came from the kitchen window. I was immediately sorry I had, because a terrible, scalding jealousy flooded me.

I burned with frustration, and even a little anger, as Mr. Brown drove us to school. We would have only half an hour for writing. He was beaming and relaxed, still wet from a hasty shower. His happiness was so vexing. That morning, I wished that Mrs. Brown were far away, visiting her family, anything, just away, at least for a while. I could still hear her sounds of pleasure, or perhaps it was Mr. Brown's mind wandering as he drove, one elbow out the window, the wind blowing his hair.

My mind turned a corner then. I needed to talk to the one who'd seen me. Even if what I found out was dreadful or terrifying. What could be worse than hiding and not knowing? That afternoon, I stayed in the classroom, though I stood behind the flag stand. It felt safer. Mr. Brown wrote a series of page numbers on the blackboard, and finally the young men and women began to enter. I felt my being flutter. Each tousled head that came through the door I wanted to be his, but on and on, a dozen boys entered, yet not the one.

I was appalled. The bell rang, the students whispered and laughed and tugged books out of their bags, Mr. Brown began to speak, and still the one who had seen me wasn't there. I watched that desk, near the back in the middle, imagining him, but he would not materialize. I crossed in front of Mr. Brown and stood in the open doorway, scanning the path in both directions. Only a squirrel and a gardener with a rake. I wouldn't accept it. I crossed back in front of Mr. Brown again and went this time to the windows on the far side of the room. They looked out onto the playing fields. A group of boys in gray ran over the grass, but the one who had spoken to me was not one of them. I looked beyond the field to the pavement just outside the fence, but he was not there either. And he was not sitting on the benches or standing at the water fountain. He's doing this on purpose, I thought. He is punishing me because I stayed away.

I could not be still. I crossed again and looked out the open door once more. A bird's shadow passed, nothing more. I was on the glass edge of panic, when I turned back toward the classroom and saw him, the one, standing beside his empty desk. He was watching me and when our eyes met, I had no fan to cover my face, no way to hide my feelings. I was desperate for him, and he could see it, all the way in me.

"You're late enough, Mr. Blake," said Mr. Brown. "Hop to."

He must've entered the room when I had been at the window. I think I would've been completely done in by my embarrassment except that he, too, looked taken aback. Perhaps it was something in the sight of me searching for him. He sat down, his cheeks flushed, and put his book bag on the floor. I looked away and moved slowly back to the flag stand and quieted myself. After many moments, I saw that he was sitting with his open book before him and a sheet of lined paper on top of it. He was eyeing me, not unkindly, but most gently. And when I felt an anxiety at the length of our gaze, he politely dropped his attention with a slight nod, almost a bow. This gave me the courage to move slowly along the windowed wall until I rested in a vacant desk next to his.

With the stub of a pencil, he wrote something on the paper he had over his book and slid it a few inches closer to me. I looked across the aisle and saw that he had written the words "Where have you been?"

However improper, I was amused. And, I admit, a little flattered. It made me nervous, though, that there was now something tangible that referred to me. I thought of retreating to the flag stand. He pulled the paper back and wrote again, this time letting the page hang over the desk edge like a banner so I could see it easily. It read: "Please don't be afraid. I would be a friend to you."

I can't tell a lie; the fact that he didn't speak or write like the other students in the room intrigued me. I surveyed him, but he kept his eyes on the blackboard. The brown paper cover of his English book was filled with little drawings of what appeared to be mythological beasts.

"I was hiding from you," I said finally.

He wrote on the paper again. My whole self was quivering as I waited for the page to be slipped my way. It read, "Follow me after class. I long to speak with you again."

Someone longed to speak with me.

I was startled when the girl who usually sat in the desk I was occupying walked in late, handed a note to Mr. Brown, and made her way toward us. I rushed to stand against the wall. I watched the boy slip the paper on which he'd been writing into the pages of his book. I couldn't take my eyes off him. Like a desert wanderer afraid of mirages, I gazed at my oasis, but he was real. It pleased me that he seemed to take no notice of the young lady who now sat across the aisle from him. He shifted in his chair, pretended to listen to Mr. Brown, and then my cherished preserver glanced over at me, without turning his head, and winked.

When the bell rang, he slowly closed his book. The other students had already slung their bags onto their backs and were migrating toward the door. The young man gathered his belongings and turned halfway back toward me. With a flick of his head, he beckoned. I followed him closely up the aisle, out the door, down the pathway. He kept his eyes straight ahead of him. When he came to the recycling bins where we had stopped before, there were a boy and a girl there, holding hands and talking. He paused for only half a moment and then kept walking. He came around the side of the library and stopped suddenly, stepping into the phone booth beside the caged vending machine. The booth was the older style that stood like an upright glass coffin. He dropped his bag at his feet and looked me in the eyes as he picked up the receiver.

"What's your name?" he said. I was breathless. "What should I call you?" he asked.

It wasn't that I had forgotten; it was just that no one had asked me in a long time.

"Helen," I said.

He glanced around to see whether anyone was eavesdropping. Then he pushed himself back into the corner of the cramped space and gestured with one hand, inviting me into the glass booth. I was shocked, but I moved toward him, and he closed the sliding door behind me. It wasn't until then that I realized he could talk now without others hearing.

"Helen," he said.

"Mr. Blake," I said.

He smiled, a brilliant moment. "Not really," he said. "My name is James."

There was such an odd silence, he staring into my eyes, and me, well, I was so lost; I could scarcely speak. "How is it you see me?" But I wanted to cry, *Thank God you do.*

"I'm like you," he said. When I only blinked at him, he added, "In spirit."

"You're Light?" I couldn't believe it.

"Light." He adopted my term instantly. "Yes."

"That's not possible."

"I only borrowed this flesh," he said. "I couldn't see you before I was in a body." As someone passed by the booth, he jerked the phone back to his ear, having let it slip absently down to his chest. "Are you still there?" he said into the phone, but he was smiling. "Miss Helen, if you'll pardon me asking, why did you hide from me yesterday?"

"I'm not sure why. I was afraid."

"Please don't be."

He seemed so clever, the way he moved among the Quick as if he were one of them. "How long have you been dead?" I asked.

"Eighty-five years."

"How old were you when you died?" I asked. I wanted to know everything about him.

"Twenty-nine."

I had forgotten that even if he'd died at a hundred and nine, he'd look seventeen in Billy's body. Perhaps I blushed, if that's possible, for now he watched my face with great interest.

"Are there others like me, then?" I asked. The idea that I might be ordinary to him hurt me inexplicably.

"No," he said. "Now that I'm in a human body, I can see other spirits, but none like you."

There was something about him that continually disarmed me. "Mr. Blake . . ." I hesitated. "That's not your name, is it?"

"It's Deardon," he said, "but it would be a crime for you to call me anything but James."

He'd left me speechless again. He was truly exasperating.

"Please," he said.

"James . . ." The word felt strange. "Why did you—" I stopped myself. "How did you take Mr. Blake's body?"

"He vacated it," said James. "He left it, mind and soul, like an empty house with the door open." He seemed excited to tell me his strange adventure.

"When his spirit left his body, why didn't he die?" I wanted to know.

"His body didn't die," he said, still fascinated by his own luck. "His spirit chose to leave. It's difficult to explain. Instead of the ship going down taking the crew with it, the crew abandoned the ship, but the ship was still seaworthy." Now he looked embarrassed. Something in my expression had shamed him.

"It seems wrong," I said. "Like stealing."

"Better that *I* have him rather than—"An untold and eerie story flashed by behind his autumn eyes.

"Than what?"

"Well, left adrift, something evil might pirate him away." James had let the phone slip down again. I raised my hand to my ear, and he smiled and raised the receiver again.

"How long have you been inside there?" I asked.

"Since September ninth."

That was a fortnight. "Then how is it you saw me only last Monday?"

"That was my first day back," said James. "Billy's body was so sick, I was in bed for a week."

"What was wrong with him?" I asked.

James looked sorry to tell me. "He took so many drugs he almost died."

"But how could you tell he was empty?" I wanted to know. Plenty of the students in Mr. Brown's classroom looked fatally bored.

"It was the way his body resonated when he left it. It sort of rang."

"It rang? Like a bell?"

"No." He thought for a moment. "Bodies with souls in them are solid, like a beam in a house. And bodies that are empty make a very small vibration, the way the wind can blow past the gutter on the roof and make the rain pipe hoot like an owl."

"You heard this boy hooting?" I was sure he was teasing me.

"I noticed that he sounded hollow. Like holding a seashell to your ear," he said. "I doubt that anyone who wasn't Light could hear it."

This was becoming as curious as Wonderland. "How is it that I have seen more years than you, but you know all these things that I don't?"

James laughed. "It's being in a body again," he said. "For once I saw through a glass darkly, but now I see the world clearly."

"How did you find this body?" I sounded more demanding than I intended.

"I saw him almost every day. He came to my haunting place to hide from his friends or take pills or smoke." James watched a student thump past the booth, his shoulder rattling the glass door. "I knew there was something wrong with this boy, that he sounded empty sometimes. I wasn't sure what it meant. He seemed hollow, but he was living, not Light," said James. "I was held to my haunting place, but I felt responsible for this boy because I could tell he was in trouble, and yet I couldn't warn anyone." James took a deep breath, remembering. "So I followed him home that afternoon. On other days, I'd seen the way he came in and out of his flesh when he put poisons in his blood. His spirit seemed to go to sleep for an hour or two and he'd start to ring empty. But this day, he closed himself in his room and took pills and sniffed powder and even inhaled fumes from a bag. This day, when his spirit left his body, it didn't come back."

I felt a chill encircle my heart.

"I watched for seven hours," said James.

The pathways outside the phone booth quieted. Students and faculty had migrated to the parking lots. I was running out of time before I would have to leave with Mr. Brown.

"Then I felt something wrong pulling at the body, something evil," said James. "I tried to wake him up, but his spirit wouldn't come back, so I went inside him, and I tried to scare away the evil. The trouble was, it wasn't afraid of me. I couldn't drive it away; I couldn't even open my eyes or move, the body was so sick. The evil didn't quail until Billy's brother came in and called for an ambulance. Then it disappeared." He sounded as if he had finished the story.

"What happened?" I said.

"We went to the emergency room, Mitch punched a hole in the waiting room wall, and I stayed in Billy's body while they flushed the poisons out. It was frightening."

I must've looked horrified.

"It wasn't that bad," he said. "We're all right now."

"Did the evil that tried to get Billy look like a person or a creature?" Perhaps I had read too much about Middle-earth over

Mr. Brown's shoulder, but I thought it was important to know the shape of the enemy.

He shook his head as if he'd never want to describe such a thing to a lady. I was fascinated by his adventures, but they still seemed so unreal.

"Do you have any of Billy's memories?" I asked him.

"No, I don't. And that does make life in a stranger's body rather tricky."

"Where is your haunting place?" The more I heard, the more I wanted to know.

"It's a park a few miles from here. There used to be a two-story house there. That's where I was born."

"You remember your life as James Deardon, then?" I said.

"Not at all, when I was Light," he said. "But since I've been inside a body again, some things have been coming back to me. I don't know why."

"Do you remember how you died?"

"Not yet," he said. "But I remember more things every day."

"But you must've been with your family at first," I said, "if you were haunting their house."

"The house had burned down long before I was haunting that land. Before I was in Billy's body, I didn't even know why I was stuck there. I just knew I couldn't get more than a hundred feet away."

"How did you know you were stuck?"

"If I tried to walk more than a hundred feet down the side-walk . . ." He thought for a moment and shortened the descrip-tion for me. "It hurt too much. I'd have to go back."

A queer recognition shook me. "Is it like black icy water crushing you?"

He gave me an odd look. "Mine's more like a light that burns and a wind that cuts you."

We looked into each other's eyes, picturing each other's hell. *What a strange goblin God must be*, I thought, *to torment James*. He was just to punish me, for I sensed that I had truly sinned. But not James.

"You spent almost a hundred years on an acre of land by yourself?" I asked.

"Well, after a few years, they built a park," he reassured me.

I suddenly felt like crying. "You didn't have lamps at night or books."

"*Some* people read in the park," he said. "Horror stories mostly."

"No poetry," I said. "No Shakespeare. No Austen."

As if to cheer me, he said, "I read a comic book of *Frankenstein* sitting next to a ten-year-old girl once."

"That's too awful."

"It's all right now." James saw that I was on the verge of weeping and fumbled in his pocket. Then he smiled. "I was going to offer you a handkerchief, but I haven't got one and even if I did . . ."

That made me laugh.

"What do you recall about life as James?"

He straightened up as the janitor walked by our glass booth. "Very little. We had an almond orchard and a weather vane of a running horse." He thought for a moment. "When I was small, I had a rocking horse named Cinder because his tail got burned off when he sat too near the fireplace."

I felt cold and thin as tin for a moment, made fragile by a half memory of a child at play. A blonde head bent over a little wooden lamb on wheels.

"My dog was named Whittle," he told me. "My cousin taught me to swim in the river. One year we made our own raft and nearly drowned." He laughed, then saw something that worried him in my face. "What's wrong?"

"What else?" I didn't want to hear about swimming.

"My father carved me soldiers out of basswood." He switched the receiver to his other ear. "That's all that's come back to me so far."

I wished I had a picture of James in his true body.

"And what do you remember from before you were Light?" he asked me. "Tell all."

"Nothing." Then I realized that wasn't true. "Only my age, my name, and that I was female." He waited for more. "The rest is only images. And feelings. I won't go inside closets," I said.

The way he was gazing at me made me curious. "What do I look like to you?" I heard myself asking. Immediately I was embarrassed, but James wasn't.

"You look beautiful," he said. "You have dark eyes and light hair." He stopped but continued to stare.

"How old do I look?"

"A woman, not a girl." He shrugged. "I can't tell."

"I was twenty-seven," I said. "What am I wearing?" I added, "I can't see myself in a reflection."

"I know," he said softly. I had almost forgotten that he had been Light as well. "You're wearing a gown with a striped ribbon here." James drew the neckline of the dress on his own chest.

"What color?" I wanted to know.

He smiled. "It's difficult to explain. You're not like a painting. You're like water. Sometimes you're full of color, sometimes you're gray, sometimes almost clear."

"And when I'm full of color," I said. "What then?"

"Then your eyes are brown," he said. "Your hair is golden and your dress is blue."

One slow, hard pulse of cold clay beat through my heart. I leaned closer to James, banishing the fear.

"What did you wear before you were inside Mr. Blake?" I wanted to know.

He laughed. "I don't know. I couldn't see my reflection."

I laughed too; the feeling, so unfamiliar, made me giddy. Were we actually joking about our deaths?

"Is the dress blue now?" I asked. "Or am I clear as water?"

"Now?" He stared a moment more, still holding the phone to one ear. "You're silvery, like the Lady of the Lake."

I had so many more questions for him, but I couldn't stay.

"Tell me about haunting the school," he said.

"I need to leave now."

"Wait." He reached out to take my hand but couldn't. I was startled by the flash of warmth. He took a moment before speaking.

"Miss Helen, you have a way about you. When I watched you with Mr. Brown, the way you read over his shoulder, how you listened to him recite poetry. I don't have the words," he told me.

"It was as if you were the only one in the world who could under-stand me. And now you're looking at me and speaking to me." He spoke very confidentially into the phone. "It's like a miracle."

Perhaps it was because Mr. Brown was preparing to drive off, perhaps it was because James seemed to be speaking from my own heart, or perhaps it was simply that I had gone for 130 years without being heard or seen, but all at once I felt faint. I dropped my gaze.

"Did I say something wrong?"

"No." But I was fluttering madly like a winged thing about to fly apart. Then a pang of ice told me Mr. Brown was moving too far away.

"Please be there tomorrow," said James.

When you are Light, you may move through solid objects with no more effort than it would take to add sums in your head. But at that moment, if James hadn't opened the glass door, I'm not sure that I would've had the strength to pass through it.

Three

I sat on Mr. Brown's roof through the tortured slowness of the night, thinking of questions to ask James. I watched the stars arc across the sky, slow as grass growing, and was at Mr. Brown's bedside when the dawn broke. I wasn't put out by Mrs. Brown any longer, not since I had someone of my own. Just as Mr. Brown started to rise, however, she slid her hand up his bare back. As he fell under the covers again, I gave a cry of frustration, the soundless fury of which disturbed only a sparrow on the windowsill. I blustered outside to wait in the back seat of the car.

I thought better of it when Mr. Brown appeared at last, rushing to button his shirt and run a hand through his hair. He had spent almost his whole writing hour in bed, but I couldn't be unhappy with him. As he turned back toward me to pull the car out of the driveway, he looked just a little like James—an angle of his jaw or the curve of his lashes. My heart unwound. He was, after all, my Mr. Brown, and he loved his wife, and at last, I had someone to talk to after so many years of wanting to talk with him and not being allowed. I remembered then how I used to whisper to my previous host, my Poet, while he was dreaming.

That morning as Mr. Brown opened the box and took out the pages of his unfinished novel, I rested my hand on the back of his chair and leaned in toward the shell of his ear.

"I know you can't hear me," I said to him. "I wish that you could." I moved my fingers to his shoulder. I rarely attempted to be in the same space as the Quick. It was always an odd feeling, like falling. This time it felt like sliding down a waterfall. At that moment, he set the papers on his table and looked out at the empty desks. He let the arm I was touching drop, his hand in his lap.

"My friend," I said. "I want to tell you something." I felt foolish, and at the same time confiding in him made my heart pulse like the fanning of doves' wings. "I've found someone," I told him. "He can see me and hear me."

Mr. Brown turned to the door as if he had forgotten something and was considering going back to his car.

"I wish you could be happy for me," I whispered in his ear. "You're my only friend." Then I realized I had another friend now. What a queer idea.

Mr. Brown looked out the windows on the left, then the door on the right, as if he might see a familiar face looking in.

"I just wanted to tell you," I said. Then I withdrew my hand and the first bell rang, startling him. He put the papers of his novel away without writing a word.

That day as I waited for James, I felt not in the least afraid. As he walked in and slyly scanned the room, he found me sitting at his own desk. He tried not to laugh and I pretended not to notice him. He walked calmly up to me, rubbed his chin for a moment in mock contemplation, then continued past me toward the back of the room where he sat in the very last seat. I stayed where I was until every student was settled, even the young woman next to me. Finally I drifted back toward him. At the sound of Mr. Brown's voice, I stopped, standing in the aisle right in front of James.

"Mr. Blake?" called Mr. Brown.

James had been smiling up at me. Now he looked through me, or tried to. I ruffled with pleasure at the idea that I could block his view. He ended up leaning far to the left in order to see around me. "Sir?"

"Anything wrong?" asked Mr. Brown. There were several empty desks between us and the next occupied seat.

"Claustrophobia," said James.

Mr. Brown shook his head and commenced with the lesson. I moved to the desk to James's right and sat. He looked toward the front of the room, as if listening to the difference between an adjective and an adverb, then reached over, took hold of my desktop, and dragged the whole chair a foot closer to him. The deafening scrape made Mr. Brown stop lecturing, and several heads turn back toward us. James sat with his hands folded on his book and what appeared to them an empty desk beside him. As Mr. Brown continued with the lesson, James slipped the same paper he'd been writing on the day before out of his book and turned it over. He took a runt of a pencil stub from his pocket and wrote: "How long have you been Light?"

"One hundred and thirty years," I told him, speaking quietly, though there was no need.

"Were you born here or did you die here?" he said softly but not softly enough. The girl who used to sit beside him turned and glared back at him.

"Write," I whispered.

"Which?" he wrote and tilted the page toward me, though it was not necessary. I was leaning as close to him as a cat at a mouse hole, ready to pounce on every word.

"Neither," I whispered.

He said aloud, "Then why—"

"Mr. Blake?" interrupted Mr. Brown. This time both the girl and the boy in front of us turned back to frown at him.

James jumped. "Sir!"

"Something you'd like to share with the rest of us?"

"Not for the world," he said.

I took my right hand and touched the fingers of James's right hand, the one that held the pencil. He made the smallest sound, a faint intake of breath, and looked down at this. I folded my fingers into his. For some reason, perhaps because James was inside this boy, my hand didn't pass through. In a fragile way, I could hold his fingers. I wished I could grip the pencil, as well. I could feel that falling sensation I felt whenever I touched the Quick, but this time there was something different to the touch. I could feel his *knowing* that my hand was there. I could feel him seeing my fingers. I could feel him thinking, *My God, I can feel her.*

The afternoon sun slanted warm on his face like firelight. He wasn't breathing at all now. I placed my other hand on his shoulder and stroked his right arm from the top down toward his hand, willing him to relax. He let me draw the tension out of him, and when I felt his resistance subside, I started gently to move his hand. He breathed now, and I could feel his heart pounding. He looked at the word he had written, that I had written: *Write*.

"My God," he whispered.

"Shh," I warned him as I let go.

He glanced back up at the classroom, but no one was watching.

"That was amazing," he wrote. Then he waited, trembling a little, his hand holding the pencil lightly, waiting for me. I put my hand into his and wrote through him, "How true."

"Why do you haunt this place?" he wrote.

I took his hand and wrote, "I don't. I'm attached to Mr. Brown."

James took a moment to read this twice, and then wrote, "Why?"

I took such a long time without moving that he looked up into my face. I finally took his hand and wrote, "Literature."

To my surprise, James gave a short laugh.

"Why don't *you* give it a try, then?" called Mr. Brown. "Mr. Blake?"

"Sir?" James sat up straighter in his chair.

"Care to offer a sentence with an example of an adverb?" Mr. Brown watched him doubtfully.

"Breathlessly he watched her hand," said James.

Mr. Brown blinked at him. "Okay."

As a student in the front row asked a question and Mr. Brown turned his attention elsewhere, James looked down again.

"He's my host," I wrote.

And James wrote, "Lucky man."

Next I wrote, "Have you ever seen Billy's spirit since you took his body?"

James thought about this for a moment. I watched him hold the pencil, rereading the last line. His hand was a fine thing, lean and long-fingered, as strong as a farmer's but unscarred.

"Only once," he wrote. "I thought I saw him watching me for a moment the first night I slept in his room."

I took his hand, hesitating slightly before beginning to write, wondering whether he'd realize that I paused not because I couldn't choose the words but rather because I wanted to just feel his fingers for a moment. I wrote, "Did he speak to you?"

"Alas, no," James wrote in answer.

Again I took control of his pencil. "So you go home to Mr. Blake's family at night?"

I took another moment before letting his fingers go. He kept his eyes on the page and wrote, "Such as it is."

Then I wrote on the bottom line of the page, "No room."

He frowned at these two words for a second. Suddenly he was fumbling so wildly in his bag for his notebook, I thought the paper would fly into the next row. He tore out a fresh page and slapped it down and wrote, "Sorry."

I laughed.

"Mr. Blake, you seem to be taking lots of notes today," said Mr. Brown. "Do you remember an example of where not to insert an adverb?"

James just stared at him.

"To desperately hope," I whispered.

James let out a breath. "To gratefully believe."

"Well," Mr. Brown said. "Claustrophobia certainly has improved your grammar skills."

"Yes sir, captain sir."

The class laughed.

"At ease, Mr. Blake."

"Helen," James wrote on the paper.

I was fascinated by the look of the word. A picture flipped past my mind—"For Helen" scripted in fading ink on the linen frontispiece of a small leather volume. One moment, then the vision snapped shut.

"Don't go home with Mr. Brown," he wrote. "Come with me."

I read the words and didn't take his hand right away. He waited, keeping his eyes on the paper. Finally I touched his fingers, and it may have been my imagination, but I sensed that he could feel me trembling and knew before reading the words. "I'm afraid of leaving my host."

With my fingers still entwined in his, James wrote, "You must've changed hosts before."

The young man seated in front of James twisted around, surveyed the distance between them, and threw the paper in his hand backward at James. It swooped and landed in the aisle. James bent and retrieved it. It was a lined sheet of paper, wrinkled and torn on one corner. In handwriting that was not James's, the paper was labeled: "W. Blake, September 4, eleventh grade English." The page contained only a few lines of messy black ink. In green ink, at the bottom, in Mr. Brown's hand, were the words, "5/10 points. The assignment was to write a full page of descriptive prose. Please rewrite and submit for full credit."

James glanced up. No one was paying us any heed. The students were looking over their graded papers, and Mr. Brown was still handing pages to the last few students. James whispered, with some embarrassment, "This was before me."

It was odd to think that just two weeks before, Billy's body had been sitting in this classroom, and I hadn't cared. Now, because he was James, this same body drew my eye like the moon in a starless sky.

James was reading the five-point assignment with a weary expression. I leaned over to see as well.

It read: "I'm describing the library where I'm sitting. It kind of stinks, like old stuff. The librarian watches me suspisiously. Books are boring. I used an adjetive and an adverb so now I'm glad and I leave happily." Mr. Brown had made a small green check mark beside the two misspelled words but had made no more specific suggestions.

"You'll have to rewrite it for him, I suppose," I said.

He smiled at me now. "I need a tutor," he whispered.

"What?" The girl in front of him was looking at James with annoyance.

James turned the page over and wrote, "Help me."

This made me feel restless, for some reason. I excused myself and took a walk, back and forth against the rear wall. I strolled up the outside aisle by the windows, then stopped and stood beside Mr. Brown, who was doing a review of the Dickens story before the students were to take turns reading aloud. I knew that James was watching me, but I didn't meet his eyes. I needed to just be still with my host for a moment. I hovered behind Mr. Brown, listening to a girl flatly read of a boy dying in the arms of his cousin under a tree. But the next to have a turn was James. He didn't read like the others. He understood the words. His voice rang so true, it tolled in every corner of me. I had to flee the room.

Under the tree where I had hidden before, I waited. Finally the students appeared, James so full of color now, not at all the pale creature from the first day we'd seen each other. He strode toward me, his green bag over his shoulder and his hair blowing. I couldn't take my eyes from him. He stopped under the tree and let the book bag drop as he knelt, pretending to tie his shoe.

"You have to come with me," he said quietly, without looking up. "Can't you see I'm on my knees?"

I said nothing.

"You move about the school freely," he said. "You don't need to stay in the same room with your host, do you?"

To move about freely sounded so appealing.

"Well, shadow your professor if you must," he sighed, standing up but still not looking at me. "I'm going to the library." He put his bag over this shoulder. "Of course, if you don't like libraries, I understand." With that he walked off down the path, merging with the rest of the bodies.

Except for the librarian and a couple of mice, I spent more time in the school library than anyone. Of course I followed.

I moved past the librarian's desk and between the large tables, three in a row, but no James. I began slowly to snake my way up one aisle of books and down the next until I found him waiting for me at a small study table tucked in the back of the room. There were four chairs there. James looked up at me and slid his book bag off the chair beside him.

The library was quiet but not silent. There were whispers,

gentle footfalls, the squeaking wheels of a cart in the next aisle. I sat. No one was nearby.

"Tell me all about yourself," he whispered. "I want to know everything."

"I thought you wanted me to help you write."

"Tell me about your hosts," he whispered. "You must've had several. Were they all men? What cities have you lived in?"

"We don't have time," I said.

"All right." James took a notebook from his bag and tore out a clean sheet of paper. "A full page," he said aloud. "Of descriptive prose."

"Hush," I warned him.

"About the library," he whispered. He took out the pencil stub from his pocket and poised it over the page.

"Will you write like Mr. Blake or like yourself?" I inquired.

He wrote and whispered the words aloud as he did. "I am in the library. It smells like old stuff."

"It smells familiar," I suggested. "It smells like words." Because his left side was to me, I couldn't easily take his hand to write.

"Books are boring," James said as he wrote.

"They line the walls like a thousand leather doorways to be opened into worlds unknown," I offered.

He thought about this and then wrote with a smile, "I hate books."

"A sea of dreams trapped in a span of pressed pages," I said.

"Very well," James said. "Shall we make Mr. Blake a little more enlightened?" His sudden smile at me, like an arrow, struck deep.

He crossed out the last two sentences and wrote, "Books are okay, I guess."

I laughed. Next James wrote, "As I look around the quiet room, I see a thousand leather covers like doorways into worlds unknown." He paused and then wrote, "I hear . . ."

"Silence," I suggested. "Eternity."

"A silence like the mind of God," James wrote. He gave one small laugh, then wrote, "I feel..." He paused, then continued with, "a presence in the empty chair beside me."

"James," I scolded.

"But it's true," he whispered.

"What does Mr. Blake really think of the library?" I asked him.

"From what I've derived, he thinks it's unpleasant because there's no music and you aren't allowed to eat," said James.

"I should be going," I told him. I could feel Mr. Brown preparing to leave, stopping in the hall to talk with another teacher. Soon he'd drive off without me if I didn't hurry. A skittering panic moused up my spine. I had minutes, no more.

"We've only just started," said James. "You can't quit me already."

"Very well, then, but be serious," I said. I tried to reach out and take his right hand in order to control the pencil, but he laughed and moved to avoid me. "Do you have a suggestion, Miss Helen?"

"Stop," I whispered.

James looked into my eyes to make sure I wasn't truly angry. "Why do you whisper?" he whispered.

"Because a library is a sacred place," I told him.

"The library," he wrote, "is a sacred place."

"You're supposed to be Mr. Blake," I reminded him. "At least misspell a word here and there."

James thought this over and then erased *sacred* and replaced it with *sacrid*.

I could feel Mr. Brown moving into the far corner of my reach. The pain crept into my bones, but I tried not to let it show. I craved more time with James. But I also knew that it was important not to let my desire pull me down, as when I had dropped away from my host during a Shakespeare play.

"I'm leaving," I said.

"She threatens to take her pulsing goddess light from this place," he wrote. His teasing charmed me. As I reached again for the pencil, he hid his hand under the table, laughing at my frustration. Another warning chill made me recoil.

"If you have an idea, let's hear it." He glanced at me and must've seen some discomfort in my eyes, for his smile fell.

"What the fuck are you doing?"

We both looked up. The instinct to lift a rifle at this animal made me stiffen. But it was just a boy with a scar on one cheek, wearing a stained army jacket. He frowned at James. "What're you doing, turning into a schizo?"

"Hey," said James, deflated. He slid the page off the table and put it and the pencil in his pocket as the boy sat in the seat across from us.

"Where've you been?" the boy asked. "It's like you don't know us anymore."

"I had the flu," said James. "Puked my guts out for days."

"Grady said you OD'd," the boy told him, looking him up and down, trying to determine what was different about him.

"Pretty close," said James.

I rose and began to flow slowly away. I could feel the flutter as I passed through James—he had put out his arm, pretending to stretch, as I was leaving. We were as close to touching as one spirit and one mortal could for a moment. I started to imagine putting my arms around him but was stopped suddenly by a wall of cold blocking me. Blinded, I reached up and felt wet mud, the slime of a leaking dirt cellar or the bottom of a grave. I had let Mr. Brown leave me behind. I pushed against the coldness, and it gave way in messy pieces, the chill now running down over me like rain on my face. I had no voice with which to call out. I dug through the mud, hearing students laugh, buses, trash can lids rattling. I felt cement under my feet, and then the darkness was pierced with white. I was sitting in the back seat of Mr. Brown's car, the sun blinding me in the rearview mirror.

All evening, I hovered as Mr. Brown and his wife made dinner together, listened to television as they paid bills, read, and talked in bed. After they had turned off the light and settled into each other's arms, just as I was passing through the wall into the garden, Mr. Brown's voice stopped me.

"I thought of a baby name."

"Boy or girl?" she asked.

"Erin," he said. "Could go either way."

I had never heard them discuss children except as a distant possibility during their courtship. The idea frightened me. By their words I knew that this was a conversation that had been visited many times, most likely while I gave them time alone in bed. All my past hosts had been childless. I had not been drawn to children over the decades; nor had I been repelled by them on trains, in parks, laughing in the nurseries of homes my hosts visited, but this was different. This would be the flesh of my host. A child in my every room and in each hour of my existence.

"Spelled how?" asked Mrs. Brown.

"A I R O H N G," he said.

She laughed in the dark.

"Silent G," he explained.

I stayed perfectly still, half in and half out of the bedroom wall.

"Maybe for a girl," she said. "Got any other boy names?"

"Chauncey."

Mrs. Brown let out another laugh. "We'll have to fork it out for those karate lessons so he won't get thrashed every day."

"Okay, how about Butch?" said Mr. Brown. "For a girl."

It was dark, but I saw him stop her laugh with a kiss.

"Let's get started then," she said.

"I thought you wanted to wait so you wouldn't be a blimp in the summer."

"I don't mind, as long as you wait on me hand and foot."

I fled the rustle of sheets and hovered in the living room. Something stronger than logic tore at me. I drifted restlessly through their other rooms, sometimes shifting a curtain or making the floor creak without meaning to. I was a caged panther. I sat on their roof and stared at the stars, but I couldn't explain my terror. Was it some instinctual knowledge that an infant would be aware of my presence? That thought knotted at my throat. Would a baby be frightened of me? Some deep voice answered yes, you are a danger to children. I realized suddenly that I no longer felt welcome in Mr. Brown's house. I was an intruder. I tried to remember feeling at home in the houses of my other hosts but instead saw a hideous flash of a cellar door and a shelf of baskets. I flew to the car, thinking I might feel safer there, but as I sat in the dark garage, huddled in the back seat, I began to weep. I wept a waterless river, sobbing without relief. I thought of running away to the classroom or the library, but I knew I could not. They were too far away. I couldn't go alone. I was a prisoner, crying bone-dry tears until the morning.

Four

THE NEXT MORNING, I meant to watch Mr. Brown write, but as I circled his desk, I kept thinking about James and worrying about a baby at the Browns' house. When the first bell rang, I looked down at the manuscript. Mr. Brown had written and erased the same sentence so many times, the paper had worn through.

By the time James's class began to arrive that afternoon, I was fairly humiliated by my own need for comfort. I sat in the desk in the last row and wouldn't meet James's eyes as he sat down beside me. I could tell, by the way he was watching me without speaking, that he sensed something was wrong. Mr. Brown was leafing through papers on his desk. He stopped on one and silently read it back and front.

"Listen up," he said then. "Here's a good example of description." Then he read aloud: "The library smells like old books—a thousand leather doorways into other worlds." Mr. Brown paused and glanced up at the room, but especially at James for one moment. "I hear silence, like the mind of God. I feel a presence in the empty chair beside me. The librarian watches me suspiciously. But the library is a sacred place, and I sit with the patron saint of readers." Mr. Brown paused as he stared at the page, and then read, "Pulsing goddess light moves through me for one moment like—" Here Mr. Brown paused again. "Like a glimpse of eternity instantly forgotten. She is gone. I smell mold, I hear the clock ticking, I see an empty chair. Ask me now and I'll say this is just a place where you can't play music or eat. She's gone. The library sucks."

Two boys laughed, but it was a quiet, half-hearted sound that died in the silence. Mr. Brown was staring at the page, though he had read every word there. Perhaps he was staring at the white spaces in between. I turned to James, who was looking down at his hands. Finally Mr. Brown put the paper on his desk with deliberation.

"Why was that a good description?" he asked the class.

" 'Cause the library does suck," one boy near the front snorted.

Mr. Brown ignored the giggles and looked from face to face with a kind of awe, as if he had never seen his students, or anything as fascinating, before.

A girl in the front row raised a hesitant hand. Mr. Brown nodded at her. "Because he said how it smelled and sounded, not just how it looked?" she asked.

"Good." Mr. Brown almost laughed this syllable. "What else?"

Now James had slid down in his seat as if shy of the attention, though Mr. Brown had made no reference to him. I leaned toward him with every intention of merely whispering in his ear, but when my lips neared his temple, I could not stop myself. With one hand on his chest, I pressed a brief kiss to his brow.

To my surprise he gasped, arching in his chair, his left hand flying to his chest where I had touched him. I jumped back, unable to tell whether his expression was one of pain, fear, or ecstasy. I retreated to the back wall. I knew he had turned to find me, but I was ashamed and would not meet his gaze. Instead, I hurried out of the room and hid just outside the open door. I could hear Mr. Brown's voice, and I tried to let the familiar sound soothe me.

"So we have sight, sound, smell, detail, simile, metaphor, and feelings. Good."

"Who wrote it?" one boy called.

"If the author wants to tell you after class, he or she may choose to do so," said Mr. Brown.

I did a most childish thing then. I hid when the students left Mr. Brown's class, not behind or under the tree where James would seek me out but high in the branches. I needed to think. I shadowed Mr. Brown so closely when he left that no light could have slipped between us if I'd been solid flesh. I held to him like a baby to its mother's skirts until he was in his car. Then I sat beside him, something I never did. I always sat in the seat behind. As he started the engine, I saw James mounting his bicycle. I touched Mr. Brown's arm.

"Follow him," I said. I couldn't tell whether Mr. Brown had obeyed my command, until he turned the car south instead of north. We drove behind the bicycle, now a block ahead of us. As James came to a red light, one foot touching the curb for balance, his hair blowing and his green bag on his back, we caught up to him. After we turned on Rosewood, we passed a small park with a swing set and a statue of a deer. At the corner of Amelia, James's bicycle swooped left, and a moment later Mr. Brown's car rolled dreamily after him onto the tiny residential lane. The houses were small, wooden, and worn. James stopped in the driveway of the third one, both feet on the ground, his black shirt blowing in the wind as he turned toward us. Mr. Brown stopped his car right in the middle of the street and looked perplexed. He turned and saw James staring at him. The window rolled down with a soft hum.

"Mr. Blake," he said.

"Yes, sir," said James, who brushed the hair out of his face. I stayed hidden behind Mr. Brown.

"Good writing," he told him.

"Thanks." I could feel James searching for me.

"See you tomorrow." Mr. Brown raised the window. "How the hell did I get on this street?" I looked back, as we glided away, to see James walk his bicycle toward the garage. It was a light blue house, peeling, with ivy growing up one side and a fig tree in the lawn. The number over the door was 723. The side mirror on the bike flashed as he rolled it into the darkness of the garage. I made a wish as if I had just seen a falling star. I wished that James were my host. A thrill burned through me like a fast wick. Seven twenty-three. I repeated it over and over like an incantation.

When we arrived at Mr. Brown's house a few minutes later, a dreadful thing happened. When he entered the house, I could not. I was as barred from moving through the doorway (or the wall, for that matter) as a leaf would be when blown up against a solid pane of glass. Instead of flowing through the door as he closed it behind him, I bobbed against it. I floated to the window where I could hear faint sounds from the kitchen. I could touch the outer walls in my benign way, but I could not enter. I didn't mean to, but I cried out, like a child fallen down a well. My spectral voice frightened the crows in the oak nearby, and this sobered me, for a while. I paced round and round the small house, looking in at every window. As when I wished to be one of the actors I watched on a stage far below, I had made a grave error in judgment.

I tried to thrust my arms through the wall and cleave to Mr. Brown again, as I had with my Knight, but I couldn't. If you love me, I thought at him, invite me in. But I knew better. It wasn't a matter of love. It was only nature. I hadn't so much broken the rule of proximity as the mysterious rule of devotion. I had wished for another host. My spirit had wandered off, and this had severed our tie like a blossom cut from the vine. The old pain would be returning soon. Stubbornly I bumped against the same window time and again, like a moth with no memory. I found that the bedroom window was half open, but still I could not enter. I waited there, my face at the brink of the opening, my hands gripping the window frame like prison bars, waiting for my hell to come for me.

Mr. Brown came in and sat on the bed, looking troubled. His wife followed and went to the mirror, taking a clip from the dressing table and looking at herself in the glass as she twisted and fastened up her hair. She saw Mr. Brown in the reflection and asked, "What's wrong?"

"Nothing," he said, but when he tried to smile, she turned and looked at him.

He shrugged. Mrs. Brown came over and sat beside him. "Really," she said.

He lay down on his back, gazing at the ceiling. "I don't know."

She lay on her side by him, raised up on her elbow so she could observe his expression. "Tell me."

He looked so worried, but he played absently with the fingers of her right hand as he spoke. "It's like I have the feeling I lost something or I forgot something. It keeps bugging me."

Mrs. Brown leaned over and gave him a short kiss on the shoulder. "It'll come back to you." Then she said, "Did you mail that package to my sister?"

"Yes."

"Well, that was probably it."

"It doesn't feel like that," he said. "It's like when you know you dreamed about someone, but you can't remember what happened in the dream. I feel as if I can't remember . . ." He stopped. Mrs. Brown stroked his chest, drawing soft circles over his heart.

After a moment he said, "What if I've forgotten a person?"

"Like your first grade teacher, you mean? Someone like that?"

"Is there a moment when you'll never be able to remember something again?"

"No," said his wife. "Your mind will never lose anything forever that's worth keeping." She gave his temple a playful push, and he let his head fall to one side. "It's all in there."

Something happened then. Any other night, he would have put his arms about her or tickled her. This time he simply looked back at the ceiling. His wife stood up and said, "Snap out of it, Babe." But he didn't laugh. She paused as she unbuttoned her jeans, frowning.

"Maybe I lost my muse," he said. "I wonder what I did wrong."

Her eyes flashed at him, a ripple went through the gentle

stream of her nature. A shock wave she hid by turning her back on him as she got undressed. She was shaken, and I knew why. He had broken the illusion that *she* was his muse. She knew that he was smitten with her, but now she feared that she was not enough. Mrs. Brown slowly folded her T-shirt and laid it over her jeans on the dressing table chair.

"I think I'll take a shower," she said. And on any other night, he would have followed her into the water, but tonight he lay staring at the ceiling.

It was my fault. I had stepped off one stone in the river before finding another. He sat up as the water started running in the next room and looked toward the open window. He stood and walked to me now. Leaning a hand on the wall on each side of the frame, he studied the darkness, the breeze that wafted through me, stirring his hair. I was inches away, but he was alone. It was not like talking to him when I had touched his shoulder alone in our classroom. He couldn't feel me anymore. If only I could appear to him like the ghosts in stories. The soles of my feet began to feel like ice.

I backed away, willing his eyes to eventually lock with my own, but of course he was blind to me, and I couldn't bear it. I had never left a host who wasn't dying. I was losing my beloved friend, and he wasn't going to heaven without me. He was going to live his life without me. I turned my back on him and fled. Once I had run from my hell and managed to make my way back to my host's doorstep. I began walking in what I hoped was the right direction. As I felt the pain crack through my bones, I held the number I had memorized in my mind like a compass. Seven twenty-three.

I was in the freezing waters again, being pulled down in the dark, the demons roaring above and mud flooding my throat. I reached out, trying to tear down the dirt wall, but it was a plank, like the side of a rough coffin. I clawed at the wood, and it started to crumble in little rotting chunks. Water shot between the boards with a scream.

An animal, a black deer, loomed over me. It stood so still even as the wind was blowing leaves and sticks around in a wild maypole dance. I realized then, it was only a statue of a deer. I could see, behind it, two swings flapping in a crazy jig. I was too fragile to move. I felt as if I would be blown to pieces if I tried to rise, so I stayed close to the ground and let everything else riot over my head. My hell and a storm were strangely mingled.

I couldn't actually hear anything except the shriek of the wind and all that it carried, but I knew that someone was calling me. I looked around and on the street corner, I saw a figure. He put a hand up to his head, perhaps blocking the wind from his eyes. No, he was holding back his blowing hair. He started running toward me. When I saw that it was James, I struggled up but was thrown into the madness of the dance and caught in a tree over his head. I saw James stop on the sidewalk below and look about as if I had disappeared.

I was then sucked into the sky, and I could see nothing. All I could hear was wind and all I could feel was wind, but I was thinking over and over, seven twenty-three, seven twenty-three. Finally, I smashed into the grass of a small yard. Ivy shook on a pale blue wooden wall, and then James was standing beside a fig tree that was jerking in the wind. He was scanning the street, but as I pulled myself toward him, he caught sight of me and stared.

I crawled closer, trying to keep myself from sliding down the hole in the earth that dragged like a whirlpool at my feet. He seemed terrified. I must've looked like a monster, covered in mud, tearing at the grass. He held a hand out to me, but I didn't want to pull him in.

He dropped to his knees and tried to clutch at me with both hands, looking panicked when he couldn't. Finally he threw himself on me, and I couldn't help but embrace him. Don't let me pull him down with me, I was praying. A moment later the wind had softened to a mild hiss.

Kneeling beside me, he waited until I looked at him, then he slowly rose and began to move backward toward the small blue house, one foot behind the other, like a tightrope walker. I rose as well, concentrating on the wind ruffling his hair. With my other salvations, it had always been clear, the uniting of spirit and host. This felt different. I followed, so weak I felt as if all the color had been drained from the world. He climbed the porch stairs backward, one step at a time, and I followed. I kept my eyes on his face, perfect as a sculpture. He opened the door and backed in, then moved to one side and beckoned me to enter, as I had longed for Mr. Brown to do. I followed him into the house, and he closed the door.

It was only then that I noticed the noise. There was loud music and many voices, much smoke, and little light in the small living room. A dozen men and women, all holding bottles of beer and burning cigarettes, moved about in unsteady, sweating clusters, swearing and laughing and taking little notice of James. Only one of them, a strong, tattooed man with no shirt, looked over.

"Where'd you go?" he called.

"Nowhere." He had to yell to be heard over the din.

"Do your homework," the man called.

"It's Friday."

"What?" The man frowned, holding his beer-bottled hand to one ear.

"Okay!" yelled James. He ducked down the tunnel of the hall. He stopped at a door with a hole as big as a baseball almost broken through it. He opened the door and waited until I had glided in before closing it. It was a small room, lit with a dim overhead light. There was a large square bed, far too big for the cramped space, a tiny desk and chair cluttered with magazines, clothes and cans, and the walls were almost completely covered with pictures, mostly from magazines, but there were also some larger pictures pinned and taped up, even on the ceiling. Some pictures were of almost nude women, some were of guitars and musicians, some of cars, and a few of athletes caught in midjump. The space over the desk was papered, every inch, with cartoon drawings of dragons, insects, and monsters. Each was signed with the initials BB.

I knew that these walls were full of color, but everything seemed gray. James watched me look about. He still seemed to be trembling, though the wind was far away now, only a tame howl outside the closed window. Even the overpowering squeal of music from the other room was just a muffled hum. This space seemed so alien, I had to stare.

"This is Mr. Blake's home," I said.

"Did you leave him?"

The truth was more that I had lost Mr. Brown than left him, but I didn't want to say it out loud. I felt a brick-heavy sorrow in my chest threaten to take me over, until James smiled.

"Haunt *me*," he said, and he shrugged in such a light, odd manner, I felt instantly as if I must be taking myself far too seriously.

"Don't be foolish," I told him.

He pulled his book bag off the desk chair and motioned me to sit.

"I'm your host now, aren't I?" he asked.

"I suppose that's true." My host. My James. "I don't know what to do now, I confess," I said. "It doesn't seem quite proper, this . . ." I was at a loss.

"I don't know much at all about anything," said James. "But I know we should be together, you and I. That's all I can be sure of."

Together, he'd said. I wanted to know exactly what he meant.

"How could we not?" he asked, sitting on the rumpled brown blanket on his bed. "It's as if we were the only two of a species or the only two people on earth who spoke the same language. How could we not be with each other?"

I was shocked at his words, the last of a species. There was something carnal in the sound.

"I've never cleaved to a host that . . ." I hesitated. "Well, that was aware of me."

This made him smile.

"You'll tire of me," I said, afraid all at once of being hated. "I couldn't bear that."

"Miss Helen," he laughed, "you must be joking." But then he thought on it again. "You may tire of me," he said. "That's far more likely. Are you afraid of that?"

"No, not of that," I said.

The door banged open with a flood of reckless music, and a

woman staggered in, with a man following. The man put an arm around her waist and a hand into her shirt. She wore a short black skirt and a black lace blouse that was smoke thin. She blinked at James. "Hey, Billy."

"Hey, Rayna," said James, sounding tired all at once.

The man looked over her shoulder and frowned at James, not bothering to remove his hand from her breast. "Goddamn it."

"Do you mind?" said James.

"Sorry," she laughed. "We can go somewhere else."

"Like where?" asked the man. He had one earring and a beard like a pirate.

"How about the bathroom?" said the woman, as she closed the door again.

"I apologize," James said to me, blushing. He went to the door and put on the chain lock. He sat back down on the bed with a sigh.

"Which ones are in your family?" I asked.

"Only the man who spoke to me when we first walked in. That's Billy's brother, Mitch. He doesn't talk about it, so it's difficult to know, but I think our mother died and our father's in jail."

"I see." It seemed like such a bleak life, but who was I to judge? I was not much more than a wisp of vapor. "I'm sorry," I said.

He smiled. "It's all right." Then he looked around the room. "Last week I tried to change the pictures and clean up the mess, but when Mitch saw it, he thought that I was having a mental breakdown and was so upset, I went back to the clutter."

I laughed at this, feeling more comfortable whenever James seemed happy.

"I have a secret treasure, though." He pulled a box out from under his bed and opened it. "Promise not to tell."

"I do."

He took out one item after the other and laid them on the bed. A copy of an art history book with a sticker reading $1.00. A tattered photography magazine. A worn paperback of short stories. A dog-eared copy of a collection of Robert Frost poems. Lastly a journal with a feather as a bookmark and a dark purple pencil stuck in the elastic band that held it shut. I laughed in recognition of what a treasure ought to be.

"I'd like to smuggle in my own favorite music, but Mitch sold Billy's stereo and computer to pay for the emergency room when the boy almost died, so . . ." He shrugged.

I noticed then a piece of lined paper folded up in the treasure box. I could tell from a few handwritten words visible there that it was the page on which he and I had written. I was aflutter with pleasure—*I was part of his secret treasure.*

An odd thing happened then. As James was looking at me, his face went pale. He seemed ill. He went to the door and took off the chain. He came back to the bed and carefully returned the treasures to the box.

"I'm afraid I was being selfish," he said at last. "This must be like a prison to you."

He looked in my eyes and realized that I didn't understand. "You lived in a world of books and beautiful music and paintings on the walls at Mr. Brown's house, didn't you? I must be mad to think you'd want to stay with me in this cave. I'm so sorry."

I was taken aback. I watched him slide the treasure box back under his bed.

"Caves were the first libraries," I reminded him. "And the first art galleries."

Now he blushed and that achingly healthy peach in his cheeks brought all the color back into the world for me.

"Still, Miss Helen," he said, "I've done a very wicked thing. I've lured you away from a wholesome place into a dark one because I didn't want to be without you. I will understand completely if you do not choose me."

I was so unaccustomed to attention, it made me bold. "The most compelling thing in my world, sir, is to be heard and seen by you."

He looked at me a long moment. "Then I am most beholden to you."

The door banged open again and his brother Mitch leaned in. "Phone."

James just looked at him.

"One of those little assholes is on the phone," he said with irritation. "You want it?"

James jumped up and followed him out of the room. I was alone, surrounded by the walls of pictures. I studied Billy's artwork over his desk, torn-out notebook pages with creatures rolling bloodshot eyes and gnashing dripping fangs—muscled legs and smoking nostrils. The edges of the pages rippled in the draft of my curiosity. Then I noticed a picture from a magazine, taped to the wall beside the bed. A young woman in a white cotton dress, and nothing more, stood under a waterfall. I was startled at the way the cloth clung to her and became transparent. Her head was tilted back, her eyes closed, her mouth open. I had seen enough of these types of images on boys' shirts and book covers, but in such close proximity to where James slept, I was shocked. A hot sensation almost like jealousy boiled up my legs until I remembered that the decorations were chosen by Billy and not James.

When James came back in, he looked concerned. He was about to close the door when Mitch slammed it open with one hand.

"You're not going anywhere tonight," he said.

"I know," said James, standing between me and his brother.

"And I better not see that little shit over here."

"He's not coming over," said James.

" 'Cause you're grounded until I say so," said Mitch.

"I know," said James.

Mitch just scowled at him for a moment. "You don't have to stay locked in here," he told him.

"I have a headache," said James.

His brother's face darkened. "What'd you take?"

"Nothing," said James, obviously frustrated.

"You lie to me and I'll kick your ass."

"I'm not lying," said James. "I just don't want to hang out with your friends."

Strangely, this seemed to calm the man. He shook his head and closed the door. James slipped the chain across again and came back to the bed to sit.

"My apologies," he said. "I have so many things to ask you, I don't know where to start." He sat cross-legged now.

"How brave of you to become one of them," I said. "I think I would never have the courage to even try."

He regarded me for a long moment, the way Mr. Brown used

to study a paragraph of prose that he loved, refusing to turn the page when I wanted him to, dwelling on his favorite turn of phrase.

Rembering Mr. Brown, and my struggle through the storm, sobered me at once. A wave of anxiety came over me as I imagined being on my own tonight as James slept.

"Do you want to sleep?" he asked, as if he could read my thoughts.

"Did *you* sleep?" I asked. "When you were a spirit?"

"Not really," he said. "But you can rest safe with me. I'm not like the others you've been with. I'm akin to you."

He motioned me to the bed and I obeyed, trembling all through.

"Be still," he said, so I lay down. James sat in the chair and slid the box out from under his bed again, choosing a book. On the ceiling over the bed was the one picture in the room that seemed halfway like James. It was a photograph of a wolf standing in the shelter of dark pines, his coat thick for winter, his gold eyes focused on the photographer.

> Whose woods are these I think I know.
> His house is in the village though.
> He will not mind me stopping here
> To watch his woods fill up with snow.

I could hear the wind outside and James's voice inside, calming me. The noise down the hall was gone.

When I became aware again, I found that the overhead light was out, but the tiny lamp beside the bed was lit, giving off a faint glow like a candle. I found James asleep on the floor with a jacket rolled up as a pillow under his head. The music and voices were filtering in from the rest of the house. I knelt at James's side.

"Go to the bed," I whispered.

He didn't open his eyes, but his forehead wrinkled as if he were concentrating on deciphering a dead language. I moved closer to his ear and whispered again, "Get in bed, James." He slowly rolled over and sat up facing the bed. Still he didn't open his eyes. He pulled himself up on the mattress and was asleep again instantly. I watched his face, beautiful and pale gold in the lamplight, and his hands, relaxed, half-open, his long fingers so still. I watched his chest rise and fall almost imperceptibly. Finally I reached over to put out the lamp, but, of course, I couldn't.

Five

<hr />

I was all at once aware of a falling feeling so deep that I gasped. I had, apparently, been sleeping on the covers beside James, and he had rolled out of bed, right through me, and was now on his feet, still half asleep. He squinted at the small room, lit with the sunrise and the bedside lamp. He turned toward the bed, and we stared at each other, James with his hair wild and the crease of the blanket on his cheek; me, lying on his bed, startled but uncreasable.

He gave a small wave of apology and crept quietly out of the room. I was stunned. I'd been asleep. It was almost as strange as having been seen. When he came back a minute later, I was still sitting on his brown blanket, also disturbed by the idea that we had been sleeping in the same bed.

He closed his door and ran a hand through his hair. "Did you rest?" he asked me.

"Why could I sleep last night when I hadn't slept since my death?"

He seemed still very tired as he sat on the mattress beside me. "Perhaps because you aren't alone now." Then he shrugged. "The only problem with being Light is you have no mentor to explain it all. You discover the rules by breaking them."

He rubbed his eyes as if Billy's body still needed rest. Without planning to, I put a hand on his shoulder. As he had the time I kissed him, he took a sharp breath and his back straightened. I pressed him toward the blanket and he lay down again, between the wall and me. When I took my hand away from him, I asked, "Does that hurt you?"

He shook his head.

"Does it feel cold?"

He gave a half laugh. "It feels like . . ." He thought better of it. "No, it doesn't feel like anything I've ever felt before. It's wonderful."

I lay down beside him, then. It seemed almost scandalous in one way, and yet in another it seemed as natural as two blades of grass brushing each other in the wind. We lay, looking at each other, and he reached over and touched my closed hand. I opened it, a flower blooming in a sudden heat, and he lay his palm against mine. At that moment it began to rain outside, the hiss of it like a curtain of sound around us. As his flesh touched my spirit, the feeling of falling turned into a feeling of flying. I was soaring through time toward him.

"Why can we touch?" I wanted to know. "When I touched Mr. Brown, he didn't feel me."

"Because you're not just touching Billy's fingers," said James. "You're touching me inside him."

He lifted his hand off mine and looked at it. He placed his

hand on his cheek. He looked at it again, then sniffed his palm.

"You smell like jasmine," he marveled.

"And how is it that you can smell me?" I asked.

"Ghosts have scents," he said. "I suppose it's some residue from the past. Like a memory."

"What other ghosts have you smelled?" I felt a ridiculous surge of jealousy.

"You don't understand. There are two kinds of ghosts." Again he delighted in sharing with me the peculiar knowledge that apparently came with body theft. "There are ghosts who know they're dead and ones who don't. Before I took over a body, I couldn't see either kind." He smiled. "But I still have seen only one like you, who knew she was Light."

"And the ones that think they're still alive," I said, "what do they say to you?"

"Nothing," said James. "They can't see me or anyone. Not even each other."

"What do they do all day," I asked, "and night?"

"They usually repeat some task from the past. They walk home from school, they clean the windows of a building that's not there anymore, they look for something they lost or someone they lost."

It seemed so sad. "How many are there?" I asked. "Can you see any now?" The idea made my skin prickle.

"You mean this guy?" James nodded to the foot of the bed. When I gasped, he laughed at me.

"That isn't funny."

"You're right." He tried not to smile. "There aren't as many as I thought there'd be when I saw my first in the hospital hall-way," James said. "I've seen only a dozen or so since then."

Although I knew that he was not seeing an apparition in the room with us, I still felt unnerved by the idea that one might appear at any moment.

"Where do you think Billy is now?" I asked. "You said you saw him only once. So he's not attached to his brother or the house."

James shrugged. "I don't really know, but I don't think he's attached at all." He looked around the room at Billy's sketches taped to the walls. "Maybe he's wandering, like a runaway child."

I wondered what it would be like to fly from house to house and face to face at will. It sounded liberating but at the same time lonely. I felt overwhelmed suddenly, the way I had in the phone booth, and I moved away from him, into the corner. Too much was new too fast.

"I'm sorry I tricked you," he said. "About seeing a ghost."

I couldn't explain my cowardice. The tension whined like insects around me.

"How many hosts have you had?" he asked me, hoping to distract me from any escape plans, I could tell.

"Five."

"How did you choose them?" he asked.

I told him briefly of each host and how I had claimed them. I left out the envy I'd felt for what Mr. Brown had shared with his bride. The idea of describing my coping with their love life made me want to fold up like a fan and hide.

"And now I'm host number six," he said.

"Yes." But I felt confused again. "I need to be alone a little," I told him.

And he simply said, "Of course."

I melted out of James's room and wandered through the rest of his house. The rain had slowed to a fine mist. In the living room a man in overalls and a kerchief tied around his head slept on the couch with his arm over his eyes. There were cans, bottles, and crumpled paper all over the floor and furniture. In the kitchen, dishes filled the sink and the faucet dripped. In the other bedroom, Mitch slept, with one shoe off and one shoe on, his pants unbuttoned, sprawled on top of his covers. There was a tiny empty bathroom with the light left on and a small back porch where the roof dripped rainwater onto a shiny black bag of trash. I wished it were not Saturday but Monday so that I might go to school with James and see my Mr. Brown. No, he's not yours anymore, I reminded myself. You have a new host. My *James*.

I heard a stirring from the hall. Mitch was walking unevenly to the bathroom. I kept my distance, drifting into the kitchen. There some pictures tacked to a corkboard beside the back door stopped me. In one of the photographs, a child of twelve, a dark-haired boy, was holding a four-year-old brown-haired lad upside down by the feet. The little boy was screaming with laughter, and the big boy was mimicking a body builder's triumphant growl. What stopped me was not only the little laughing face, which must have been James's, or I should say Billy's, but more it was the slightly blurred woman's hand and leg that were caught in the margin of the scene, the owner's face missing from the memory. Their mother, in the wings, as often mothers and grandmothers are, ready to catch the children should they need saving, but otherwise invisible. Her hand was a pale flutter, her leg slender and bare, wearing a white shoe, the corner of a light green skirt caught in the frame just above the knee.

"Damn it," Mitch grumbled from the bathroom. The door must've been standing open. "The fucking toilet's broken!" I heard a hollow sound like porcelain scraping on porcelain and next a sound that made me cold all through. An animal danger thundered down the hallway. I was afraid, but I rushed there. Mitch ran to James's door and kicked it open. James, who was just unbuttoning the shirt he'd slept in, jumped back in surprise and, bumping into the bed, sat down on it. Mitch pulled a hand back and slapped him so hard across the face that James flew back on the bed and his head thumped the wall. Mitch held a clear bag of white powder in James's face and shook it.

"Are you a fucking idiot?" he yelled. "What the hell is this?"

James was breathing hard and didn't seem to see anything yet. He put his hand to his face and tried to sit up. Mitch slapped him again. I cried out, but I don't think even James could hear me. He scrambled back away from Mitch up against the wall, blood in the corner of his mouth. Mitch shook his striking hand, as if James's face were poison.

"I should just call the fuckin' cops right now," Mitch screamed at him. "You wanna kill yourself, go live in the goddamn street." The anger burned red on his face.

"I'm sorry," said James.

"Fuck you, you little shit," Mitch yelled. There were veins standing out on his neck and arms. He paced back and forth for a moment, his fist flexing on the plastic bag.

"I told you I got messed up that night," said James. "I can't remember everything."

"You are so full of shit!" Mitch kicked the chair so hard it slammed into the door frame and slid out into the hall.

"I forgot about that one," said James. "I didn't use any, I swear."

Mitch stormed out again. I could hear the groggy voice of the man in the kerchief who'd slept on the couch. "What's the matter with you?"

"Shut the fuck up," said Mitch. Then the sound of water running in the kitchen.

The fury ebbed out of the room. I waited, watching James touch his jaw gingerly, dabbing at the blood with the back of his hand. He glanced at me, ashamed.

"Are you hurt?" I asked.

He sighed. "I'm all right." He rose stiffly and brought the chair back into the room, placing it on its feet beside the desk. Then he looked me in the eyes for a longer moment. "I'm sorry you were frightened."

I didn't know what to say. He noticed that his shirt was open and modestly closed the middle button.

"I should shower." He excused himself and I sat on the bed.

Down the hall, the water pipes began to hoot as the shower started. The bedroom door opened wider as Mitch stepped in. He moved with stealth now and not anger. He went immediately to the dresser and opened one drawer after another, starting at the top, looking under the rumpled clothes and feeling the sides and top of each compartment.

Mitch opened the closet and rummaged through the clutter

on the floor within. He pulled out two scratched army boots, thrusting his hand into each one. I watched him as he looked inside the lampshade by the bed. I stayed very still until he suddenly turned, kneeling, and put his hand where I had been sitting on the blanket. I stood on the bed and backed into the corner as he reached between the mattresses and felt around. His face tensed and he pulled out something hidden there. As soon as he saw the magazine, he laughed and put it back. On the front I caught a fleeting glance of a woman in a tiny bathing suit stepping out of a pool. Mitch was smiling as he felt under the bed.

He pulled out James's treasure box and looked inside. Frowning again, he brought out the art book. He shrugged and returned it. He was just starting to open the poetry book when the man in the kerchief came into the doorway.

"You're turning into a narc," he pointed out.

Mitch pushed the box back under the bed and stood up.

"Why're you still here?" Mitch wanted to know. "I gotta be at work."

"I need a ride."

Mitch and his friend left Billy's room as the sound of water in the shower stopped. I slowly sat down on the bed, for some reason still so careful not to cause the slightest stir even though the two men were now well away, their voices in the kitchen.

When James came into the doorway, he was wearing a towel like a kilt, and his hair was still dripping. "I need some clothes," he said in apology and skulked to the dresser.

"I'll go," I said, and I was through the wall at once, lingering in the bushes outside the house, near the bedroom window. The sun was trying to push through the clouds, and every leaf was wet and clean. I did something then I'd never done. I watched my host dress. I didn't go back into the room, but, like a guilty thing, I stayed at the window sill, a peeping tom, watching James throw his towel onto the corner of the bed and pull a pair of gray shorts from the top dresser drawer. He stepped into them and I meant to stop, but it wasn't just the novelty of his nakedness that gripped me. It was all of him. He let the door stand open to the hall, so unmindful of the other men, yet he dressed quickly, as if not wanting to keep me waiting and as if he would be too modest to have me arrive back before he was covered.

I felt quite the sinner, but I couldn't help myself. I had to watch him step into a pair of pants and pull a sweater over his head. Was it actually the shape of his chest or the muscle of his arm that attracted me, or was it just James? He started to pick up his shoes from the floor but changed his mind. As he left the room, I moved back through the wall and found him in the living room, dropping into the couch there, picking up the tiny box that controlled the television.

"Do we have any food?" James called loudly. "Maybe I should go to the store."

Mitch came into the kitchen doorway. "There's half a pizza left. You don't go anywhere. Clean this place up, if you want something to do."

The other gentleman came from the hall, tucking his shirt into his stained trousers. "Stop bitching," he laughed at James. "We have to go to work. You get to sit around here and jack off to MTV."

There was a slight pause before James spoke, as if he were al-

ways translating from one language to the other. "Screw you."
James turned on the television to a movie with cars chasing each
other and muted the sound. He slid down on the couch until he
was almost reclined. Mitch and his friend picked up keys and
denim jackets, and the friend took a half-empty bottle of beer
from the small table in front of James.

"Have fun," he said.

"I'll be thinking of you, Benny," said James without looking
at him.

Benny stopped with the beer almost to his lips. "What did you
say?"

Mitch shoved a tattered cap into Benny's hands. "Ignore him."

James waited until the two men had closed the front door behind them, then he sat up and turned the television off. He
watched the door until he heard the sound of a car engine moving away down the driveway. Then he looked around the room
and found me loitering in the corner.

"He'll be gone for hours," said James. "Wait for me." I
watched him rush from room to room, gathering trash to the
garbage can, dishes to the machine in the kitchen, clothes and
towels to the machine on the back porch.

"If I do any more than that in one day," he said, "Mitch will
think I'm losing my mind."

I watched him put on shoes and take an apple from a drawer in
the icebox. "It's a drawback to the flesh," he said, "having to eat."

A drawback? I hadn't tasted an apple in 130 years. Truthfully,
until that moment, I hadn't missed it. But now I listened to
the crunch as James bit into one and saw the juice spray in a

momentary mist. It was then that I noticed a rose-colored bruise on his cheekbone from his brother's hand. And a fainter gray one on his jaw that I hadn't noticed.

Before I could reach over and touch the place, James turned. "We should get away from here." He locked the house and I followed him across the lawn and down the pavement under a dark sky with one odd shaft of gold that slanted down to some unseen place in the distance. He took a leisurely pace, eating his apple.

We passed the tiny park with the statue of the deer where the swings were decked with shouting children, and chatting women surrounded the picnic table. James turned left at the corner and crossed the street. He tossed his apple core into a pile of raked leaves and looked at me.

"How fast can you travel?"

It had never occurred to me to wonder. "How fast could you travel when you were Light?" I asked.

"Race," he smiled, and suddenly he was running. He was laughing so hard when he saw me on the end of the block up ahead that he had to stop and rest with his hands on his knees. He walked the rest of the way to me and said, "Double or nothing." He pointed to the baseball field a block farther and panted, "Top row of the bleachers, west end."

The park was nothing more than a baseball field, but it was alive with activity—the bottom two rows of bleachers were full of parents, grandparents, young siblings, watching twenty little children in uniform play ball.

James was sprinting toward them. I was so taken with the sight of his lean form as his clothes were pressed to him by the wind that I waited until the last moment to arrive before him. He scrambled to the top bleacher seat beside me, gasping for breath, his hair in his eyes.

"You win," he said. I could tell that he delighted in the power of the human form. I tried to remember the feeling of running with my own legs under me but could feel only envy. He sat taking in the scene. The crowd on the lower benches took no notice of him. On the field, two men coached a tiny boy who struggled to lift a wooden bat that outweighed him.

"Helen," he said, without turning to me. The sound of my name startled me. "I can't explain how it feels to be able to ask you questions no one would understand but us."

"I know."

"The trouble is," he said, and a wave of pain came over me, turning my heart to wood. He was ending our connection, I could feel it, the sound of tragedy. "The trouble is," he said, choosing words carefully, "I find that my feelings for you are changing." Although the people sitting below could not hear him, he lowered his voice. "It's hard to have you with me but not be able to take your hand or kiss you."

This froze me, not just my voice but all thoughts.

He looked down, his expression dark. "I would never turn you away, since I was the one who invited you, but I might have been wrong. I don't know . . ."

It was bewildering, the thrill that he loved me together with the fear of his saying goodbye. I fought to recapture my voice.

"This probably seems absurd to you," he said. "I'm sure your feelings for me are not of this nature."

"I can't lie to you," I said. "I do care for you. But I'm older than you."

"You forget, I'm not a boy," he told me. "I'm only in a boy's body."

This was difficult to remember—James was so young at heart. Now he looked me in the eyes.

"I would court you with a passion, if things were different. You'd never get me off your porch swing."

I laughed at this, but I was still feeling hurt. I sensed that he was preparing to leave me. I remembered this feeling from before I was Light. A man says something meant to be flattering to balance his real message. He'd court me if he could, but the trouble is . . .?

"I'm a coward, though," James sighed, looking back at the field. Another small boy was trying to dislodge a white ball from a red plastic stand, with no luck, as his fans called out words of encouragement.

"I don't have the courage to be without you, now that I've been with you," said James.

"Do you mean to say that if you had more character, you'd leave me?" I thought he might laugh, but he was very serious.

"Please tell me what you want," he said. "I'll do whatever you want me to do. If you find any comfort in being with me, then please forget what I've said. You deserve to be happy. What can I do?"

Don't send me away, I thought.

He looked at me again. "What do you want?"

"I want to taste an apple," I said. *And your lips*, I thought.

There was a sudden surge of cheers as the white ball hopped and bounced across the grass, and the small boy at home plate turned, surprised, to his parents' calls before scrambling into a run toward first base. James was looking over the field, his face gone pale, the pink bruise standing out like a rouged kiss.

"Did I say something wrong?" I said.

"Do you believe I stole this body?" he asked me.

"You told me you saved him," I said. "You didn't chase him out."

"Do you want to save someone?" he asked. His voice was even. He put no emotion into the words. He waited, not looking at me.

Not even when I longed to turn the pages of Mr. Brown's book or bite into James's apple did I conceive of this. It seemed to make no sense. It would be like a knight saying to a scullery maid, "Would *you* like to slay a dragon, as well?"

"I couldn't," I said.

"What if you could?" he asked.

My fears were strong, but the idea of actually being able to touch his hand, flesh to flesh . . .

"But I'm not like you."

He laughed and gave me a side glance. "Not like me?"

"I *want* to be brave."

"I'll help you," he said.

I was trembling again, the way I had when he had first spoken to me. "Tell me what it was like," I asked him. He studied me, gently. "Saving Billy's body, I mean."

The cheers and laughter rose as the children pulled off their hats and went to greet their parents on the grass below.

"*How* did you go inside him?" I wanted to know. Something in my voice surprised and aroused James. I saw the pulse at his throat quicken.

"I lay down in his place, in his body, and fought to stay there until I felt his flesh," he said. "From the inside."

"Can you go out again whenever you want?"

He looked apologetic. "No. There's the rub. I have to stay until the body dies or someone else wants in."

"Someone else?" I was shocked. "Someone like us?"

"Or Billy, if his spirit is still alive somewhere."

"Or something evil," I said.

He didn't comment on that.

"How do you know you can't get out?" I asked.

"I changed my mind after the fourth day and tried to leave." He looked as if he didn't want to describe the outcome. "It was like the pain that would come if I tried to leave my haunting place," he said. "Only worse."

We were alone now. A bird in a tree across the field screamed, piercing my thoughts like a blade.

"I need to think," I told him and let myself sink under our bench. Hiding beneath the bleachers, I watched him walk across the green and imagined James watching Billy, in the same way, before he took possession of his body.

Six

Like a banner, flying but captive, I floated behind him and then sat on the Amelia house roof, next to a rotting softball, for hours until I saw Mitch's car, a patchwork of rusty mixed parts, turn the corner. I dropped through the ceiling to find James lying on his bed, awake. He smiled without surprise to see me appear in the corner.

"You do that so well," he said.

"Do what?"

"Materialize." He laughed.

"Were you not able to pass through objects?"

"In my clumsy way." He looked me up and down, and I wondered whether I was clear or colorful at that moment. "Not with your grace."

I hadn't thought on it for years, but when I was newly attached to my Saint, I practiced moving through her walls and tables and rose bushes, sometimes slowly, like a smoke ring, and other times instantly, like a flash of lightning. It became less and less distracting, and soon I could wander through her rooms with no more thought than bird song moving through a lace curtain.

"Perhaps it's easier for those of us who haunt people rather than places. We're always having to traverse through doors to keep up with them."

Before James could answer, the bedroom door banged open, and Mitch stood fuming in the hall.

"Where the hell did you go?"

James sat up. "Nowhere."

"Bullshit," said Mitch. "I called when I got to work."

"I didn't see a message—"

"I didn't say I left a fucking message, I said I called. So, where were you?"

"I took a walk," said James.

"Do not lie to me." Mitch shook his head.

"I'm not. I walked to the rec center and watched some little league."

"Did I say you could leave?"

"I didn't think you'd care if I took a damn walk. I locked the house."

"Who were you with?"

"No one," he lied, and Mitch could tell.

"I swear if I find out—"

"I'm not getting in trouble," said James.

"I work all day and you sit on your ass watching baseball."

"You're right," said James. "That's not fair. I should get a job."

"You're not quitting school, asshole."

"I meant on the weekends."

"I know what kind of work you used to do."

"You choose the job then," said James. "No shit."

This quieted Mitch. He frowned at his brother, then walked away.

"Did you have enough time alone?" James asked me now.

Mitch came back into the doorway. "Are you talking to yourself?"

"Why do you care?" said James.

"Chris is home for the weekend, wiseass. We're going out tonight."

James looked blank. "Okay."

"Did you really get brain damage?" said Mitch. "You don't know what the hell I'm talking about, do you?"

"Your friend Chris?"

"Rayna's brother. Ring a bell? He's on furlough."

"Well, have fun. I'll be fine."

"Yes, you will," sighed Mitch. "I want you where I can see you tonight. You're coming with us."

During my meditations on the roof, I had nearly decided to let James help me board an empty body, but I was still afraid that it wasn't something my Light spirit could manage. Perhaps James was different. He'd haunted a place instead of a series of hosts. What if that quality had made him stronger than I? I was afraid that if I leapt into a body, I would fail and plummet into my hell, never to see him again. There was no way of knowing.

"Take me to your haunting place," I asked him. I craved to retrace his steps.

"I did," said James. "Where the baseball field is, that was my haunting place."

"Why didn't you tell me?" I felt almost annoyed.

"I thought it would make you sad," he admitted.

And it might have, looking down at the grass and imagining a garden there with a two-year-old James running barefoot or looking out at the playing field and imagining a Light James walking the bases in the dark.

A sudden desire rocked me. I longed to know everything he remembered. Every scent and sound. Every color he could conjure from this life past. I dreaded my own, but I had a deep hunger for his memories.

"Tell me everything you can recall about your life as James."

"I've told you everything I remember."

"You said you remember new things every day," I said. "What did you remember today?"

He thought for a moment. "I remember the sound of our rocking chair," he told me. "It creaked on the left side."

While I watched him prepare for an evening with Mitch, he performed an act as if he were a silent comedian. Although it consisted of nothing more than showing me the fronts of Billy's T-shirts, one after another, it made me laugh so hard, the pictures on the wall beside me fluttered like moths. The images on the shirts—everything from a skull with a snake crawling through the eye socket, to what had to be a puddle of vomit—were in such opposition to James's personality, I was charmed to the core. When he finally pulled off the navy sweater he'd worn all day and tugged a plain brown T-shirt over his head, he was laughing, too. The weave of this shirt was so thin, I could see the shape of his collarbone, the curve of his muscle.

"I apologize in advance for any offense my companions this evening may cause," he said, putting on his jacket.

"Thank you," I said. "But I did live in a men's dormitory with Mr. Brown for two years."

"Did you?" He looked impressed. "Stout-hearted Helen."

After many warnings from Mitch to hurry up, James had to wait for *him* at the front door. When Mitch finally appeared, pulling on his denim jacket, he eyed James suspiciously.

"What did you do, comb your hair?"

"Isn't that what you told me to do fifty friggin' times?" said James.

Mitch shrugged. "Never worked before."

I followed the two of them into the patchy car, sitting behind them in the back seat.

"What're we doing tonight?" James asked.

"Rusty Nail." Mitch pulled out of the driveway and roared down Amelia. "Maybe a movie. Why?"

"I don't care," said James. "Is it too windy back there?" James asked as he rolled down his window. He turned and glanced at me in the back seat. I was too startled to answer. It felt flattering to have him forget that wind couldn't muss my hair. Then James looked at his brother.

"What?" said Mitch.

"I mean . . ." James put his elbow out the window. "I don't want to make stuff . . . blow around." Mitch still looked perplexed. "In the back seat," James added.

"If it wasn't so expensive," said Mitch, "I'd have your brain scanned."

"Shut up," said James.

Mitch shook his head. "Light me a cigarette."

The Rusty Nail was a large, barnlike building with a huge neon sign blazing the name in red light on the outside and an infestation of cowboy and mining antiques floor to ceiling on the inside. A butter churn, cracked and useless, hung mounted high on one wall—a relic from my forgotten days as outdated as a Roman chariot.

The bar was veiled in smoke and the dining room clashed with noise. Mitch and James found Rayna, the young woman from the night before, sitting in the bar with her pirate by her side. Apparently his name was Jack. Others were with them: Chris, a muscular man with a shaved head and a tattoo of a shark on the back of his hand; his sweetheart, Dawn, who had short black hair and wore a short black dress; Libby, Dawn's sister, a buxom girl with black curls and a red shirt with a green dragon on it. They were already drinking.

"Who's this?" asked Libby, giving Chris a push.

"You met Mitch before," he said.

"No, this one," she said, watching James.

"That's his brother, Billy," said Rayna. "Too young for you," she warned.

"Hell, no such thing," said Libby.

I hovered away from them, staying in the corner beside a buffalo head that hung on the wall, as they slid into a large booth. James, who sat on the end, scanned the room until he'd located me. I had been to many restaurants with my hosts, especially Mr. Brown, but with James it was different. He was so conscious of me.

Libby sat between Mitch and James, her hand on James's thigh, the shiny nails, like little crimson beetles, hopping on his knee. He lifted the hand and placed it on her own lap, as if it were a dead rat. She smiled at him and gave him a playful swat on the wrist as if he had been the one flirting.

The others ate and laughed and smoked cigarettes. James sat as far from Libby as he could without falling out of the booth.

Libby stretched, the dragon on her shirt expanding in a mute roar over her breasts. "Are we going dancing?" she asked. "I wanna have fun."

Then there was a discussion about movies, and finally they were moving toward the door and putting their coats back on.

"We got five in our car," Rayna told Mitch. "Can you two take Libby?"

I followed them at a distance as they split into two groups in the parking lot. The older men went to inspect Jack's new truck while the women cornered James against the rusty car.

"Is Mitch okay about Jill dumping him?" asked Dawn.

"I guess," said James.

"Who's Jill?" Libby asked.

"Ex-girlfriend."

"What's this bruise?" asked Rayna, tilting James's face toward the streetlight.

"Nothing."

Libby stood with the other girls but stared across the parking lot at Mitch like a carnival gypsy about to guess his weight.

As they left for the movies, Libby sat in the front with Mitch. James got into the back seat. I joined him. He was so relieved, he slumped back as if exhausted.

"What's wrong with you?" asked Mitch, watching him in the rearview mirror. "Never mind. I'm sorry I asked."

"Want me to sit back there with you?" Libby offered, turning around in her seat and winking at him.

"No!" said James. "No, thank you."

As we drove under the flashing street lamps, James had his hand resting on the door handle. He fingered a tear in the upholstery. He looked at it closer and pulled on the corner of something. It looked like a square of paper. James slid it out. It said Trojans on it. James laughed and felt in the tear again. This time what he pulled out was a tiny envelope. He went white.

"What's wrong?" I asked.

He opened the envelope and looked in, then closed his eyes in pain. He glanced quickly in the rearview mirror. Mitch had his eyes on the road.

"You seem tense," said Libby, putting a hand on the back of Mitch's neck. "I give great back rubs." Then she leaned toward his ear and her hand slid down his arm and out of view. "I give great all kinds of rubs."

The car swerved and Libby giggled.

"Christ," said Mitch. "What're you doing?"

James tried to push the envelope back into the hole in the lining of the door, but it wouldn't go in far enough. Next came the sound of a siren. Lights began to flash in the opposing lane.

"Oh, God," Mitch moaned, slowing and letting his head drop to the back of the seat.

"No," James whispered.

"Is that for us?" Libby sounded shocked.

Mitch parked by the curb and put his head in his hands.

"Don't worry, sugar," said Libby. "I'll talk to him. I can be very persuasive."

The police car parked, facing Mitch's vehicle, pointed the wrong way, lights blazing in through the windshield like a lighthouse warning.

"Do not mess with him," Mitch warned Libby, rolling down his window.

"Good evening," said the police officer. James ducked down behind the seat. "Is everything all right with you folks?" the policeman asked.

"Sure," said Mitch. "Was I speeding?"

"No, sir. Could you please show me your license and registration?"

James motioned me closer and whispered, "Tell me when the other one looks away from our car."

I passed through the door and found that a second man was sitting in the police car.

"Would you mind stepping out of the vehicle?" said the first officer.

"What did I do?" asked Mitch.

"Just step out."

I moved to the patrol car, watching the second officer, who sat inside, chewing gum and filling out a form on a clipboard. Mitch got out of the car, and the first officer shone a small flashlight in his eyes.

"Have you been drinking tonight?"

"One beer," said Mitch.

"Who's with you, sir?"

"Just a friend and my kid brother."

I watched the second officer lean down to take a plastic bag out of a box on the floor. I called to James, "Now!"

James's car door opened. He dropped the tiny envelope down the sewer drain.

"Is that your brother?" asked the first officer. He shone the flashlight in the back seat. "Please step out of the vehicle, sir."

James climbed out of the car. The second officer joined his partner, and they looked at everyone's ID, searched the car with flashlights, gave Mitch and James breath tests to see whether they were intoxicated. Neither was.

"Why didn't you give me a test?" Libby asked, as if insulted.

"Well, ma'am, it seemed quite likely that you had been indeed drinking but that you were not under age and that you had a designated driver."

"Guess what?" she said, as if bragging. "I was the one that made him swerve." She laughed. The officers just stared at her.

"You know what I mean," she said, coyly. "I was getting a little friendly."

"In my opinion," said the first officer, not even inspecting her dragon, "that would seem like a very bad idea." He tore off a ticket from the pad he held and handed it to Mitch.

"Please stay in your own lane in the future," he told Mitch. "And please respect your driver," he said to Libby. Then he squinted at James. "You look familiar."

"He has one of those faces," said Mitch. "Thanks."

Mitch made Libby sit in the back seat alone. I waited beside the car, and when James glanced up through the window and motioned to me, I passed through the car door and sat on his lap.

This was a very strange sensation. I could feel a tingle drum up and down my body everywhere we were touching. I wasn't sure what it felt like to him, but he held the door handle and the back of the car seat tightly. At the theater parking lot, when the others got out of the car, I stood by his door, but James didn't get out.

"Now what?" asked Mitch.

"I'm coming," he answered. He opened the door and stood up slowly. I walked beside him, the others far ahead. He didn't look at me.

"Was that Billy's treasure you found in the car?"

James sighed. "It's frightening not knowing what the boy might have done that'll come back to bite me." His voice was low, but Mitch turned and looked back at him. James shrugged as if he didn't know what he wanted. I admired his mastery of twenty-first-century body language.

In the theater, Dawn and Chris sat together, Jack and Rayna sat together, Libby sat down, and Mitch looked around for James.

"I gotta take a leak," James said. Mitch gave him a wary glance but sat next to Libby when he left. I stayed behind, lingering in the aisle. Rayna offered everyone thin strings of red candy. Libby ate some, chewing with her mouth open, watching Mitch.

"Did anyone ever tell you you look like a movie star?" Libby asked him.

"No."

"That guy from—what's the name of that movie? No, wait, not him." Libby furrowed her brow. "You look like that other guy."

"Who's that actress you look like?" said Mitch with unnoticed sarcasm.

"From the Levis commercial?" she said, delighted.

"No, that other chick," said Mitch. "Ask Rayna."

James returned but stepped into the nearly empty row behind Mitch and the others. He sat one seat in from the aisle and I took the empty seat beside him. When the lights went dim, he leaned back, looking over at me.

Mitch turned around and glared at him. "What's with you?" he whispered.

"Shh," Libby hushed him.

James watched the screen now, but he put his hand on the armrest and I pressed my fingers into his. He had taken off his jacket and I watched the brown shirt rise and fall as he breathed, the movie light shifting shadows over the shape of his arm. The two couples cuddled together, Chris and Dawn head to head, Rayna held a string of candy in her teeth and let Jack nibble it until they were kissing, Libby turned to look at Mitch every few seconds, but Mitch never moved. And James sat still as well, except during a scene in which the man and woman who had been robbing banks and running from policemen were nude, making love to loud music. I dropped my gaze, choosing to look down at James's hand.

I missed silent movies. The music was more integral, like a sound painting. Emotions were not lost but heightened because of the muteness. When you read the actors' eyes, a secret language formed in your mind. If truth be told, more often than not, I watched the audience instead of the screen while attending silent pictures with my Knight. As the light dappled across the forest of faces, I could watch them create inside their hearts each a different story from the same images. It was a shame the way modern movies smothered their stories with songs and loaded every moment with noises and words. Little was left to the imagination.

James watched the screen but shifted uncomfortably to the sounds of moans and cries. Libby whispered something in Mitch's ear, and when she looked back at the screen, Mitch turned and watched her for a long moment.

Libby went with her sister, three of them crammed in the back of Rayna's car. She rolled down the window as they were about to pull away and waved. "Call me some time," she yelled. She grinned with white baby-sized teeth, her black curls bobbing.

Mitch just watched her, looking ill.

"That Libby is a trip," said James as we stood beside the rusty car.

"No kidding." Then he looked at James. "When we got pulled over, why the hell were you hiding in the back seat, for Christ's sake?"

"I wasn't hiding," said James.

"You can't lie worth shit," said his brother. "Don't ever play poker for money."

We drove back to Amelia Street, me in the back seat, James with his arm on the open window.

"Thanks," said James.

"What for?"

"For buying me dinner and stuff."

"Well, when I get you that great job, you can start taking me out."

"Okay."

There was silence again.

"So, what did Libby do to make you swerve?" asked James.

"Not another fuckin' word about her," Mitch groaned.

James laughed.

When I had followed them into the house, Mitch went off to bed and I sat at James's desk. Amid the monster cartoons, there was a new drawing now. It looked nothing like the snarling creatures around it. It was a light pencil sketch of a pair of eyes. An itching pleasure curled into me when I realized who the model must have been. James took a white undershirt and shorts with him to the bathroom and came back wearing them. He sat on his bed.

"So you slept last night," he said.

"Yes."

He lay down on his blanket close to the wall, leaving a space for me. I sat with him.

"Did you have a wife when you were James?" I tried to pretend I didn't care one way or the other.

He hesitated. "I don't think so." Then he asked, "Did you have a True Love?"

"No," I said. "Just a husband."

"I'm sorry." He didn't ask me for details, and I wouldn't have been able to provide many even if he had.

"I wonder why you didn't get all your memories back when you went into Billy's body," I said.

"Maybe it takes time."

I knew *I* didn't want to remember everything. "What was the very first thing you remembered when you became Billy?"

He smiled. "How the knothole in our porch steps looked like a cat's eye."

"I don't think I'll know how to take a body," I confessed. But I wanted with a full-moon fever to touch James.

"Tomorrow we'll look for someone who needs saving," he said quietly.

I reclined, facing him.

"You'll love it," he told me. "When you step into the flesh, you can smell grass again. And drink water. You can grip a stone and throw it. Everything will be fine."

He sounded so sure, I couldn't help but believe him. I had my arm at my side, and now I lifted my hand to his, where it rested on the blanket. Without intending to, my hand passed through him from the thighs up to his heart before I pulled away, tingling. He gasped and his eyes widened in amazement.

"I'm sorry," I said, worried that I had inadvertently stopped his heart. Then I saw his hand move to his shorts and press the hardness under his clothes against his body. His face flushed. I leapt out of the bed to the corner of the room.

"I'm sorry," he echoed. "It's all right." He took the pillow and covered himself with it.

"It's my fault," I stammered. I wanted to fly away.

"I didn't mean to offend you," said James. "You surprised me."

"I'll be back in the morning," I told him.

"No, no," he whispered. "Rest in the bed. I'll sleep on the floor."

I shook my head. "Please," said James. "Otherwise I won't be able to sleep."

He stood, still holding the pillow in front of him. I moved to the bed and lay down, both embarrassed and secretly flattered. A flitting memory of warm skin under a cool sheet made me blush. I lay there and watched him, glad to be in his bed rather than alone on the roof. He turned out the light and stretched out on the floor, tucking the pillow under his head now.

"Maybe tomorrow," he whispered, "you'll taste an apple."

Seven

As THE TWILIGHT before dawn began to form objects out of what had been invisible, the window frame cast a cross on the wall, turning the little room into a chapel. On the floor beside the bed, James sat up with a start, like a dog that hears gunfire. He looked at me where I sat on his mattress. "Don't go anywhere," he said.

While he showered, I wandered through the house. Passing the bathroom door, I heard the echoed hiss of water running, and, as I passed Mitch's room, I heard a voice. I couldn't understand the words, but there was a kind of anguish in the tone. I moved through the wall and found Mitch sleeping with a sheet over him up to his bare chest. I could see his tattoos better now: around his left arm, a Celtic braid; around his right, a chain of thorns; and over his heart, a single sword no bigger than a butterfly. He seemed deeply asleep, but then he spoke.

"You bastard." His face, eyes shut hard, went from anger to pain in one instant. A sob shook him, and he swung his right arm over his body as if trying to free it from something. Then he sat up with a cry and opened his eyes.

"Shit," he muttered. He rubbed his face where tears had not had time to run and shook himself. Looking at the clock, he sighed.

"I hate Third Sunday."

James found me waiting in his room. He appeared in his towel and took clothes from his drawer and closet. He smiled at me. "Close your eyes now."

I sat facing the windows, watching him in the reflection there. I didn't realize he knew I was peeking until he'd buttoned his pants and then pantomimed a strong-man pose looking at the window before he put on his shirt. I turned to him, unable to truly feel ashamed.

We came into the kitchen and found Mitch drinking a cup of coffee. "You ready?" he said to James.

"What for?"

"Third Sunday," said Mitch. "Just 'cause you didn't go last month doesn't mean you get to blow it off. I'm not hanging out with Verna by myself."

James paused. "Verna. Okay." Obviously he didn't remember this monthly ritual. "You get off work okay?"

Mitch frowned at him. "What?"

"You work on Sunday mornings."

Mitch gave him an odd look. "They know about Mom," he said. "I've had Third Sunday half-day for four fucking years. What's the matter with you?"

"My name is Billy, and I'm a recovering drug addict."

This made Mitch laugh, almost spitting his coffee on his shirt.

James seemed pleased. They made breakfast together, not speaking much. As they ate toast and eggs, Mitch began to wind down, like an abandoned clock, his eyes fixed at a distance. By the time they were getting in the car, Mitch was so pale, James asked, "You okay?"

"I hate Third Sunday," was all Mitch would say.

We drove for several minutes in silence, past the business district and toward the suburbs. As we were entering the next town, Mitch pulled into a small shopping center.

"Be right back," he said. The small grocery store Mitch entered was the only shop open.

"I have no idea where we're going," James said to me. But the next moment, Mitch was walking back toward the car with a bouquet of pink carnations.

"We must be going to his mother's grave," James whispered.

Mitch got in, looking taut, and tossed the flowers on the seat between them.

"Nice color," said James.

This made Mitch laugh again, for some reason. James watched him as we drove on. A few blocks later, we pulled into an apartment building lot, and a freckled, beaming woman of perhaps fifty waved to them from where she sat on a cinder block wall. She had a rubber-tipped cane and a shopping bag.

"Here's Aunt Verna," said James, fishing for information.

"Aunt?" Mitch shot him an annoyed glance.

James watched the woman limp toward them, leaning into her cane. "Wasn't she Mom's best friend?" he asked.

"Do we have to talk about this?" Mitch reached behind him to open the back door.

"Hey, boys." Verna got in, sitting forward to see James's face better. "You look okay," she smiled.

The car pulled back out into traffic. The woman buckled herself into the seat beside me. She wore her auburn and gray hair back in a ponytail and dressed like a house painter.

"How are you, Mitch?" she asked.

"Getting by," he said.

As we neared a huge lawn lined with headstones on the right, James stiffened, his eyes scanning each row of graves, but Mitch didn't pull into the gate of the cemetery. We passed it, and the county hospital, pulling into the parking lot of the third building. The sign read: St. Jude's. It was a cement slab, made no cheerier by the clown-colored flowers choking its entrance.

James looked confused, Mitch looked ill, and the woman with them looked quite happy, as if she were going to a party. They parked in a space marked VISITOR, and I followed them toward the entrance. The boys politely slowed their pace for their friend.

"Billy, could you take this?"

James took the woman's bag, and she shifted to pushing with two hands on the cane. When they entered the glass doors, Mitch and the woman went immediately to the front desk and signed a sheet of paper on a clipboard.

"Good morning, Karen," said Verna.

The girl behind the counter smiled. "How's the knee, Verna?"

"Could be worse," she said.

I hovered behind James. "Maybe Billy's mother isn't dead," he said. These sounded like hopeful words, but I could feel a foreboding in his voice.

Mitch started to follow Verna down the hall to the left, but he turned back to James.

"Hurry up." He gestured not so gently with the flowers and a bit of petal flew off.

James went to the counter, picked up the pen attached to the clipboard by a thin chain, and printed on the line below Mitch's name: William Blake.

I saw that the girl, Karen, seated behind the desk, was hiding a book under a file folder. Not a hospital text but a dog-eared paperback with a creased corner to mark her place. For one disconcerting moment, I saw my own hands tearing the brown paper off a small blue book as if having to wait one more second for a new novel would drive me mad. As quickly as the vision came, it was gone.

We followed his brother down the hall, and now it was James who was looking ill. We came through a white door into a sanitized room where a woman in a nightgown printed with tiny Eiffel towers sat motionless in a mechanical bed. Mitch dumped the flowers on the tray beside the patient and took refuge in the chair against the wall, the farthest away. Verna went right to the bed and kissed the staring woman on the cheek, wiping off a smudge of lipstick, the only color in the face. "Hi, Sarah," she said.

James stood in the doorway.

"We're all here, sweetie: Mitch, Billy, and Verna." Verna dragged the chair beside the bed right up to the metal rails and took the limp hand. The nails were cut short and there was a wedding band on the third finger.

"I brought you some surprises." She motioned for James to bring the shopping bag.

James did and stayed close to the bed, lingering at the foot.

"I have the alumni newsletter and a letter from Belle and a recipe I think you'll like." Verna rummaged in the bag and brought out a thin magazine. "The boys brought you flowers. Pink, your favorite."

Now James glanced at Mitch, but he was brooding and did not look up. There was such a strong pulse to his anger, the room was pounding with it.

"Why don't you read to your mother?" Verna gave James the magazine and the chair. "I'll put these in water."

She took the flowers into the small adjoining bathroom, and James looked at the cover of *Alumni News* without opening it. He reached over and gently touched the hand of Billy's mother.

"Class of seventy," said Mitch quietly.

James flipped through the pages until he found the right year. "Announcements," James read aloud. "The planning committee for the thirty-fifth reunion will be meeting in February for a weekend in Lake Florence. Please contact Vicky Hanson if you would like to volunteer. V Hanson at home dot com." James glanced at the waxwork woman.

I moved slowly to the other side of the bed and looked at Billy's mother. She would have been very beautiful if she weren't ill. I reached down to touch her arm but was startled by Verna passing through my body to display the white plastic pitcher of flowers on the bedside table. I retreated to the doorway.

"Deaths," James continued to read. "David Wong died of heart failure August first in Livingston, Vermont. He's survived

by wife Greta Zenner Wong, their two children, and four—"
James stopped reading as Verna touched his shoulder. He let her
have the chair.

"Thank you," she whispered. Then in a much cheerier voice,
she scanned the page. "Let's see. Business. Mark Hogan has
opened his third BMW dealership in Seattle and would welcome
any Colfax alums to apply for jobs. Especially those who made
fun of his sixty-five Ford pickup."

James kept watching Billy's mother. He paused at the end
of her bed again and leaned forward, lightly touching the shape
under the covers that was her foot. Her eyes were open, but she
didn't blink.

"Remember Mark Hogan?" Verna asked Billy's mother.
"They called him wing-nut because of his ears." Verna read a letter out loud from a friend named Belle about her daughter divorcing a gambling addict and their dog Chloe's leg amputation.
James sat in the chair on the other side of the bed from Verna,
unconscious of me since we had entered the room. The longer the
visit stretched, the more it wore on Mitch. He leaned forward,
resting his elbows on his knees, staring at the floor, rubbing his
fists together as if he were waiting for a jury to convict him.

After an hour, a nurse paused in the doorway: The visiting
session was over. By that time Mitch was slumped back in his
chair, a hand over his eyes as if he'd been trying to sleep. Verna
packed her bag.

"Next time I'll bring that short story about the yard sale," she
promised. "It was a hoot."

Mitch got up, battle weary, aching with the weight of his
armor.

"Bye, sweetie." Verna kissed the patient's cheek again. "Say goodbye, boys."

"Bye, Mom," said Mitch without looking at her. He was already out the door.

James waved at the silent woman, a small boyish gesture. "Bye, Mom." He stayed beside Verna, carrying her bag. She seemed to have even more trouble walking out than in. Mitch was waiting in the car by the time they were signing out at the desk. I trailed behind, mesmerized by Verna's lurching gait.

"You take the front," said James opening the door for her.

When he was in the back, James finally looked at me. I knew he wanted to speak, but he glanced in the rearview mirror and changed his mind.

"She loved those flowers," Verna said to Mitch.

Mitch turned on the radio and played music all the way to Verna's apartment building. As soon as the music came on, James leaned toward me and whispered, "She wasn't ringing." When I looked perplexed, he added, "She's not empty. Their mother is still in her body."

I was horrified at the idea of this type of hell. "Without being able to speak or move?"

As we passed the graveyard again, the stones flashing by seemed to catch and hold his eyes like the pendulum swing of a hypnotist's watch. "Seven," he whispered.

"Seven?" I asked.

"Ghosts in the cemetery."

"What?" asked Verna.

"Nothing," said James.

When Verna got out, James got out too and gave her his arm.

"Want me to walk you to your door?" he asked.

She gave him a bemused look. "No, I'll manage."

James bounced into the front seat. I stayed in the back.

"Bye!" She waved, but the car was pulling down the street before James could answer.

"Okay," Mitch sighed. "Light me a cigarette."

When we arrived back at Amelia Street, James pretended to watch television as Mitch read the sports section of the paper. Finally Mitch got his jacket and picked up his keys.

"Can I take a walk if I stay out of trouble?" James asked.

"I guess."

"Since I got brain damage and all," said James, "can you remind me, how long am I grounded for?"

"To be announced," was all he'd say.

I watched James eat a peanut butter sandwich.

"I've always wondered what that tasted like," I said, sitting across from him at the kitchen table.

"Well, now I know what to get you for Christmas." When he'd finished, he drank a full glass of orange juice and said, "Let's go hunting."

"Where will we go?"

"Where people go in September on a Sunday afternoon," he answered. "The mall."

It was strange following James while he rode his bicycle. He'd look about now and then but couldn't focus on me. He locked the bike to a rack outside the huge shopping plaza, and we wandered into the cavernous clatter. The mall was choked with people and echoing with babble. Music of various kinds mixed in disconcerting waves. Mr. Brown hated shopping, so I hadn't been in this sort of place for several years.

James moved slowly against the current, "hunting." Wrinkled faces with thick saucer eyeglasses, baby faces half-hidden by plastic pacifiers, bearded faces with mirrored sunglasses, blue-lidded faces with rings in their noses, spotted faces with braces: All swam past me, misunderstood like foreign words. James walked the length of the vast mall and back again three times with me in tow. He sat on a stone ashtray, his brow dark, watching a flock of youngsters as they ate at little round tables. Finally he rose and began walking again, staying in the center of the wrong side of traffic. I was feeling much less nervous now than I had the night before. It seemed so farfetched, finding an abandoned body, that I felt I had nothing to fear yet. It would take us days to find someone to save.

"That one," he whispered.

Near the entrance to a large store, a woman of perhaps thirty crouched down to tie her running shoe. Her chopped brown hair covered her face; she wore sweatpants and a hooded jacket. I hid behind James as he slowly approached her.

"She's empty?"

"Listen," he whispered. "Don't you hear it?"

As she stood up, the hair fell back to reveal a thin face with a shadow of tension around the mouth. She walked into the store, and we followed three paces behind. I did begin to hear a faint buzz, but I couldn't tell whether it came from the woman or the lights from the jewelry cases.

"What should I do?" My nerves twisted in me like wires.

"Cleave to her," he whispered. "And when she's alone, go into her."

I didn't want my spirit to cleave to anyone except James, but a body seemed to be the only way to truly be with him. "What if there's an evil that isn't afraid of me?"

"She's not on drugs." James stopped when the woman hesitated in an intersection of the aisles. "It won't be like with Billy. She's an athlete—she takes care of her body."

Now the woman turned left, and we circled after her until she opened a door marked "Ladies" on the far wall. James turned and pretended to check the price of a bathrobe on a rack beside him. The empty woman was alone now.

"I'll be right here," said James.

Against my better instincts, I passed through the restroom door just as she was locking it. It was a tiny room with one toilet and one sink, a metal bin, and a warning sign posted for shoplifters.

The woman looked at herself in the mirror as if she'd forgotten why she was there. Perhaps she had an athlete's body, but her face looked far from healthy. It was pale and dark under the eyes, lined with small scars as if she had once been attacked by a cat. I wondered whether I could fit behind those lips and make them smile again.

I didn't need to cleave to the woman, as James was only a few feet away outside the door, but I would soon lose my chance to be alone with her. Although still afraid, I stood beside her at the mirror and touched her left hand where it rested on the edge of the sink.

It felt nothing like touching Mr. Brown or James. Her flesh

had a prickling heat like frostbitten toes being revived in a hot bath. With her right hand, she turned on the tap, then leaned down and took a handful of water, swished it in her mouth, and spat. Then she took a long drink and straightened up. I moved closer, my right hand on her left hand, my right arm in line with her left. She looked in the mirror again, a drop of water on her chin. I could feel the definition of each of her fingers, though our thumbs were on the wrong sides. The hot tingle of her rose up my arm.

The woman was looking into her own eyes, but she frowned now as if she didn't recognize herself. She pulled her left arm in front of her and my right was drawn with it. I moved deeper into her, my right eye now looking out through her left into the re-flection that showed only one woman. Where the darkness around her mouth met the corner of my lips, I felt a tremor. I tried to move out of her, but I was stuck. From the back corner of her heart, a memory flitted by—the woman as a girl of ten, spit-ting into a bathroom sink, gagging and drinking water as she wept, her brown braids hanging in the bowl. Flashes of her hands trying to hold the door handle still in her dark bedroom, but the knob twisting in her grip. Her stepfather mutely smoking a ciga-rette on the porch as her mother scolded her for wetting the bed again.

It was gone as suddenly as it had come. The woman in the mirror was looking me in the eyes, one of my eyes inside one of hers, the other in midair and invisible. She was seeing me, I could tell because her lips curled. But it wasn't the woman who was smiling. That child had fled this body when she was still a teenager. What looked back at me was not a woman at all.

There was a knock at the door. The handle shook. But a twisting doorknob couldn't make this flesh tremble or cringe anymore. These bones now housed something unshakable that rose like a puddle of tar and then, from a hiding place in the woman's belly, fanned up black like the head of a cobra.

"Helen!" James was on the other side of the door and sounded scared. "Don't do it!"

I felt a stinging anger rise through my fingers, bringing with it the urge to take that hand and scratch the cheek where half my face was hidden, tear it bloody. It frightened me so much that I tried to dive out of her. The hand I possessed only jerked into the air and then gripped the sink as I fought for the use of it.

"Helen!" James pounded on the door.

The creature raised its right hand into a fist, pulled back, and broke the mirror. At this sound, James threw his shoulder against the door. Only one shard of glass dropped into the sink—the other pieces reflected monstrous deformities but stayed on the wall. With a disgusted grunt, the creature flung me from the body, and I flew through the wall and into a rack of clothes outside the bathroom. My fear caused the hangers to gently swing around me. I looked out from the circle of cotton nightgowns and saw James step back in surprise as the ladies room door opened and the woman in the hooded jacket walked out, her right hand bloodied on two knuckles. She kept glancing behind her as she strode off, ready to fight.

I moved to James's side and the relief in his face did nothing to calm my panic.

"I'm so sorry," he whispered. I followed him into a corner behind a rack of slippers. "I thought she sounded empty." He had to catch his breath. "The machines in here confused me. It won't happen again. I am so sorry." Finally he looked me in the eyes for a long moment. "Was there someone inside her?"

"Something dark."

"Are you all right?"

"Yes." He knew I was lying—I was still quaking. All I wanted to do was be alone with him and far from everyone else.

Finally we walked out of the store and into the mall again, moving slowly back toward the entrance where we'd started. Without warning, James stopped in the flow of walking people so that a couple holding hands had to part and walk around him on either side. I looked around, not knowing what had caught his attention. He stepped off to the side, up against a huge potted plant.

"There," he whispered, nodding in her direction. "The girl on the bench. Wearing yellow."

I saw a teenaged girl, wearing a yellow linen dress and brown shoes, sitting with a small brown purse under the hands in her lap. She stared at the floor.

"She's empty," he whispered.

"Are you sure?"

"She has a pure ring."

The girl, her blonde hair neatly combed and hanging to her shoulders, looked familiar.

"She goes to Billy's school," James whispered. "Her name's Julie or Judy or something like that."

Then I heard it, a faint sound like a finger moving on the lip of a crystal goblet. And it was coming from this girl. A pair of

women crossed in front of her, bumping into her knees with their shopping bags, but the girl didn't even blink.

"She's safe," he whispered. "I promise."

I couldn't make myself move away from him. "Stay with me," I said.

"As long as I can."

Slow as a snail, I moved to the girl in yellow and stopped a few feet in front of her. She was breathing shallowly, her eyes a lifetime away. I sat next to her. James was watching us from his place beside the plant. I was wondering how difficult it would be to learn the slump necessary to imitate the way twenty-first-century women sit and stand, but this girl had prim posture, almost as if she were wearing a corset.

"Jenny!" A slim woman in a gray dress and high heels came up to the girl. "Let's go, honey." The girl Jenny looked up at the woman, smiling mechanically, and rose smooth as smoke from the bench.

I thrust my hand out and grasped the girl's arm. It didn't feel like touching Mr. Brown or James, but it didn't feel like the dark woman, either. It felt cold like a pincushion of ice. But as Jenny moved, I was pulled along. I floated after her, looking to James for guidance. He nodded encouragement, so I clung to Jenny as she walked with her mother briskly out of the mall and into the parking lot.

"I found something I think will work for the door prize," said the older woman. "It's a Bible Atlas."

"That sounds great, Mom." I was chilled by the dead tone of Jenny's voice.

"Your father's picking up the cake. We'd better get home and change. We're supposed to be at the park at four and it's after three-thirty."

Jenny's mother pressed a button in her purse, and the lights of a maroon car blinked on and off. The vehicle that gave a short beep had a fish symbol and a small sign that said ABORTION IS MURDER on the back fender. The two stepped up to either side. James rolled by on his bike, waved a hand as he passed, and called, "Hi, Jenny!"

Both of them stopped and looked. Jenny's mother watched James disappear between two rows of cars. "Was that a boy from school?" she asked.

"I don't know," said Jenny.

Eight

———

"I IRONED YOUR BEIGE SHORTS, honey," said Jenny's mother. "Unless you think it's too cold."

"That sounds fine," said Jenny.

I was stowed away in the back seat, tasting terror like a metal bit. What had I done? I was cleaving to a host I would never want to choose. What if we'd made a mistake again and something waited inside her?

"Did your blue sweater come back from the cleaners?"

"I think so." Jenny looked out the window, but her eyes were focused on the glass rather than on what lay beyond.

"Teri and Jeff are going to sing a duet." Jenny's mother tapped her heavy diamond ring on the steering wheel as she drove. The car felt like a hearse—large, clean, and the outside sounds were strangely blocked out.

"They have such nice voices," Jenny droned.

"I should get my camera," said the mother. "Remind me."

"Get the camera," Jenny murmured.

———

"I mean before I get back in the car, silly," she laughed.

The garage they pulled into was nicer than Billy's house. It was huge, large enough for two cars and a boat, though it was empty when we pulled in. There was an immaculate counter with a shiny sink, a spotless white freezer, and a tool shop board with every hammer and saw perfectly outlined in white paint on the wall. There was a poster of a descending dove on the door and an ivy plant with a cherub wind chime beside it hanging from the ceiling.

Jenny's mother pushed a button under the steering wheel and waited for the mechanical jaws of the garage to close behind them before she got out of the car. While the garage door was only halfway down, I looked back, hoping to see James and his bicycle. If he had followed us, I could change my mind and fly to him. But he wasn't there.

"Hop hop," said the mother.

Jenny followed the woman into the house with her purse clutched to her middle. They came through an enormous sparkling kitchen, then Jenny passed her mother, who stopped at the dining room table to look at the headline on the newspaper neatly folded there.

I followed Jenny into her bedroom and watched her undress. I couldn't imagine trying to step into her flesh while she was in motion. She moved like a sleepwalker, folding her dress and slip daintily before setting them in the laundry hamper. She put her hosiery in a zippered net bag and stored her shoes in a box on the closet shelf.

Standing in her matching white panties and bra, she paused as if in a trance. *She's stopped,* I thought.

"Are you ready?" her mother's voice called from down the hall.

Jenny blinked and began to move again, like a machine responding to the turn of a crank. She found shorts and a sweater on hangers and put them on. Another box in the closet held white canvas shoes, and from a dresser drawer filled with socks neatly rolled together in little balls, she took a white pair.

"Are you almost there, missy?" called her mother.

"Almost," Jenny called back. She pulled the socks on, right and then left, sitting on the edge of the bed. Then the shoes, tying the laces in symmetric bows. Now she sat staring again as if her pilot light had blown out. Again she was still, but I was too scared to touch her.

I looked around her room, decorated in little-girl white lace and yellow roses. The dressing table, the rug, the desk: Everything was spotless. The walls were bare except for a painting of praying hands and a poster of Jesus with children gathered at his knee.

The girl sat as if hypnotized, and I stood in front of her. She was so young. It would have seemed more appropriate for us to choose a woman of my own age, but we needed an abandoned ship, and after all, James was in a body just as young. I was nervous. If I somehow floundered and could not cling to this child from the inside of her flesh, perhaps I would fall back into hell. She very well might be the last thing I saw before an eternity of pain.

Sitting beside her, I touched her hand, the delicate, tan fingers on the white lace bed. She must be empty, I thought. I didn't feel that falling sensation or the heat of danger, only an absolute stillness, like touching a statue. I recoiled, but she so generously lay down on her back now, as if surrendering, that I had to try. I reclined into her cold space. She seemed quite hollow, but there could still be a blackness hiding. A terrifying shuddering overwhelmed me. It was so violent, I jumped up again and looked down at the girl. She took a deep breath and sat up.

"Five minutes," her mother called.

Jenny rose and went to the dressing table. There was no perfume or makeup there. Only a brush and comb and a white Bible. She took the brush and slowly pulled it through her hair, smoothing the locks with her free hand as she made each stroke. Now she pulled the few gold strands of hair out of the brush bristles and, laying the brush back in place, dropped these into the white wicker wastebasket.

I followed her into the bathroom that stood open to the hall and watched her clean her teeth with a pink toothbrush.

Do it, I told myself. But I couldn't.

"Don't forget the camera," Jenny called as she rinsed her brush, watching nothing in the mirror.

"Thank you!" Jenny's mother came into the doorway. "Let's hit the road."

Jenny smiled but only with her lips. Her eyes were not even living.

"You look very pretty, honey," said Jenny's mother, as she drove.

"Thank you," said Jenny. "You look nice, too." The mother had changed into a cotton dress and matching cardigan, but I don't think the girl had even looked at her clothes. I sat in the back seat, feeling like a coward.

"Did Brad Smith ask you out?" said the mother.

"No," said Jenny.

"He's probably shy. I think he will. His mother already talked to me."

They pulled into the lot of a large park where fifty cars were already waiting. A vast pergola sheltered three rows of picnic tables covered with thin plastic—one set of two tables was crammed with dishes of all shapes wrapped in silver foil, like a graveyard for food.

"Cathy, where's Dan?" a woman asked Jenny's mother.

"He went to get the cake. He should be back by now. Are you sure he's not playing softball?"

Jenny walked to the closest table where a woman with a bottle was feeding her baby.

"Hi, Jenny," said the woman.

"Hi." Jenny blinked at the baby. "Hi, Randy."

I followed Jenny to the grass field where several people sat on blankets and beach chairs, calling out to the others who were playing ball on the makeshift diamond. The only man in a dress suit came up to bat. Someone called, "Go get 'em, Pastor Bob." Jenny clapped her hands mildly but was staring into the sky and missed seeing Pastor Bob hit a fly that was caught by the second baseman. I wanted to touch her again, but there were so many people.

A dozen women set out stacks of paper plates and boxes of plastic forks. When a gray-haired woman in a red baseball cap rang a hand bell, everyone migrated to the picnic tables, but no one sat down. The pastor, sweating but smiling, held up a hand and everyone closed their eyes. Everyone but me. Pastor Bob closed his eyes as well. It was silent except for a baby crying.

"Dear Lord," the preacher boomed. "Thank you for your many gifts. Bless this food to our good and your will. Protect all those in your flock who cannot be with us here today. In the name of Christ Jesus, Amen." The Amen was echoed, even by Jenny. When the preacher lowered his arm, he laughed and said, "Ladies, tell us menfolk the plan here."

As the woman with the bell pointed out how the food line should work, a man in a green polo shirt came hurrying up with a large pink box. Jenny's mother frowned at him.

"Where have you been?" she complained. "I was worried."

"Oh, it was my fault. I forgot to gas up the van. I had to walk a mile to buy a gallon."

She gave an unsure laugh but accepted the kiss he planted on her cheek.

"Hi, Puppy," he said to Jenny. Then he was gone, taking the cake box to the food table.

"Hi, Daddy," she said, not noticing that it was too late for him to hear.

I watched as Jenny walked through the line, taking a tiny bit of each dish onto her plate, smiling and nodding as the boy who sat beside her talked and talked. She ate very little and wiped her mouth with a paper napkin after every bite, meticulous as a ballerina practicing at her barre.

When the trash was cleared away, the pastor had the men bring most of the wooden benches, the folding lawn chairs, and the blankets to the grass. They put these in a large circle and everyone gathered. Some men stood behind the circle. No woman stood. The shadows were lengthening across the park. The pastor told the story of Daniel surviving all night in the pitch dark surrounded by hungry lions.

I stood behind Jenny. Her posture was neat, but her head was down, as if she were in prayer. She sat on the end of a bench with her mother beside her and her father at his wife's feet, sitting on a towel. Beside Jenny a little boy lay on the lawn with his head in his mother's lap, falling asleep as she stroked his hair.

"And we have the faith of Daniel," Pastor Bob was saying. "Don't we? Because we know God will shut the mouths of our enemies. When we obey His will, we can trust Him to protect us, can't we?" A few voices answered softly, *Amen.* "Let us pray."

Jenny's eyes closed and her hands folded. I decided I couldn't wait forever. I stepped over the sleeping child and sat where Jenny was sitting. The ringing sound of crystal vibrating was all around me. I felt as if I had pressed myself into cold marble. I stayed in her, and in a moment, I started shaking. It was frightening, but I wouldn't let myself run. I tried to see James in my mind's eye, smiling at me. The ringing stopped with a popping sound. I felt like an ice sculpture starting to crack into pieces. Then it happened. I felt the shape of her, the shape of myself, inside the fingers and shoulders and knees of her. I even felt the snug shoes and the difference between her warm arms inside her sweater and her cool legs exposed to the breeze. I could feel the tickle of Jenny's hair brushing my cheek. My hand went to my mouth when I heard myself cry out in amazement. I opened my eyes to see every face in the circle turned to me, and then the ground flew up and I was in the dark.

"Give me that blanket."

I could hear excited voices. Rose-colored flashes appeared as my face was passed over by shadows and then sunshine glowing through my eyelids. *My eyelids.* I opened my eyes and saw a cluster of heads hovering with concern.

"It was during the prayer," someone whispered.

"Maybe it was the Holy Ghost," came another voice.

"She just didn't eat enough," said Jenny's father. He picked me up under my arms and knees. "Let's not get too excited."

I was overwhelmed by having so many people pay attention to me. I couldn't speak. The feeling of the father's strong arm around me, the texture of his shirt felt through my own skin. I was still shaking.

"Oh, honey," I heard Jenny's mother coo.

The father set me down on a bench by one of the picnic tables. I couldn't help myself. I began to cry, sobbing into my hands and, to my surprise, making tears, the salt of a forgotten sea.

"Maybe she saw a vision," someone said.

"She's just embarrassed," said Jenny's mother, stroking my hair anxiously. "Everyone go back to prayer meeting. I've got her."

I finally took a deep breath and stopped crying. Jenny's mother, Cathy, tucked the blanket on my lap around me tightly and gave me a tissue. I wiped my wet face with the fragile paper and looked at her.

"What happened, Jen?" she asked.

"I felt so strange," I said, startled by the sound of my words spoken in Jenny's voice. My teeth were chattering.

"Are you about to start your period?" she whispered.

"I don't know," I said.

"It's okay," said Cathy. "We'll check your calendar when we get home."

"Mother?" I just wanted to say the word and see her respond.

"What, hon?"

I laughed, which was apparently an odd thing to do.

"Do you need something to eat or drink?" she asked, looking concerned.

"Do you have an apple?"

"I don't think so." Cathy scanned the somewhat ravaged food table. "Lime jello? How about some grape punch?"

"Yes, please." My back was to the grass field. I could hear two soft voices singing a lullaby hymn. I turned around now to see the pastor and Jenny's father, Dan, hovering on the outskirts, listening. A man wearing a police uniform stood with them, a baby sleeping on his shoulder.

Cathy brought me a bright yellow plastic cup half filled with dark liquid. I held it with both hands. I had seen plastic before but never felt it. It was as smooth as it looked but had a faint, peculiar scent. I found that if I squeezed the cup and released, it made a popping sound. Cathy gave me a strange look as I drank the punch.

"Oh, my," I whispered. It was shocking how glorious it tasted.

"You're going to bed early tonight," said Cathy.

I was too fascinated to be afraid now. Everything was astounding. Being touched. Smelling people, their sweat, and perfume, and even the soap they used to wash their clothes as they gave me hugs goodbye. The power of all those eyes, shining right into mine. The weight of things, like the punch in my cup. The weight of me as I stood and moved. I was lightheaded with curiosity. I wanted to run and sing and walk down a street where people would turn a shoulder to pass without colliding with me.

Unlike the woman at the mirror, I saw no flashes of Jenny's past, no glimpse of the trauma that had caused her to flee. Like Billy's body, Jenny's came with no memories at all. I remembered then that James said it wasn't until he was inside Billy that he started to remember his own life as one of the Quick. I felt Jenny's heart start to race at the idea. I was a little afraid of what I might recall about myself. But nothing came to me at first.

"Dan," Cathy whispered loudly. "Let's go."

After he exchanged a few quiet words with Pastor Bob, Dan came and took my hand. "Want to ride with me or with your mother?"

"I have no preference," I said.

Cathy took the blanket from my lap and folded it. "You ride with me."

"See you at home." Dan headed for a white van, and Cathy put her arm around my waist.

"I can walk," I said, for although I found the warmth of her arm against my body comforting, I wanted to walk free. I stretched and even tried a little hop in my step. I marveled at how strong my legs felt. The way my strides made my hair swing delighted me. I laughed out loud.

"Well, I guess we're feeling better," said Cathy, uncertainly. It wasn't until we were sitting in the car that she asked, "Jen, you didn't . . ." She hesitated. "Have a vision or anything, did you?"

I just looked at her for a moment. "Not that I remember," I said.

Once at home, I hurried to Jenny's room, closed the door, and looked in the mirror. I could still hardly believe it was true, but I was indeed this hazel-eyed girl with blonde hair and slender tan fingers. I sat on the bed and took off my shoes. I wiggled my toes, staring at them as if I'd grown wings. I hopped up and made a few turning jumps, landing on graceful bending legs. Quickly, I took off all my clothes, even the matching underwear, hypnotized by my naked form in the closet door mirror. I felt the soft smooth breasts and the tiny hollow of my belly button. I came close to the glass and held up my hair to examine the shape of my ears. What a gift, to be suddenly young.

For a moment, while I studied the maze of Jenny's ear and the line of her neck, I saw another throat, like a ghost image an artist has painted over. This throat was paler, the ear a little rounder, the hair behind it curled instead of straight. I'm remembering, I thought. But I was startled out of my vision by a rap on the door.

"Are you decent?" Cathy called from the hall.

"Just a moment." I looked in the closet, then opened the dresser drawers. I took the top pair of neatly folded pajamas and stepped into the bottoms. "I'm coming," I called, buttoning the top.

I opened the door and Cathy went immediately to the top desk drawer, pulling out a small date book. "Let's see," she said. "No, you shouldn't start for another week and a half." She replaced the book. "Tell me when you've washed up, and I'll come read with you." Then Cathy looked at the room and frowned. "It looks like a tornado hit."

"I'm sorry," I told her.

She shrugged and went down the hall. I grabbed the clothes and put them into the hamper, except for the shoes, which I put back in the box that I had seen Jenny take them from. Then I went into the bathroom where I had watched Jenny brush her teeth. This was a strange and wonderful task, scrubbing my teeth with a brush, tasting peppermint. And what a peculiar thing, the need to urinate and the sensation of doing so. Everything was new, as if I had never even been in my own body when I was Quick. I came back to my room and sat at the dressing table, brushing my hair over and over again, I was so taken with the feeling. Not only was I Quick again, I was young. It was unbelievable.

"All ready?" Cathy asked, standing in the doorway with a small magazine in her hands.

"Yes." I moved to the bed when she sat on the edge of it. She pulled open the covers, so I slid in, delighted by the cool smoothness of the sheets. Cathy put the magazine down for a moment and with the sides of her hands thumped the covers on either side of my legs to hug me in like a cocoon.

"Nice and snug," she said. "Should I choose first?"

"Very well."

She gave me an odd glance. I tried to think of how Mr. Brown's students would reply. "Okay," I said.

Cathy opened the small periodical and flipped through a couple of pages. "Here's one called 'The Miracle of the Missing Key.'" She cleared her throat and began to read. "'By Amy Christopher. My father tells me that I am alive today because an elf once stole his magic key.'" Cathy spoke with the inflection of a nanny reading to her infant charge. "'I know it wasn't an elf, and I know in his heart he knows it too. It was an angel of God that saved me when I was only ten months old.'"

It was a pedestrian piece, but I would've forgiven the writer anything. Someone was reading *to me*. Cathy smiled when she finished. "Your turn."

I took the magazine. It was called *In His Time*. I turned the pages with pleasure. I stopped on a short poem.

"'Narrow the Way.' By Prentice Dorey," I read aloud.

> Always my grandfather stood at the gate,
> A sweat stained hat in his powerful hand.
> Always he pointed the stranger the way
> To the bridge he had built on his ancestors' land.
> He'd run his long fingers through gray thinning hair,
> When the river was high or the storms had rushed in,
> And pointed the way to each wagon or cart,
> Never barring the path, never seeing their skin.
> One farmer asked him if the trek would be safe.
> He told him, "Stay to the path's what you do.
> Don't look down. Don't turn back. It's narrow, that's true.
> But if you keep going then God gets you through.'

I teetered on the verge of tears but laughed instead. Cathy gave me an odd look as she took the magazine.

"Don't forget to say your prayers." She kissed me on the cheek, and I could smell rose-scented lotion and something like lemon in her hair. "I'll send your father in."

I was so intrigued by reading even a trite poem that I jumped out of bed as soon as she had left the room and looked for Jenny's books. To my amazement, there was no bookcase in the room. There were only a handful of books standing between two thin metal bookends on top of her dresser: four schoolbooks (science, history, government, algebra), *Be a Better Baby Sitter*, and a Bible dictionary. I felt a pang, as if the universe had played a trick on me.

I jumped back under the covers as I heard footsteps in the hall. Dan came into the room and smiled at me. "Feeling better?"

I nodded. He crossed to the bed and kissed the top of my head. His skin smelled of soap, but his shirt, for some reason, smelled of gardenias.

Nine

I STAYED IN MY ROOM, far too excited for sleep. I wanted to wait until the others had gone to bed before exploring, so I sat down and read Jenny's American history book. I had read history books with my hosts over the years but had still never gotten used to certain terms, such as *antebellum*—the time before the War Between the States. It did not seem so very long ago to me. I myself predated the war. Like the use of the term *antediluvian*, which divided time into two parts, before the great flood and after, *antebellum* implied a separation of time. I had been left behind in the former pages of history. But Jenny's body was my escape into the present world.

Finally the house had quieted into the tiny clicks and creaks audible only when humans are at rest. I made a furtive path through the silent dining room and into the night kitchen. I was afraid to turn on the overhead light, so I lit only the small bulb over the top of the stove. A bowl of green pears sat like an offering on the altar of the huge counter. I took one and bit into it, so instantly intoxicated that I had to sit down to finish it. I cast about in the cupboards and found a plastic jar of Country Fair peanut butter. I opened and smelled it, laughing out loud. I found a spoon in one of the drawers and tasted the paste. Even more glorious than grape punch.

Next I explored the icebox. After sniffing a piece of bread wrapped in foil, I crushed a corner of the odd wrapping. So thin, the silver skin was almost weightless. The whole kitchen had a peculiar cleanliness about it. Except for the pears, every morsel of food was sealed away from the world. Cans of vegetables, jars of sauce, rice trapped in a rubber box. I missed the way Mrs. Brown let onions and avocados swing in chain baskets in the pantry. And then I remembered the kitchen of my childhood, where everything seemed to be part of the food. The flour and the table were one. The pot that hung in the dark fireplace always smelled of soup. The cotton bags of beans and potatoes were free to breathe the same air. Cathy's kitchen seemed to treat food with suspicion. I preferred even Billy's untidy kitchen to this strange room. At least at Billy's house, a mouse could survive for a night or two.

I was startled by my own reflection in the tinted glass of the upper oven door. I didn't recognize myself, for a moment, because of Jenny's face looking back at me. I tensed as I realized that Jenny's spirit might be somewhere nearby. James had seen Billy once. Could Jenny be watching me? I looked in every corner, but I was alone, of course. Why would she or Billy want to stay here and watch the lives they had deserted?

It was then that I noticed a set of city directories, one with yellow and one with white pages, stacked on top of each other under the wall phone. I considered looking for the name Blake, but I was afraid. It was late, and I thought I might wake Mitch.

I darkened the kitchen and sneaked through the house, exploring every room except the master bedroom. Jenny's home was as neat as a church sanctuary and like a church had no bookshelves. Finally I found the study, next to Dan and Cathy's room. To my relief, there was an entire wall of books. I turned on the small desk lamp and started to read titles. On the top shelf, all the books were about business practices and strategies, contract law, and conducting research. The next row down held "how-to" books—how to increase sales, how to influence people, how to repair your own car, how to improve your public speaking skills. On the next shelf was a series of books on audiotape—steps to success, improve your memory, *The Bible Diet*, the New Testament, and several tapes labeled "sermon" and then the date. The next row down, the entire row, was filled with books about golf or crafts, separated into his and her sections. The bottom two shelves held a set of New House Encyclopedias. Not one novel. Not one book of poetry. Disappointed, I gave up.

As I lay in the comfort of clean sheets, I remembered the poem I'd read to Cathy. The image of rain swelling a river, rows of crops turning into long thin islands, the soil around roots softening until a tree might be ripped out of the earth and fall. Finally, human sleep, that sweet and heavy drug, held me down for the rest of the night.

"Rise and shine!" Cathy thumped on my door the next morning, frightening me out of bed. So unaccustomed was I to the slumber of the Quick, I could barely open my eyes.

During my Light years, I had been in rain, under waterfalls, close to faucets and bathing showers hundreds of times, but now, as I turned on the shower tap and felt the explosion of cold water stinging like ice on Jenny's skin, I was terrified. I jumped back from the showerhead, cowering on the little rug. The sound and sensation of freezing water brought my stomach into my mouth. I swallowed the sourness back and reached into the tub. I hit the small lever that channeled the water away from the shower above and let it gush from the lower tap. Still frightened, I reached into the stream of liquid. Now it was warm as breast milk. A moment later it was hot as soup. I adjusted the knob and kept my hand in the water but my body outside the tub until I could breathe again. Finally I lowered a second lever, the same mechanism as the Browns' bath, and the water began to fill the tub. I stepped in carefully and let the water rise only six inches. Using my cupped hands, I washed myself, even my hair, in baptismal dips, trying to chase the images of rotting wood out of my mind.

It took all my wits to manage simple things, such as using a pink plastic razor or an electric hair dryer. Behind the mirror on the wall, I found a cupboard of little bottles. I read the tiny printed instructions from the doctor: TAKE ONE TABLET THREE TIMES A DAY AT MEALS. And the descriptions of each pill's purpose: FOR PAIN OR FEVER. I was reminded how the lives of children had changed so in the last hundred years. Once boys and girls were sent from the room whenever adult subjects were to be touched upon. Now they saw murders and rapes every night on television. Perhaps this was why Mitch had to search Billy's drawers for poison and why Jenny's bathroom had to be stocked with little blue pills for anxiety, little yellow pills for stress, and little white pills for sleep.

I believe that I successfully applied all the daily products I found in Jenny's bathroom and apparently chose an acceptable outfit—a dark green dress and a light brown sweater—to wear to school, as Cathy made no complaint. It was when I began to look in the kitchen cupboards for food that she regarded me curiously.

She opened a drawer and placed a metal can in my hands. "Where's your book bag?"

I returned to Jenny's bedroom and found a tan and brown plaid canvas bag under my desk. I put all four schoolbooks into it and the brown purse I had seen Jenny with in the mall the day before. I came back into the kitchen, sitting down and opening the can of my breakfast with some difficulty. I drank a sip and smiled. I had almost forgotten chocolate. I looked over to see Cathy staring at me in disbelief. She held out a plastic straw, wrapped in white paper. I took it, removed the paper, and slid the straw into the drink.

"What's got into you?" she asked.

"Do I always have this for breakfast?" I said, forgetting that it would sound odd.

Perhaps misunderstanding me, she replied, "I can get the strawberry next time, if you like it better."

I sat sipping, thinking of pine trees for some reason. But a moment later, Cathy gave me a pat on the shoulder as she passed.

"Prayer Corner." It was obvious that she expected her daughter to understand this command. I left the can behind and followed her down the hall and into the room past the master bedroom, the one with the enormous television screen. I had peeked into this room the night before while in search of books but had taken little notice of the three white chairs set in the corner. This morning, they were lighted by a bright bulb from above. The chairs faced one another and sat only a foot or two apart. On one chair sat a Bible, on one a brown leather book.

Cathy picked up the Bible and sat in the chair it had occupied. When I hesitated, she patted the brown book.

"We don't want to run late," she said.

I lifted the book and sat. Cathy closed her eyes, placed her hand on the Bible, and took a deep breath as if she were listening to a lovely symphony I couldn't hear. I looked at the book in my own lap. It was imprinted with the word *diary*. I opened the cover, and the frontispiece was labeled *May 15 to*. The ending date was left blank. The binding would have held perhaps a hundred pages, but I found that almost half the sheets, the ones at the front, had been torn out. Not cut out or carefully removed but ripped out, leaving the binding thread stretched and jagged parchment teeth agape. The first page remaining was dated July 7. Despite what was printed on the cover, the words neatly written in blue ink on this first page were not a diary entry, but a long quotation from the Bible.

"Exodus twenty—Then God spoke all these words saying: I am the Lord your God who brought you out of the land of Egypt, out of the house of slavery. You shall have no other gods before me."

It was the Ten Commandments. Jenny's handwriting, for I was sure it was hers, having seen the notes in her schoolbooks, was small, neat, and deliberately dark. I flipped forward a few pages and found a Scripture passage from Proverbs.

"A child who gets his own way brings shame to the mother."

Dan appeared so suddenly that I slapped the diary shut. He sat in the third chair, smiled at Cathy, and then they both closed their eyes. Fascinated, I watched. Moments crept by in silence. When Dan spoke, I jumped so badly the diary slipped to the floor.

"Heavenly Father." His voice boomed around the room, far louder, I thought, than God would require. "Open our ears to your word. Cleanse our hearts of sin. Turn our will to your will. In Christ's name, Amen."

I quickly dipped down and retrieved the diary from the carpet as Jenny's parents opened their eyes. Dan crossed his legs and took a pen from his dress shirt pocket, offering it to me without bothering to make eye contact. I took the pen and Cathy, who had been cheerfully patting it like a baby on her knee, passed the Bible on to her husband. He found the page he wanted and began to read aloud. I watched his hands, spread across the cover of the book, his fingers hard and tanned. He wore no wedding band.

"You yourself have seen what I did to the Egyptians, and how I bore you on eagles' wings, and brought you to myself."

As he read, I watched Cathy's shoe. She swung her crossed leg, her foot tapping the air soundlessly. Her ankle was thin as a girl's, her shoes flat, black, and strapped like a child's Sunday school slipper.

"Obey my voice," Dan read, "and keep my covenant, then you shall be my own possession among all the peoples, for all the earth is mine."

When he was done, he handed the Bible back to Cathy. "Proverbs twenty-two three."

———

Cathy dutifully flipped to the correct passage and swiveled in her chair to face me. She breathed in to begin reading but stopped when she glanced up at me. "Proverbs twenty-two three," she prompted. Dan looked over as well. I finally understood that I was to write in the diary in their presence. I opened the journal and flipped to the first blank page. Now my heart started thrumming. Could I print like Jenny? I fumbled trying to open the pen, discovering that it needed to be twisted to reveal the writing point.

"Proverbs . . ." Cathy prompted again.

I began to take dictation, printing with small neat letters as close to Jenny's hand as I could manage. Dan was the one swinging his foot now as Cathy read.

"The prudent sees the evil and hides himself." Cathy waited while I worked. Although the passage brought me no joy, the pen itself was a wonder. The best invention since the printing press.

"'But the naive go on,'" read Cathy, "'and are punished for it.'"

I completed my writing and tentatively offered the pen to Dan again. He took it and stood, glancing at me as he did. "Up."

Hesitantly I rose. He stood, hands on hips, never looked me in the eye but scanned me: my face, my body, my legs. He gave Cathy a small metal square from his pocket as she glared at him.

"It's a school dress," she said. "It didn't shrink." Cathy startled me by leaning over and checking the distance from my knee to the hem of my dress with the little measuring tape.

"She's growing," said Dan.

"She's not getting taller," Cathy complained.

"Turn," said Dan, as Cathy gave him back the tape. When I

hesitated, Cathy moved her hand in a circle, so I imitated the gesture and turned all the way around once. Dan scanned my body again. "Take off your sweater."

Cathy seemed insulted, as if inspecting Jenny's clothes was her job and she was being demoted. "You saw this dress last week," she told him. "The light doesn't show through, the straps are hidden, there's no jiggle."

"Cathleen." His tone warned of a danger close at hand. I began to peel back my sweater, but Dan waved us away. "Have a good day, ladies."

As Cathy drove me to school, it finally began to occur to me what a fish out of water I was. Because of her books, at least I knew that Jenny was in a history, a government, a math, and a science class. I felt a bit lightheaded with nerves, and the odd cherry-scented perfume Cathy must've put in her car didn't help. We passed two girls, one in a cheerleading uniform, walking to school.

"What do you think about cheerleading?" I asked Cathy, hoping this would tell me whether I was expected at a practice.

"We went over this in junior high. The uniforms have bare midriffs and the choreography is inappropriate."

She pulled up to the curb in front of the high school.

"Have a good day, hon." She tilted her perfectly groomed head toward me, so I gave her a kiss on the cheek.

When I got out, I leaned down and looked at her through my open door. "Do I look all right?"

"You look fine."

"What about sports?" I said.

She blinked at me. "You want to play in a sport?" she asked. "You gave up ballet lessons so you'd have more time to study."

"Never mind." I smiled and let the door close.

I tried not to make eye contact with the other students, embarrassed not to know their names or which ones would expect to be my friends. I went to the administration office and waited at the counter until the receptionist, Miss Lopez, hung up the phone. Mr. Brown called her Olivia.

"What can I do for you, Miss Thompson?" she said.

"May I have a copy of my class schedule?"

She looked curious. "Who's it for?"

To my surprise, a spontaneous lie rolled off my tongue. "Church."

"No problem." Olivia glided her rolling chair to the computer on a table against the wall and typed in a few words. The room smelled of glue and spilled ink.

I felt my heart skip a beat as a familiar voice struck my ear.

"Any messages?" asked Mr. Brown. He leaned over the counter as Olivia handed him one small slip of paper from the slot marked M. BROWN on the wall.

"Thanks," he said.

I looked up at him. He stood right beside me reading the note, holding his briefcase, wearing the blue shirt he so often wore on Mondays. He looked like he always had to me, but now I could feel the faint heat of his body, smell the leather of his case and even the soap he'd showered with, like sage. I was stricken by his solid, textured complexity. I could tell he hadn't brought his novel with him. When he had the box squeezed into his briefcase, the latch nearly wouldn't close. Today his briefcase was light and empty. For this I felt sorry. But I was thrilled to be standing so close to him. I took a breath, meaning to speak to him, but remembered suddenly that he wouldn't know me. He may not even know Jenny. Without glancing up, Mr. Brown turned and walked out. Although I had become as tangible as he, I was just as invisible to him as I had been before. Olivia was on the phone again.

Next I glanced out the window. There was James, standing on a stone bench, scanning the crowd of students. Blood surged into my cheeks.

"Here you go," said Olivia, handing me the sheet of paper.

I practically ran out of the building and into the quad, but James was nowhere to be found. *I* was the one scanning the crowd now.

I knew the school, the numbering of the rooms, and the names of some teachers but not many students. Two girls I couldn't place greeted Jenny as they passed, but I only smiled. I sat dumbly through a lecture on sediments, Building A, room 100. I jumped so when the passing bell rang that the boy sitting behind me laughed.

I was making my way through the crowd toward Building C when I saw a familiar head in the distance, the dark hair blowing. James was turning around, stretching on his toes to see over the others. I was paralyzed with excitement, standing perfectly still until he had turned toward me. He froze when he saw Jenny's face. I watched while he wove through the crowd in my direction. Finally I started to weave too, losing sight of him at once because I was not tall enough.

When he sidled around a group of girls and was suddenly standing only a few feet in front of me, I stopped short.

"Helen?" he asked.

I nodded. There was an odd moment when I didn't know whether we should pretend that we were just meeting each other. It lasted only a heartbeat. Both our book bags hit the ground, and he pulled me into his arms so hard the breath went out of me. It was overwhelming, actually feeling his face pressed to me and his arms so hard and his heart beating. The scent of his hair. The heat of his skin unlocked my tears. I heard a few students make rude noises and one girl laughing. James let me go, but took my hand, pulling me along through the crowd. I had to run to keep up. He swung me behind the recycling bins where we had first spoken, took my face in his hands, and kissed me, struggling in wonder at my realness—probing at the muscle and bone and moist moving warmth of me.

We stopped when the bell rang again. This could have been an hour or five minutes, I couldn't tell. He was pressing me against the wall and put me on my feet now. We were both out of breath. James glanced toward the pathway to see whether we were being watched, but the few students visible there were running to their classrooms. I had no restraint. He was better than food. Tasting him only made me hungrier. I threw my arms around his neck again and breathed him in.

A jolt of memory hit me—my fingers in wheat-colored hair and a whiskered throat with a tiny half-moon scar. The sensation was chilling. I shook the image off, and there was only James, his dark hair fallen over one eye. I slid my hands under his shirt, feeling the smooth heat of his back. I pressed my face to his chest, but he took my hands and held them in front of him.

"Wait," he said. "What class do you have now?"

It took me a moment to remember. "Government."

He was still breathing hard. "What about third period?"

"Library Practice."

"What about fourth?"

"Study hall."

"Meet me right here before study hall."

Our book bags were, fortunately, still lying on the ground where we had abandoned them. He picked mine up and put the strap over my shoulder.

"James," I said. I just loved the way it felt to say that word out loud.

He smiled. "Do you know where your classroom is?"

"I've been at this school longer than you have."

"I forgot." He glanced quickly around and kissed me again, his hand on the back of my head. He pressed into me deep, as if he had to make sure I was real. Next moment, he had turned and was running up the path.

I managed to find my next class, but when I walked in, everyone stared.

"I'm sorry I'm late," I said, giving a small curtsy. Someone laughed and the teacher made a mark in her attendance book, but that was the extent of my punishment. I sat in the back and never heard a word. All I could think of was the way his skin was so tender over the hard muscle of his throat under my lips. And the clean cool forest scent of his hair.

I held my textbook open, but the words were as meaningless as mouse prints. I stared at the white space between the pages. I noticed how childlike my slim wrists and small hands appeared. It seemed scandalous for such a young body to be clicking with desire. Had I been many years older when I had first felt this way? When the bell rang next, I walked to the library, searching for James with a savage thirst but not finding him.

Library practice consisted almost entirely of shelving books. I rolled the loaded cart up and down the aisles. A handful of students taking independent studies sat at desks or at the long tables in front, reading or writing. One was sleeping. When I had shelved my books, I chose an armful of novels and poetry. I deposited them on the front counter and peered over the pile. "How many may I take out?"

When James found me waiting beside the recycling cans, I was standing next to my bulging book bag. He kissed me for a long moment, holding my shoulders, perhaps to keep me from pressing my whole body against his. Then he tried to lift my bag.

"My God," he said. "What happened?"

"I found out one may check out twenty books at a time from the school library."

"They make soft-cover books now, you know." He handed me his own bag and picked up mine with both hands. "Come with me."

I followed him behind the auditorium to where a fire exit had been propped open with a wooden ruler. He opened the door for me, making sure no one was watching. It was very dark. I touched his face, but he said, "Wait." Taking my hand, James led me into the school's theater, through the narrow pathway backstage that was lined with ladders and tall canvases stretched on wooden frames. It sounded hollow as a cave and smelled of mildew and wood shavings.

At the base of a built-in wooden ladder, he took both our bags and pushed them under a table. He pointed up and, without hesitation, I started to climb. At the top was a platform already spread with a thick black curtain like a velvet bed. The floor was as wide as a rowboat and, although I could stand without crouching, James had to duck his head. It was like a tree house. I had never explored it in my spirit form. I stepped out of my shoes and felt the cloth with my bare feet. The stage, twenty feet below, was a beautiful lake of darkness.

"Miss Helen," said James, "I don't want to compromise you."

He stood, his head bowed and one hand holding the crossbeam above him.

"If I am in any way taking advantage of the situation . . ."

"As far as I know," I said, "we are the only two of our kind in the whole world. Who could be more mated in God's eyes?"

That was all he needed to know. There was a confusion of clothes among our kisses. He was trying to the take my dress off over my head while I struggled with his denim pants, which had far too many metal buttons. One of my shoes slipped off the platform and hit the stage, with a bang like a rifle shot.

How strange it was to open his clothes without shame. I was often shocked when modern women in books and movies became the aggressors, pushing their partners onto beds or stopping elevators between floors. Even Mrs. Brown would startle me by her sudden seductions, rousing Mr. Brown's interest so quickly that I hardly had time to escape. Although I could not recall who had taught me as a girl or what words had been chosen, I knew the etiquette — the bride waits, seen but not heard, ready to open at his command. His pleasure is the goal, and hers, if any, is the secret. But this was new. Everything seemed new with James.

Now I marveled at my own boldness. When we lay down in the bed of black drapes, there was only skin between us. He put his hand down to guide himself into me, and a sharp pain made me gasp.

"Is this your first time?" he asked.

"No."

"I meant for Jenny."

"Oh." I could feel his whole body trembling, but he waited. "I don't know," I said.

"Am I hurting you?" he asked.

"I'm all right."

With relief he pushed in. A small sound from my throat came back to me, a sister echo out of the cathedral darkness. A deep recall made me squirm into the shape of him and cling. All around us the shadows pulsed with the rhythm of his sounds, a whisper breath with each thrust. My answers as soft as bird talk. The invisible depths above shifted with hidden ropes and dark lights like the hushed sway of limbs in night trees. As I pressed his lower back to me, my vision went white and a wave of sweetness rushed everywhere, even into my scalp. I didn't know I had cried out until I heard the echo. James covered my mouth with his, then broke off the kiss when his body arched. He lifted me off the cloth with his arms around my waist.

"James," I said.

He didn't answer. He rocked with me for a moment.

"Was that your first time?" I asked.

He finally started breathing again and blinked at me. "I don't know." Then he laughed.

We lay braided together, but our teeth started to chatter. Our skin was wet and there was a draft in the loft. He pulled his shirt and my sweater over us like blankets. I felt almost dizzy, imagined the loft was rocking on a river, taking us downstream under a moonless sky.

"How did you take the body?" he asked me.

I shocked myself by laughing about it. "I went into her at a church picnic during the prayer."

"You didn't."

"They thought I'd had a holy vision."

"Where do you live?" James asked me.

"I don't know," I said, having forgotten to take notice. "I don't know my phone number either."

How amazing, how unexpected, that after my heart had stilled and my body had relaxed, he was still holding me, so intent on my every word and gesture. Why I had anticipated loneliness afterward, I couldn't say.

"Have you started to remember things yet?" he asked.

"Only glimpses." I didn't like the feelings that went with most of my moments of recall. "Tell me what else *you* remember," I said.

"Let's see." He was staring at me, tracing the shape of my jaw and collarbone with his fingertips. "This morning I remembered that my mother had half her finger missing, here." He held up his right hand, the index finger bent in half. "When she did up her apron, she flipped the ties in this funny way." He tried to demonstrate the little dance of her hands. Then he put his face to my neck and breathed in.

I jumped when the bell rang.

"We both have second lunch," he said, kissing my throat. "We can stay here until one o'clock."

"And miss lunch?" I sat up. "I still haven't tasted an apple."

We dressed each other and then James climbed down first, holding one of my shoes. I climbed down the ladder barefoot. He had found my missing shoe on the stage, because at the bottom of the ladder, James knelt in front of me and placed both on my feet.

When we'd picked up each other's book bags again, he looked at me with a peculiar smile.

"What's wrong?" I asked.

"You look mussed," he laughed. "It looks as if someone has been doing this—" He put his hands on either side of my head and kissed me deeply while moving his fingers into my hair.

When we reached the courtyard, it was already filled with students sitting at tables, on benches, and on the grass, eating sack lunches and from cafeteria trays. We stopped under a tree.

"Do you have a lunch ticket?" he asked.

I searched the purse in my book bag. There was a comb, a small cloth bag, a mirror, a tissue, a thin box of chewing gum, and a wallet. I opened it and James pulled out a plastic card with a black band on the back and the school crest on the front.

"This is it," he said.

"I live on Lambert Drive," I said, having found my driver's license.

"You must have flunked your driving test," James told me. "Otherwise you'd have a photo on your license."

I put it away, pretending to be insulted by the suggestion that

I could flunk anything. Something about the license bothered me, though I didn't know what.

"So what's your last name?" he asked me.

This amused me, considering what we had just been doing.

"Thompson," I said.

"Well, Miss Thompson of Lambert Drive," said James. "Would you have lunch with me?"

In my girlhood it was rare for a bride to see her groom's bare arm or a groom his bride's naked ankle before the wedding night. The Bacchanalian abandon with which modern young people explored each other still shocked me at times—the dance of mating without courtship. Boys and girls hid in the library stacks or behind the gym and flew at each other with no promise of love or even kindness, tasting one another in clumsy attempts to steal pleasure before they could be hurt or hated.

But with James there was nothing careless, not a movement wasted. His desire was shameless, because it was offered completely. His passion was so guileless, I could not muster the least bit of embarrassment about my lust for him.

We left the book bags under the tree, and James gave subtle suggestions as we passed by the foods in the cafeteria line.

"Don't touch that," he said, as we approached three steamy trays of brown gravy over something.

"What is it?" I asked.

"No one knows."

I chose a hardboiled egg, a roll, a large red apple, and a small carton of milk. James chose a sandwich and an orange. We sat on the grass, and he watched me eat with amusement. He let me have a section of his orange, and I almost swooned. I peeled and ate my egg slowly and then my bread, lingering on every bite. I reached over and rubbed the plastic wrap from his sandwich between my fingers, fascinated by the softness. Then I tasted the milk. "It's different," I said.

"Modern cows," he explained.

A sudden, short sorrow kicked at my heart. I had been struck by several of these flashes since I'd met James. This vision was of a wooden milking stool, worn smooth with use. I was brought back by James taking a drop of milk from the corner of my mouth with a kiss. I heard a few students behind me hoot and laugh at this, but James ignored them, so I did as well.

"I should probably warn you that my family is very religious," I told him. "Don't be shocked."

"Are you implying that your family is more shocking than my family?" he asked.

"In a different way," I told him.

Biting into the apple brought tears to my eyes. Again a flash—maple leaves, large as your hand and deep orange, flour on a wooden table, smoke from a gray stone chimney. I shuddered. James stared at me, enthralled, it seemed.

"Did you love the taste of things this much when you first became Billy?" I asked.

He lay on his side, propped up on his elbow. "No," he said. "But I should have."

After lunch James decided I couldn't drag my book bag into every class.

"Where's your locker?" he asked.

"I don't know."

"Maybe it's written inside your wallet," said James. "That's where I found the combination to Billy's locker and his bicycle lock."

I looked at everything in Jenny's wallet. There was only a school ID, a lunch pass, a license, a phone card, and a twenty-dollar bill folded into fourths.

"Oh dear." I suddenly stopped. "I don't even know whether my mother drives me home from school. What if she doesn't? I don't know how to walk home. I have no idea how to get there."

James smiled. "Maybe we'll have to spend the night in the auditorium."

He came with me and waited outside while I went back in the office. Olivia, the receptionist, was drinking a cup of coffee.

"Hello again."

I smiled. "May I have my locker number and combination, please?"

She stared at me. "For church?"

"Actually," I said quietly, leaning toward her, "I'm in love and it makes me dreadfully absentminded."

She gave me an odd smile and then looked through a notebook, copying down the information on a slip of paper and handing it to me. "You be careful with your heart now," she warned. By her tone I thought she was joking, but there was a worry behind her aging eyes.

James carried my books to locker number 113. Reading the numbers, he opened the locker and we found a pen, a can of chocolate breakfast, and a straw wrapped in paper. I loaded the small space with sixteen of my twenty books, keeping *Romeo and Juliet*, *Jane Eyre*, a book of poetry, and *Wuthering Heights*.

"Why don't *you* bring home library books?" I asked James.

"Mitch would think I was crazy," he said. "Unless I put fake covers on them."

"Do you think I need to hide these?" I asked him, concerned.

"Why should *you* have to hide literature?" James wanted to know.

"You'd have to see my house."

The bell rang too soon. We agreed to meet at the parking lot at the end of school.

I sat through the rest of my classes, paying no heed to the math lessons or the film on World War II. I wanted to sit in Mr. Brown's classroom with James, but I couldn't. After school I waited for him at the edge of the parking lot, growing more and more worried every second that he did not appear.

"Hey," a girl's voice called. I turned to find a strong-looking young woman with beads in her hair glaring at me. "You going with Billy Blake?"

I was too startled to answer.

"I don't know you from nobody," she said. "But you should stay away from that one."

"Why?" was all I could think to say.

"He's a junkie and his friends are damn scary pricks, that's why."

"Oh." I just watched her as she tossed her beaded braids over her shoulder and turned to leave.

My heart was pounding. When I saw James approaching, it took all my willpower to keep from running to him.

"English class is not the same without you," he told me. I

couldn't speak and my eyes teared. "If I asked you on a date, would you go out with me?" he asked.

I laughed. "I've already been to the theater with you."

He almost kissed me, but two teachers walked past us.

"Who are Billy's friends?" I asked. "A girl warned me about them."

"I suppose they've disowned me," said James. "They got angry when I wouldn't . . ." he chose the words carefully, "when I wouldn't go on adventures with them anymore."

Suddenly I felt cold all through. There was a man across the street. The sorrow roiled off him in a sickening wave, even at this distance. He pushed a cart of grocery bags, his eyes fixed on nothing ahead, his mouth moving as if he were singing to himself. I watched him shuffle toward the corner although he had no feet. His legs tapered at the knees to a wisp that trailed like pipe smoke from his back. Looking at him made my chest ache. I felt James's hand warm on my back.

"It's all right," he whispered. "That's one of them."

"Can he see us?" I asked, my skin prickling.

"No," he said. "He doesn't know he's dead." He slid his hand to my waist.

"Can we help him?"

"No."

Suddenly the man's ghost vanished as if a curtain had been pulled between us. But this didn't scare me as much as the next thing I saw. A serpentine dread moved through my stomach as a maroon car rolled into view.

"There's her mother," I said. His hand dropped from my side.

"I don't want to go with her. I only want to be with you."

"Just think of all the amusing things that might happen tonight that you can tell me about tomorrow," he said.

"What if I need to talk to you?" I whispered as the car neared our place on the sidewalk.

"Five five five, twelve twenty-five," James whispered. "It's like Christmas. Twelve twenty-five."

I could see Cathy's face now. She was smiling until she saw me glancing at James. She stopped the car, and the doors unlocked with a mechanical sound. I turned my back on her as I put my book bag over my shoulder. "I want to kiss you," I whispered.

"I want to do more than that," James whispered back.

Feeling like a prisoner, I faced the car and opened the door, managing to smile at the woman behind the wheel.

"Hello," I said, sitting down. I slammed the door and gave James one last look. He gave a low wave of his hand. Cathy stiffened.

"Who was that?" she asked, the tension in her voice hardly masked.

"Just a boy," I said. "He's nice."

"Remember what I told you about boys flirting with you," she said.

"Don't worry," I told her. "He's a gentleman."

"Is he?" She locked the doors with a sinister snap.

Ten

———

WHEN WE ARRIVED, I crept to Jenny's bathroom and bathed as before but with a cup from the sink to pour over my head. I didn't want to lose James's scent but was afraid that someone else would notice it on my skin, deep in my hair. When I'd put on Jenny's robe and was picking up the dirty clothes, I found a bloodstain on the panties. I turned on the water in the sink and started scrubbing the cloth, using a bar of soap shaped like a rose from the dish on the counter.

"Honey?" Cathy opened the door immediately after one soft knock. I jumped, sorry I hadn't locked it. She looked dumbfounded. "Did you take a shower?"

"No." I stopped scrubbing the panties and closed them into my fist. "A bath."

"Are you feeling all right?" She looked at my hands. "What are you doing?"

"I was just washing a couple things by hand." I smiled at her, but she still looked concerned. "Is anything wrong?" I asked.

———

She just raised her brows at me and closed the door again. I slipped out with the wet panties wrapped in the dry clothes. Before I could get to Jenny's laundry hamper, I was startled to find Cathy standing over my open bag, looking at one of my library books.

"What's this?" she asked, turning *Romeo and Juliet* over in her hands.

"It's a play."

"I thought you didn't have an English class this semester."

"I don't," I admitted. "I just like to read."

Cathy looked unconvinced but placed the book back in the bag. "Put something on. It's almost homework time," she said. "I'll meet you at the table in five." Cathy left the room with a brush of her hands, as if she needed to dust Shakespeare off her fingers.

I put on clean clothes and brought my schoolbooks into the study, but Cathy wasn't there. I walked through the house and found her sitting at the dining room table with a box beside her and notepaper in front of her. She held a pink pen and smiled up at me as I sat across from her. Her box was labeled CORRESPONDENCE and was covered in a pink floral paper. This was a mother-daughter ritual, though I couldn't tell whether it was performed daily or weekly. I glanced at Cathy every now and then as I pretended to read history, government, and math. Like a child, she moved her lips slightly as she wrote—ordering her words in straight lines and her life in neat paragraphs. Although Cathy was in all likelihood thirty-five years old or more, and I had stopped aging at twenty-seven, I felt, just then, like the elder sister of Alice, sitting under a tree, watching her little sister lest she tumble down a hole. But it was only an illusion. Cathy was my keeper, and I was the one fallen into a strange land. I needed to be as clever as Alice to devise a bridge between Jenny's world and Amelia Street.

I had not bothered to record any homework assignments. I simply read to myself, random chapters, finding it difficult to retain any ideas. All I could think of was James.

"I'm finished," I said, after what seemed like hours. Cathy had four letters written and in envelopes to her left, each fastened with a round gold sticker.

"Good job," she smiled. "I'll call when I'm ready."

Without waiting to discover the meaning of this, I went back to my room and left my books there. Then I moved silently into the study and closed myself in. I left the room dim and gently picked up the phone. I dialed five, five, five, twelve twenty-five, like Christmas. My heart was racing as it rang.

"Yeah?" It was Mitch who answered.

"May I speak to Billy?" I asked.

"Who's this?" he wanted to know.

I was a little flustered. "I'm a girl from his school. I was in his English class," I said, which was true, in a way.

"What do you want?" Mitch asked.

I couldn't think fast enough. "I wanted to ask him about a book," I stammered.

Mitch laughed. "Are you sure you want Billy?"

In the background, now I could hear James asking who it was. Then his voice was in my ear, and I can't explain the relief.

"Hello?"

"I'm hiding in the study."

I could hear the rustling of James moving with the phone as far from Mitch as he could. "I think I should come call on you," said James. "I could ask your parents' permission to take you out on a date."

"I don't know," I whispered. "I'll try to broach the subject at dinner."

"Are you all right?"

"It's very frightening," I confessed. "I never know what to do or how to act. I keep making dreadful mistakes."

"I know exactly how you feel," he laughed. "I should tell you about learning how to talk and walk and sit on a couch like Billy."

I heard a sound in the hall. "Someone's coming," I whispered and hung up without even saying goodbye. I held my breath, then gave a little cry as Dan opened the door.

"Did I scare you?" he asked, frowning.

"No."

"Mom's ready for you to set."

I'm not certain why, but something in me was convinced that the thing that would make them realize I was not their daughter, rather than something significant, like not recognizing a grandparent, would in fact be something as simple as not knowing in which cupboard to find the dishes. For this reason, my long walk to the kitchen filled me with despair. By some miracle Cathy, who was cooking a beef stew, and Dan, who was looking through the newspaper, didn't notice my quiet fumblings. It wasn't until Cathy was bringing the food to the table that she stopped.

"No place mats?" she asked me. "What's come over you?"

Dan put the water pitcher on the table and then slid three blue rectangles of cloth out of the china cabinet drawer. "They're just place mats," he said, but Cathy still looked bothered. I carefully arranged each place setting on a mat, relieved that there wasn't more I had done suspiciously wrong.

By the time they had seated themselves at the far ends of the table, the tension was making my head ache behind my eyes. I sat down, close to tears. They talked of Cathy's day as the dishes of food were passed around.

"Your mother tells me you were talking to a strange boy at school." His voice was so controlled, I knew there was nothing matter-of-fact about the subject.

"He wasn't strange," I said.

"You've talked to him before?" Dan asked. They both watched me.

I didn't know whether Jenny had ever said a word to Billy before today. "I see him in the hall."

"So he's not from church?" Dan asked.

"No," I said.

"Does he even attend a church?" asked Cathy.

"I didn't ask him," I said, but I had been with James and Mitch on a Sunday morning and knew, of course, that they did not. "He might ask me on a date." I had hoped this would sound natural, but they both stopped eating.

"Don't be ridiculous." Cathy was breathless.

"I thought we agreed she was too young to date," said Dan.

"Well . . ." My heart was pounding so hard it made my vision shake with each throb. "Mother mentioned that someone might be asking me out."

Cathy put her silverware down. "Brad Smith. From youth group. And that was only to a church party, for heaven's sake."

She looked at her husband as if explaining her innocence in the crime.

"I could invite him to church," I said.

"No," Cathy shook her head. "Out of the question."

I had the absurd feeling I'd just been sentenced without a trial. "Why?"

"I thought you two had already talked about this." Dan looked at Cathy with reproach.

"We read every word of that book together. She knows she's not to date outside the church," she told him. Then she turned to me, shaking her head in that absolute way. "Never date a boy hoping he'll convert. It said that right in the first chapter."

"It's a moot point," said Dan. "She's not going to date for another year, isn't that what we agreed?"

Those who cry to be young again should think twice before they seal those prayers. My stomach threatened to send back what little I had already swallowed. I took a deep breath.

"Are people of no value to you unless they're from our church?" I asked them. It was too late. The words were out before I realized how harsh they sounded.

The shock kicked Cathy against the back of her chair as if she'd fired a rifle. "Jennifer Ann."

Dan cocked his head at me, slow as a cannon changing targets. "You know perfectly well I do business with Catholics and Jews. We're glad you go to school with children from other faiths. But if that's how you're being taught to speak to your elders, you'll be out of that school tomorrow."

"I'm sorry." Then I rushed on. "So, I may have friends who aren't Christian? I could study with a friend——"

"Unchurched high school boys," Cathy interrupted, "do not want to be *friends* with high school girls."

"What are you afraid of?" I asked her.

"That's enough." Dan slid my plate of food away from me, into the center of the table. Cathy stood and took my dinner into the kitchen without speaking, returning with a glass of water. She set the glass in front of me, the lemon wedge in it bobbing like a dead fish.

I knew that denying Jenny food was meant as a punishment, but to me it was a relief. I was too anxious to eat. For the rest of the meal, I stayed quiet, passing the bread when asked, ever silent, drinking my water as slowly as a flower might. I had to think. How was I to escape?

When Cathy and Dan had finished, I rose and carefully began to clear the plates from the table. Dan carried two of the serving platters but then left the kitchen without a word. Cathy busied herself wrapping food with nervous fumblings and loud clatters. When the table was cleared, I lingered, at a loss.

"Go to your room," said Cathy. "You're on fasting and Bible."

It seemed this was my release, and I took it. I navigated the hall as quietly as if I were Light again and listened at the study door, which stood ajar. The lamp was on inside and I could hear the ominous rumble of Dan speaking on the telephone.

Back in my room, I felt so restless I didn't know what to do with myself. I started pacing, back and forth, watching my own shadow warp and dance on the carpet. I tried to sit on the bed and read poetry, but I couldn't be still. I stood in front of the dressing table and brushed my hair over and over again, with each stroke thinking, *Only twelve hours more.* Finally I sat at the desk and opened the drawer. There was the usual assortment of paper clips, pens, and rubber bands, all neatly separated by plastic dividers. In one compartment sat a plastic button printed with the letters "WWJD?" I had seen this arrangement of initials before but couldn't remember the significance.

There was also a folder curiously labeled PROGRESS. I opened it to find Jenny's report cards clipped together in groups. The first stack had the report card for fall semester of the previous year on top. She had taken seven classes, received seven As. The next semester, spring, was the same, every grade an A. The third card down was for summer school and, of the three classes listed, two were A minus and one was a B. The date of that report card was July 6. That date flared in my memory, but I couldn't place it. I closed the folder and found myself a tablet of writing paper and a pen.

With these I began to write James a love letter, though I knew I wouldn't need to. I could tell him everything I wanted to tell him the next morning. But I sat at the small desk and wrote: "Dear sir: twelve hours is as twelve years to me. I imagine you in your home, smiling, thinking of me. That I am your heart's secret fills me with song. I wish I could sing of you here in my cage. You are my heart's hidden poem. I reread you, memorize you, every moment we're apart." Silly, girlish lines, but they wrapped around my anxious thoughts and calmed me.

The sharp knock made my pen scratch a scar of ink on the bottom of the page. I hid the paper in the top drawer of the desk as Dan opened the door. He looked from me to the Bible that lay closed on the dressing table. I folded my hands as if praying.

"When your heart is clear, go to bed."

"All right." The slam of the door made the picture of Jesus jump on the wall.

I undressed and put on pajamas, as I had the night before. When I returned from the bathroom, Cathy was already sitting on my bed with her magazine in her lap.

"Are you right with God?" she asked, her expression icy.

No, I thought, *but he's already punishing me.* Aloud I answered, "Yes." I couldn't face discovering the next step if I were to tell her no.

"You need to watch your tongue, young lady. I don't want another dinner like that one."

"Neither do I." I glanced at her magazine. "I thought *I'd* read you something tonight," I said. I got under the covers and took the library book from the bedside table.

Cathy frowned.

"It's about heaven," I reassured her.

> Why do they shut me out of heaven?
> Did I sing too loud?
> But I can say a little minor
> Timid as a bird.
> Wouldn't the angels try me
> Just once more,
> Just see if I troubled them
> But don't shut the door.

I glanced up, but she hadn't moved. As I read on, she watched the floor, her lips pressed together as if she tasted something sour. I didn't need to look at the page, as this was one of Mr. Brown's favorites.

Oh, if I were the gentleman
In the white robe
And they were the little hand that knocked
Could I forbid?

I closed the book and waited.

"What sort of poetry is that?" she asked.

"It's Emily Dickinson."

"Watch what you pick up in the library." She smoothed the magazine on her lap. "Don't you think it would be more appropriate to read something inspirational before bed?"

"You weren't inspired?" I asked her.

She raised her brows. "You know very well I mean stories and poems about God." Cathy rose and clapped her copy of *In His Time* under her arm. "Say your prayers and do not come to Him without a contrite heart." Before leaving the room, she glanced back as if expecting me to be sneaking a book on witchcraft out from under my pillow.

As I had the night before, which seemed so long ago, I stayed in my room until the house was very quiet and, as I looked out into the hall, very dark. In the kitchen, instead of searching for food, I took the telephone receiver carefully off the wall and dialed James's number. It suddenly occurred to me that I might wake Mitch, but the line was busy, a sound I recognized but that startled me with its irritating volume now that it was right in my ear.

As I replaced the phone, I remembered Dan's threat to take me out of school. I had the horrid thought that Cathy and Dan would decide to place me in a Christian academy for girls. A panic shot through me and then a loneliness. I took up the phone again and dialed a number I knew from years of hearing it spoken.

"Hello?" The sound of his voice, even for that one simple word, was so achingly dear. "*Hello?*" Mr. Brown repeated.

I thought of speaking. Just to hear him say more. Of asking for a fictitious name so that he could tell me I had dialed the wrong number, but I couldn't speak. My throat closed and the tears came hot on my face.

"I can't hear you," he said. So polite, even to thin air.

"Who is it?" I heard his wife ask. She was near. They were probably in bed reading or just undressing.

The gentle, low sound of a laugh from him cut into me. "If this is a computer—"

"Hang up," she said.

I had covered the lower part of the phone with my hand, but the sound of my weeping must have come through to him. "Hello?" he asked again. Then in a whisper to Mrs. Brown. "I can hear someone."

"If it's an obscene phone call, give it to me," she laughed, but the line went dead.

Eleven

I CLIMBED INTO THE CAR the next morning, a slight soreness between my legs making me smile. Cathy seemed distracted, which was all the better for me. She had been having a tense conversation with Dan before Prayer Corner. He lectured us that morning on the dangers of disobeying God's will. Perhaps he was still angry with me for my manners at table the night before, or perhaps Cathy had told him about my penchant for Dickinson. Whatever the reason, he was determined to make the point that willfulness leads to disaster. He chose a Scripture passage thoughtfully and drummed his fingers on his knee as Cathy read from Isaiah. Word by word, I listened and I wrote: "Where will you be stricken again, as you continue in your rebellion? The whole head is sickened and the whole heart is faint."

Now she turned on the car radio to KDOV. Unnaturally tranquil voices harmonized a song called "Blessed Forgiveness." The only time Cathy spoke to me was just as the car pulled up to school. As we drove, I remembered an odd dream I'd had about standing at heaven's door like a Dickens caroler stamping my feet to keep warm and trying to look through the tiny milked windows. A slit like a letterbox had finally opened, and a cross voice called through the opening, "Go home!"

When we got to school, I struggled with the seat belt, which seemed to be jammed.

"Don't be tricked by the devil." Cathy looked at me as if she'd just given me precise instructions on which our lives hung in the balance.

"I'll try." I had the strange image of a costume ball at which devils and angels all arrived dressed as each other.

Slowly I walked into the quad, looking for James, but I saw Mr. Brown instead. Like a bride who misses her father, I followed him at a distance, just happy to see that familiar color of hair, the worn-out corduroy jacket that Mrs. Brown kept trying to throw away, the scratched leather of his briefcase. I followed him right into the administration building and was bold enough to pursue him into the office. I hesitated at the door, waiting as he stood at the counter to read a flyer from his mailbox. I stepped in and stood beside him. Olivia was on the phone. She glanced at me, then away, then her gaze came back to me quickly. So quickly that I felt uneasy, as if she knew I wasn't Jenny.

I turned to Mr. Brown but didn't dare look up at his face. Instead I stared at his hands holding the paper, the scar where he'd cut himself on the thumb while backpacking, the tiny line of lighter skin where his tan disappeared at the edge of his wedding band. Talk to him, a voice in me urged. But what would Jenny say to him? He left the room without a word and without seeing me at all. Olivia was still watching when I walked out.

I hunted for James in the sea of students but didn't find him. Taped onto my locker was a note that unfolded to read: "Parking Lot. 11:15."

As I arrived at my geology class, a girl smiling a full set of braces paused by me. "Half day tomorrow," she said. "So Bible Study will be Thursday lunch."

I blinked at her. "Thank you." This seemed to be enough, for she walked on, swinging a flowered purse.

Class was slow as ice melting. The clock moved by in two-minute clicks, the second hand circling gracefully, but the minute hand taking a tiny step backward and then jerking forward every 120 seconds in a nightmare dance. All I wanted was to be with James. Not true. I wanted to speak with Mr. Brown, too. I had always wanted to but not as Jenny. An idea came to me suddenly.

I turned the page of the notebook I had in front of me and started to write. I didn't hear the bell when it rang. I noticed that the class was over only because the students in front of me stood and moved into the aisles. I knew that Mr. Brown had a free period, so I went to the tree outside his classroom and stood watching the open door until I had the courage to approach. I was supposed to be in government class, but there he was, Mr. Brown, sitting at his desk, his head propped in one hand, reading a stack of papers, holding his green pen at ready. The box of his manuscript was not there. I studied his face, wanting to remember every detail. I could recall the faces of the others down to each hair—my Saint, my Knight, my Playwright, and my Poet. And here sat Mr. Brown. He seemed frozen in time, as if I'd painted a picture of him, but then he turned and looked me in the eyes, lifting his head.

"Good morning," he said, right to me. "What can I do for you?"

I hoped he couldn't tell that I could hardly speak. I stepped in but stayed close to the door, my only escape route.

"You were in my class last year," he said. "Jenny, right?"

I thought I would run from the room if I didn't move forward, so I walked up to the desk, stood in front of him, and spoke. "I wrote something."

"Great," he smiled. "Whose class are you in now?"

"I don't have English this semester," I said, clearing my throat, sounding like a mouse. "I thought if I could read you what I wrote, you could give me some advice."

He was struck silent, rarely having heard these words from a student's lips. "Of course." He motioned me to sit in the front row. "Is it a poem?" he asked.

"No," I said, letting my bag clunk onto the floor beside the chair as I sat. I cherished his attention so much, but now it was difficult to bear. I kept my gaze on the paper in my hands. "Not exactly."

"A short story?"

"Well, it's short."

Be bold, I told myself. "A Letter from a Muse to Her Poet," I read. He leaned back in his chair. "Dear sir, I was called away and couldn't bring you, but now I feel haunted." He was staring at me, which made my cheeks prickle. "I know that sometimes you felt I was a part of you and that losing me would leave a hole in your heart, but that's not true." I looked up now, knowing the rest by heart. "I liked to pretend I was the core of your talent, but it wasn't me. Everything you do, the ideas you weave, the lines you write, the words you choose, it was always only you." He was still as a statue. "Please forgive me," I said. "I'm sorry that I didn't say goodbye."

We levitated in that fragile moment, then my tears came furiously and sudden. I sobbed into my hands. I heard his chair grate on the floor and felt his palm on the top of my head. But this didn't stop me. Like the new well of weeping a child finds in her mother's embrace, I dropped my head into my arms on the desk and cried even harder.

I only half-heard his questions of concern. I couldn't answer. He kept one firm hand on my arm. Finally I had emptied myself and gasped in a shuddering breath, lifting my head. He gave me his handkerchief, white, clean, folded, still warm from his pocket. I took it with perhaps too much familiarity and wiped my face.

"Please tell me what's wrong," he said. Now he was sitting in the desk beside me, and his hand released my arm. "Or if you can't tell me, I can take you to the counseling office. Have you met Mr. Olsen?"

"It's all right," I said, still shaking. "I'll be fine."

"You don't seem fine," he told me.

"It was reading out loud," I tried to explain. *To you*, I thought.

"Oh." He seemed uncertain. "It was beautiful."

"Thank you," I said, rubbing my eyes again, and then I

started laughing for some reason. "I've always wanted to talk to you about writing." I handed him back the handkerchief.

"But that's not the only thing making you cry, is it?" he asked.

I wanted to lie, but, after all, it *was* Mr. Brown. "No," I said. "But it's too difficult to explain." Oddly, I no longer felt as if I needed to talk to him for hours about his novel. I felt strangely free.

"Please try," he said.

He didn't understand that the quest was over. He had looked at me, heard me, spoken to me. That was my grail.

"I have to figure out the rest on my own." Then I smiled at him, calm and without shyness. "You're a wonderful teacher."

He looked doubtful. "I didn't teach you that."

"Yes, you did." I stood up, putting my bag over my shoulder and handing him the paper. "I'll see you around," I said, which made me laugh again. "Thank you, Mr. Brown." I left the room, and I didn't feel any need to look back.

By 11:15 James was already at the parking lot curb. He took my book bag and kissed me, then led me to the row of lockers outside the cafeteria, opening number 77 with surprising speed and grace. Although they would barely fit, he managed to pack both our book bags into the small space and forced the door closed.

"Ever ridden on a bicycle?" he smiled.

"No."

Once back at the parking lot, James freed his bike from the rack. "Nothing to it." He stepped over the middle bar and balanced the apparatus between his legs. "Hop up." He put his hands on my waist and lifted me as I gave a small jump. My heart was pounding as I sat perched on the metal handlebars in front of him.

"I'm scared." I was laughing, but I meant it.

"Trust me," said James. I gave a little cry as he pushed off, stepping into the pedals with a runner's strength, and we rolled toward the street.

"Just keep your balance," he coached.

We leaned to the right and curved into the roadway much faster than I liked. I closed my eyes as we passed a row of parked cars. But when I opened them again, a calm set into me. This was familiar but not because I had ever been on a bicycle. It was the way you travel invisibly when you're Light. I took a deep breath of cool air, the wind fluttering my hair like ribbons. We were at Amelia Street far too soon.

The garage was closed. James gave me a hand as I jumped down and let the bike rest on its side on the lawn.

"Why are we here?" I asked innocently.

He took my hand and led me up the porch steps. "We're having lunch at my house today."

"Why?"

He laughed as he felt on the ledge over the door and brought down a key. I couldn't hear the music yet, but James said, "Mitch must've left the radio on."

When James pushed open the door, we froze in the doorway. Libby, who was wearing nothing but a smile, sat astride Mitch, who was sitting on the couch, wearing nothing but his tattoos. I ducked behind James, who just stood there, confounded.

"Oops," said Libby.

"Libby," said James, as if he still couldn't quite believe it. "Hello."

"Hi," she said good-naturedly.

I backed up a step and stayed on the porch.

"What the fuck——" Mitch sounded angry.

"Sorry," said James. He turned sideways in the door frame and looked away. "What are you doing home?"

"It's my lunch hour, asshole." I could hear the rustling of clothes even over the sounds of guitars from the radio. "You're supposed to be at school," said Mitch.

"I left one of my books here," said James. "It's my lunch hour, too."

"Jesus Christ," Mitch muttered and the radio was shut off. Then I could hear him very close to James, but I stayed hidden.

"Didn't you tell Rayna you'd rather chew off your own hand than go out with Libby?" James whispered.

"Shut up, wiseass."

"Nothing wrong with changing your mind," said James.

Libby came out onto the porch adjusting her bra.

"We're gonna go get something to eat," said Mitch.

"I'll drive," called Libby. "Does Billy wanna come?"

"No, he does not," said Mitch with irritation.

"Can I use the car," said James, "if you're taking Libby's?"

"Hell no."

"Just to drive back to school and home after," said James.

There was a pause, then Mitch sighed. "Anything happens, you're dead."

Then Libby noticed me and smiled.

"This is my friend," James told her.

Now Mitch followed Libby down the porch steps.

"Hi." Libby waved with a child-sized hand.

Mitch only glanced at me on his way across the lawn. "Get your stuff, get out, and lock it," he said as he and Libby climbed into her dented red car.

"I will," James reassured him.

I stepped into the living room that I had seen before but never smelled. It had the scent of beer and pine needles. As soon as the door shut behind us, James was kissing me. He pressed hard as if he were lost at sea, drawing fresh water from my depths. He lifted me in a hug around the waist with my toes barely grazing the floor and walked me to his room. I shrieked at the cracking noise the bed frame made when we fell on it.

Again, I was amazed at my own undisguised desire. It was as if sex were something that we had just invented, a magic alchemy that only our two spirits could create.

I managed to get his shirt off, but the metal buttons on his pants were tight. "Help me," I laughed. And he did.

"What do you want for lunch?" he asked, but I couldn't speak.

Afterward, he was kissing my neck as if now he craved the salt he found there, and, to my surprise, I began to cry.

"Did I hurt you?" He brushed the hair out of my eyes.

"No." Then I noticed that I was still wearing my dress, and James still had on his socks and shoes. His jeans were around his ankles. I poked at the pants with one foot and started laughing. James just looked relieved the tears had stopped.

He kicked off the rest of his clothes and carefully took off the rest of my mine as well. I watched him all the while. The room smelled of newsprint. I felt an absurd pride at being Quick enough to smell and taste the world again. To celebrate my senses, I kissed his bare shoulder, tasting his skin.

"I want to sleep all night with you," I said.

"I'd never have another nightmare with you in my bed," said James.

"You have nightmares?"

He looked embarrassed to have spoken of it.

"What do you dream?" I asked.

"I'm always shouting at Mitch. I think it's Mitch. I'm warning him about some danger, and he can't hear me."

"I want to sleep with you all night, every night," I told him.

"Some day." He pulled the bed sheet over us and put his arms around me. Then he saw my expression and added, "Soon."

"How soon?"

"Well, we're nearly eighteen. When we're eighteen, we can make a home together."

"Why do we have to pretend to be young?" I demanded. "We could lie, couldn't we? Move to a new city and say we're twenty-one."

He looked intrigued by this scheme.

"Well, when is your birthday?" I asked impatiently. "I mean, Billy's birthday?"

"In October," said James.

"Only one month?"

"Thirteen months, actually." When he saw how shocked I was, he added, "Well, we need a proper engagement."

"Are you asking me to marry you?"

He straddled me, a knee on each side of my body, pinning me down on the mattress, and sat up, the sheet making a cape over his shoulders and leaving me bare under him. The sudden cool on my skin made me cover my breasts with my crossed hands, but James gently took my wrists, opening my arms like wings as if he were a painter rearranging his model.

"I'm on my knees," he said. "Will you marry me?"

Something in me whispered a warning: *You're too happy — in a moment, you'll wake.* But I didn't listen. "Yes, I will," I told him.

I thought for a moment he intended to consummate the betrothal, but then he caught sight of the little clock on his desk. "We have to get back."

Once we were dressed and heading for the kitchen, James reached into his pocket.

"I have a present for you." He pulled a small disk out and held it in front of his face like a monocle. It was a plastic button printed with the words YOU ARE MY HOME.

"What is it?" I asked, delighted even before hearing the story.

"It was a game in English class," he said, pinning the button to my dress. "If you could remember what character said the line, you won the button."

Now I recalled Mr. Brown playing this game with his students the year before. "Smike," I said.

"Very good," he laughed. "You and I could have wiped out the treasure chest."

We took an apple and a bottle of water from the kitchen, and James led us into the garage through the inside door. I kept stroking the button like a magic amulet. James reached under the front left fender of Mitch's car and pulled out a tiny tin box that held a key.

"What does Mitch do for work?" I asked.

"He's a mechanic." Like a gentleman, James opened the passenger door for me. I loved the way the car smelled of car, not like Cathy's. "You wouldn't know it to look at this creature of a car," he said, getting in. "He scraped it together from other people's wrecks."

"Like Frankenstein."

"Precisely." He started the engine and glanced at me. "You should drive. You need the practice to pass your test."

"I don't know how to drive," I said.

"You don't need to have Jenny's memories," said James, opening the automatic garage door. It roared painfully upward. "Automobiles haven't changed all that much." He pushed his hips back in the seat and pointed down at the pedals. "Left brake, right gas."

"This doesn't help me," I pointed out.

"What are you talking about?" He seemed almost annoyed at my reluctance. "Didn't they let women drive?"

"The car hadn't been invented yet," I told him.

James looked at me blankly for one moment, then bent forward in such uncontrolled laughter that I thought he was going to stop breathing. His face turned red, and tears were running down his cheeks.

"I beg your pardon," I said, trying to seem offended. "Are you making fun of my age?"

This didn't help. He motioned that I should stop speaking. I couldn't be angry with him, though.

"I'm sorry," he gasped. I sat and started to eat the apple. Finally he wiped his eyes on his shirt and sighed, but he wouldn't look at me. I gave him a bite from the apple and he calmed down.

"Hadn't been invented," he mumbled. Then he bit his lip, and his shoulders started to shake again.

Near the school, James parked on a side street. Just as we got to his locker, the bell rang. He opened the metal door with a clank and brought out my book bag.

"Can I come calling on you tonight?" he asked.

I was instantly shackled with thoughts of Jenny's home. "I'm not allowed suitors," I said. "I'll have to try to find a chink in the armor."

"Why does everything you say sound so appealing?" he whispered.

"Is it a half day tomorrow?" I asked suddenly.

His face lit up. "I forgot."

"But Cathy will probably pick me up early."

"Maybe she won't remember," said James. "Mitch didn't know when we had the last one."

I stopped listening and put a hand on his arm. There was a girl, walking with a group of twenty or more, all wearing red and white shirts and shorts, about thirty feet from us. She had stopped and was fixed on the sight of James. He looked to see what had drawn my attention. When he met her eyes, the girl turned so chalky gray, I was sure she would faint, but a friend came back a few paces and whispered to her. The pale girl, her eyes deeply shadowed, folded her arms against the vision of him and let her friend coax her away.

"Who was that?" I asked.

"I don't know," said James. "They're from Wilson, I think. They look like cheerleaders."

"She knows Billy," I said, which was certainly not difficult to see.

"But I don't think she likes him." James gave a small laugh, but I knew it bothered him.

"Blake," a voice called. It sent a chill through me. "We wanna talk to you."

The same young man who had stopped to talk to James in the library was walking up to us with another boy. The one following had tangled red hair down to his shoulders and a dirty denim jacket covered with words he'd written on it himself. James gently but firmly turned me in the opposite direction and gave me a little push. I walked away without looking back.

After school, I didn't see James at the parking lot. And I didn't see the maroon car. Instead I saw Jenny's father pulling up in his van. It seemed like an ambulance, it was so white. He waved, and I tried to be subtle as I unpinned my Smike button and tucked it into my book bag.

"Hi, Puppy."

"Hi, Dan." I sat down, putting my bag in my lap. Then I realized my mistake. "I mean father."

"When did you start calling me father?" he asked.

"Sorry, Dad." Then I said something that surprised me. "I've been changing a lot lately," I told him.

I believe Cathy would've been disturbed by this, but Dan's glance at me seemed impressed. "You can call me father." As he pulled away from the school, I looked back, hoping to catch a glimpse of James.

"You're not going to decide you want to be called Jennifer all of a sudden, are you?" he laughed.

"No," I said. "I'm not a Jennifer."

"You'll always be Puppy to me."

"Where's mother? I mean Mom?"

"It's Tuesday," he reminded me. "She's at Missionary Meeting. Where did you think?"

I sighed, tired of making mistakes.

"Buckle up," he ordered.

I pulled the shoulder strap across my chest and smelled there the soft scent of gardenias.

Twelve

———

"WANT TO PRACTICE?" Dan asked, when we were a few blocks from school.

"Practice what?"

"We could go to the Market Basket parking lot, if you don't mind the Previa." He winked at me, but I was terrified as soon as I understood. "What is it?" he frowned.

"No, thank you." I heard the fear in my own voice.

Dan turned chilly, tightened his grip on the steering wheel. "The righteous are bold as a lion."

He was calling me a coward, and although he hadn't ordered me to practice driving, I felt strongly that I had disobeyed. I tried to imagine what Jenny might say to mend his temper and show respect.

"I want to study hard tonight," I lied. "I have a quiz tomorrow. I want you to be proud of me."

This seemed enough. He relaxed, placing a hand on the back of my neck. It felt like a yoke of heat dragging me down.

———

When we got home, I crept quickly into the bathroom and bathed. Today there was no blood on my clothes. I didn't know where Dan was in the house. It was as perfectly still as a museum after hours. I tiptoed to the study, and then, as I neared the half-open door, I heard him talking on the phone. While trying to start back toward my room, a creak in the floor startled me.

"Well, okay." His voice shifted into a new volume. "I'll be there if I have to."

I ducked into my room and was already sitting on the bed, holding *Romeo and Juliet* (right side up, no less) in front of my face when he knocked once and entered.

"Is that your homework?"

"Yes," I lied.

"Your hair's wet," Dan pointed out.

It was a miracle that he didn't realize Jenny had no English class this term, for everything else I did that strayed from the daily routine was noticed. Every breath counted, every step measured. I struggled for an explanation, but before I could speak, he left me alone.

I had grabbed the Shakespeare in such haste that I'd knocked the book bag over. I righted the bag, but the button James had given me fell out and rolled on its edge under my dresser. I had to get down on my knees to feel beneath it. When my hand closed on the disk, I accidentally banged the bottom of the lowest drawer. There was a rattling sound there that I found curious. I pulled the button out and looked into the bottom dresser drawer. I found some scarves and stockings there and one knit hat but nothing that would rattle. I shook the drawer and heard it again.

For some reason, at that moment, I saw Mitch, his brow furrowed with intention, delving in the toes of Billy's boots, like an egg-hungry snake.

I emptied the drawer of scarves and soft gloves. The bottom was lined with yellow and white gingham paper, just like the other drawers and the shelves in the closet. I tapped on it, and it sounded hollow. Then I saw a tiny piece of cream-colored ribbon sticking out of the middle of one side. I pulled on it, and the false bottom lifted out. There, in the space beneath, was a lumpy lavender pillowslip and a manila envelope. I felt my heart jump forward to a trot. I glanced at my door, but it was closed. Slowly I took out Jenny's secrets, but I was almost afraid to open them.

It's all right to look, I told myself. Perhaps they're messages for you. Gingerly I unrolled the pillowslip. There were three items inside—a camera called a Polaroid, a package of film in a blue box labeled BLACK AND WHITE, and a small plastic bag with a few dollar bills and a few coins. I wrapped them up again, afraid someone would walk in. Next I opened the envelope. A stack of photographs slid out. The ones on top were like the picture on the film box—small, square, with black-and-white images. There were a dozen or so. I was fascinated. Not one was like the last. Some had words hand-printed under the image in black ink. One was of a pale hand, probably Jenny's own, stretched up to touch a leaf on the branch of a tree. Under it were the words *Adam's Reach*. One was of Jenny, her whole self head to foot, dressed in a thin white nightgown, looking at herself in the mirror of her closet door as she jumped, balletlike, frozen in midair, the flash of the camera in front of her face making a blinding little star where her head should have been. Another was a flock of pigeons blurred in group ascent, a flutter of frozen wings. Another was of a cat's footprints on a car windshield.

Under these were some larger photos, also in black and white, and I scrutinized them one by one. Jenny, nude, curled in a ball, sitting on the floor in front of her closet mirror, with the camera on the carpet beside her. The blackness behind her and in all the curves of her form made the lightness of her skin seem to glow. One was of her own feet, one stepping up the wall in the arch of midstride with the other lifted in a turn, like a folk dancer headed for the ceiling. Another was of Jenny—I assumed it was Jenny—with a white sheet over her head, sitting with a suitcase beside her on the bed. I couldn't tell where the camera was. This one had a piece of white tape in the upper-right corner with the words *the ghost waits* written on it. The last, the most startling to me, was Jenny's face, taken in the dressing table mirror. She rested her chin in her hands, looking into the camera with absolute peace. It was a disturbing picture because I had never seen her this way. I had seen her with myself behind her eyes, and I had seen her empty but never with Jenny's soul inside. For the first time, I wondered where she was, and the fact that it was the first time I had done so made me sorry.

It was the sound of the front door that sobered me. I slipped all the photographs back into the envelope and put both it and the pillowslip back into the bottom of the drawer. As I heard Cathy coming down the hall calling to Dan, I lowered the false bottom back in place. Just as she opened my door, without knocking, I picked up one scarf and started folding it.

"What're you doing?" she said, looking at the pile of clothes.

"Just sorting a few things," I told her.

"Do you not like Brad Smith?"

I was so surprised I didn't answer.

"You don't have to go with anybody," she smiled. "I'm chaperoning. You can ride with me."

She was talking about the boy she'd arranged to take me to the church dance. "Is that tonight?"

"Tonight?" She repeated the word and her smile faded. "What's the matter with you?"

"I'm all right." I smiled as best I could. "Let me know when to set the table."

"It's Tuesday," she said. "Paper plates for game night. Hawaiian okay?"

"Hawaiian?" I placed the scarf I'd just folded in the drawer and started folding another. "Yes."

"Where has your mind been?" she frowned.

"I have a quiz tomorrow," I said.

"Ever since you fainted on Sunday, you've been acting funny."

"Sorry," was all I could think to say.

"Are you done studying?" she asked.

"Yes."

"I'm ordering now. Meet you in the den in half an hour." Then she paused. "What happened to your hair?"

I touched my head, which was still damp from my bath. "Don't ask," I said on a whim, and it seemed to help. She left with a little laugh.

I put the clothes back in the drawer and picked up the button

James had given me. I was about to put it in my book bag when I thought, what difference would it make? I pinned it to the outside of the bag.

Cathy wasn't in the dining room or kitchen. When I found her, she was setting three folding chairs up around a card table between the two couches in the middle of the family room. Although it would've been easier to use the chairs from the Prayer Corner, she didn't touch them. They were sacred space, apparently. The large TV was dark, but soft music was coming from somewhere. She had a boxed game called Monopoly sitting out. The distance behind her eyes as she unpacked the game saddened me. It seemed as if humans had lost the ability to make their own fun. The more they were gifted with inventions, the less they needed one another. They didn't sing or play fiddle at the hearth; they turned on the stereo. They didn't tell stories on the porch; they watched television. Cathy laid out thin plastic plates with knives and forks wrapped in paper napkins like Christmas crackers, but it didn't feel at all festive.

"I'm not going to be that little iron this time," she said. "I want to be the ship."

She placed three tiny metal toys in one corner of the playing board—a little dog, a top hat, and a little ocean liner. When the doorbell rang, she called, "Dan, it's the pizza!"

A minute later, Dan walked into the family room with a pizza box lifted on one hand as if he were a waiter. He had changed into a casual shirt and smiled at us, yet I had a feeling it wasn't his wife and daughter or the food that was making him smile. He looked as if he had just remembered a joke but was not planning on repeating it. He set the pizza box down on the end table beside one of the couches. I was surprised by the beautiful smell that came with it. I had seen plenty of pizzas but never tasted one.

"I don't know about Monopoly," he said.

"We haven't played it since last month," said Cathy.

"It's just that I have to go in to the office later," he said. "I don't know if I'll have time."

Cathy stopped and stared at him. "Jenny, please go get the soda and cups."

I went quickly, feeling that Cathy wanted me out of the room. Unfortunately the cups and the bottle of soda were easy to find on the kitchen counter. I walked back down the hall at a snail's pace, listening to the voices of Jenny's parents.

"I know it's family night," he said. "I'm here. I can stay for an hour. I just need to go in and rework an account with Steve."

"You promised that Tuesday nights would be off-limits."

"I'm doing the best I can." He sounded more like her father than her husband. "I don't think it's too much to ask for you to be supportive and understanding about my work. I try to earn a good living to make sure my family is taken care of. Don't you think I'd rather play Monopoly than do paperwork?"

I stood outside the door, wishing I could sit on the roof.

"Jen?" Dan called.

Cathy still looked unhappy when I came in. Dan put a slice of pizza on each of the three plates. Cathy poured the soda. I sat between them like a pet.

"We can play Monopoly," said Dan. "I'll just give you two equal shares of my wealth when I have to leave." He reached in the box and took out the miniature iron, switching it for the ship, which he tossed into the box. "Dad, Mom, and Pup," he said.

He hadn't noticed that his wife had made a new choice, chosen a marker that was the symbol of freedom and adventure and left behind the little housewife iron. I watched her, waiting to see whether she'd stand up for herself.

"No, it's all right." Cathy looked weary. "Let's play Scrabble. That's faster."

She stood and scooped up the Monopoly game, sliding the board and pieces back into the box.

"That sounds good," said Dan.

Cathy brought another box and opened it. I understood this game better. I'd seen Mr. and Mrs. Brown play it with friends several times.

"Cathleen?" Dan intended to sound tender but failed.

She finally looked her husband in the eyes and gave him a smile I knew was a lie.

"That's my girl," he grinned, standing to give her a kiss on the cheek.

I almost made the mistake of tasting the pizza on my plate while Cathy arranged all the Scrabble pieces to lie upside down, but then Dan said, "Why don't you ask grace tonight, Puppy?"

They bowed their heads, eyes closed, Cathy with her hands clasped under her chin. I folded my hands and tried to remember a prayer. They hadn't said grace at the Brown's. It had been a long time. I closed my eyes, trying to concentrate. Then a bone-white tablecloth with blue violets painted on the corners came into my mind, and a grisly fear shook me. For a moment I could hear shutters rattling and branches drumming against the wall outside. I was standing now looking down at an empty table covered with this painted cloth. The table trembled, the flowered edges of the cloth flapped as if coming alive. I looked around the dim room—the fireplace with the hanging pot, the sink and pump, the straw broom standing in the dark corner. Although the windows were shut, the panes of glass creaked in their frames, and a phantom draft rippled the white cloth across the table. I held something heavy on my left hip.

"Not a silent prayer." Dan's voice awakened me.

I opened my eyes, relieved to find the plastic plates lying quietly in front of me.

"Dear God . . ." I closed my eyes again, grateful that I did not return to that quivering white cloth. "Bless this food. Amen."

"Amen," said Dan. I wouldn't look at Cathy, but I could tell she was staring at me. I'm sure that I did not sound like Jenny when I prayed.

Pizza was luscious. I chewed intently, studying every flavor, inspecting the piece in my hand, trying to understand the spices. It was like a recipe for catsup but more peppery and less sweet. A memory of watching a hunk of brown sugar dissolve in a pot of stewing tomatoes fled as Cathy spoke.

"Choose letters."

I chose seven squares, perching them in a row on the little wooden pew of my Scrabble rack. Dan checked his watch while Cathy folded over the top sheet of a small tablet of paper. As I tasted root beer for the first time, I must've made a surprised sound, for they both turned to me. I relaxed as the burning in my mouth tingled away and left a sweet flavor like anise and vanilla.

"Like ginger beer," I smiled. "I like it."

"Beer?" Cathy frowned at me. "What did you say?"

"She's kidding," said Dan.

I preferred the pizza to the game, but I played my turns without rousing suspicion. The phone rang, and when Cathy went to the little table by the couch, Dan paused, watching her.

"Hello?" Cathy hesitated with the phone to her ear. "I can't hear you. I'm hanging up."

She returned to the table. "I hate that."

"Wrong number?" asked Dan.

"Dead air." Cathy sat down. "Should I star sixty-nine?"

"No," he said. "If they call back, I'll get it."

She looked at him.

"In case it's an obscene phone call," he added.

The phone rang again, and Dan got up. "Yes?" he said, with the receiver to his ear. "Steve. Did you just call?" He paused. "Must've been a wrong number. What's up?" He listened. "Okay. That sounds good." Another pause. "In about half an hour or forty-five minutes."

Cathy fiddled with her letters.

"I'll try," he said, turning his back on us. "I know. I feel that way too. Don't worry." The hush in his voice made Cathy stop and listen. "Everything will work out. See you soon." He hung up and came back to the table without glancing at Cathy, who was watching him.

"You didn't draw," Cathy reminded him.

He took three letters. There was an unnatural stillness in the room as if the air had been shut off.

The game went on in near silence until Dan used his last letters to make the word *run*. There were no more tiles to choose.

"Daddy won," said Cathy, circling the score under his name.

Dan shrugged. "Game of luck." He picked up the pizza box

and the bottle of soda. "I'd better be going." Before leaving the room, he bent to where Cathy still sat picking up the game pieces and kissed her cheek. "Count your blessings," he said, quietly. She looked like she was feeling the lack of air, too.

"I know," she whispered. He breezed out of the room as if he had all the air in the heavens. I helped Cathy put away the game and clear up the plates and cups.

"How about a work night?" she asked. "We could sit together like when you were little, and I could do the bills while you do homework." She paused. "I forgot, you already did your homework."

I would much rather have hidden in my room or sneaked off to telephone Billy's house, but thoughts of James inspired me to benevolence.

"I have reading to do."

I will make a promise to God, I decided. I will try to be as kind to Cathy as James was to Mitch. This was my vow—to be a friend to Jenny's mother.

I brought a book, and Cathy brought a box covered in brown-and-cream colored paper bearing the label BILLS. She read figures from statements and invoices and checked them for accuracy. With birdlike care, she nested the little slips into piles, pecking at a tiny adding machine with her pen, scratching notes in the little margins. This was good, I thought. We were passing an evening in pleasant company, as I might have done with my Saint.

I sat across from her and, although it was almost impossible not to think about James, I read silently from *Jane Eyre*, skipping forward to her arrival at Thornfield. It was a completely liberating experience to be able to turn pages at will. It had been very frustrating, while Light, to be unable to read farther than my host would feel inclined to. How many times Mr. Brown had closed a book just when I wanted to start the next chapter. Now I was stopped only by Cathy's sound of dismay.

"What in the world?" She stared at a slip of paper, then went to the phone and dialed. After a pause she said, "It's me. Where are you?" She hung up and returned to the table, even more vexed. Since she didn't look up at me, I went back to Jane and Mr. Rochester. A minute later, the phone rang.

"Hello?" She listened. "Where are you?" And then, "Why didn't you pick up?" She twisted the cord. "I'm confused," she said. "We have two gas receipts for Saturday. One for yours and one for mine." She listened. "But you said you ran out of gas on Sunday." She listened and I was watching her, realizing that she was talking about the day I had gone into Jenny's body.

"How could the receipt be wrong? It comes out of a computer." She paused, crumpling the slip in her fist. "I'm saying I don't understand. No, I didn't say that." She paused. "I'm not saying that." As she listened, her head came down lower and lower on her chest until she was staring down at her fist. "All right," she said finally. "I know." She hung up without saying goodbye and returned to the table, scooting in her chair and smoothing the wrinkles out of the gas receipt.

"What are you reading?" she asked, her face both flushed and pale.

"*Jane Eyre*," I said.

She put the receipts away with a trembling hand. As she stood with the box under one arm, she said, "Back in a tick."

I had to keep myself from going to the phone when she left

the room. The idea that I could be hearing James's voice in a matter of seconds hurt me, but a moment later, Cathy was back with
a sewing basket and a shirt over one arm. She moved from the
seat she had chosen across from me to the seat beside me where
the light was better. The shirt she unfolded must've been Dan's.
It was white with long sleeves. There was a button missing, the
fourth one down.

First, Cathy took out a small box and opened it. There was a
treasure trove of buttons inside, every size, color, and shape. She
fished out a few small white ones, holding them up to the other
buttons on the shirt until she found a close enough match. Next
she took a pin and deftly extracted the little bits of thread left
over from the button that was gone. Here was one thing that had
changed little since my death. Needle and thread. I felt suddenly
homesick. My male hosts had not mended their own clothes very
often, but Cathy's slim wrist as she drew back a stitch reminded
me of my Saint.

I watched her from the corner of my eye, though my face was
still bent to my book. Now she stopped and stared at the shirt. She
pulled on the fabric surrounding the place where she was sewing
on the new button. Was the shirt stretched there just a little, as if
it had been torn off him in haste, or was that my imagination?
She felt the buttons below and above, to see how loose they were.
They were a little loose. Then she did what I had just been thinking I would do myself. She smelled it and, I know it couldn't have
been real, but I thought a faint scent of gardenias lifted from the
fabric. She wasn't sniffing to see whether the shirt was clean. I
believe that she would have started under the sleeves if this were
the case. No, she breathed in the collar of the shirt, blinked at it

for a moment, then gave it a hard shake as if dismissing the thought. She retrieved the dangling needle and continued to sew the new button in place.

"What's happening in your story?" she asked after a few stitches.

"Jane is starting to fall in love with the master of the house."

She nodded as if having read a dozen Harlequin novels in her youth meant she had heard it all.

"Shall I read out loud?" I offered.

Cathy smiled. "My grandmother used to have me read out loud while she was quilting."

I took this as a yes and began to read. "'Were you happy when you painted these pictures?' asked Mister Rochester presently. 'I was absorbed, sir, yes, and I was happy. To paint them, in short, was to enjoy one of the keenest pleasures I have ever known.' 'This is not saying much,'" I read. "'Your pleasures, by your own account, have been few.'" I glanced at Cathy to see if she was interested, but I couldn't tell. Her placid expression was fixed on her mending. "'But I daresay,'" I continued, "'You did exist in a kind of artist's dreamland while you blent and arranged these strange tints. Did you sit at them long each day?'"

Cathy sighed, and I believe I could have slipped into a Byron poem or a Shakespearean soliloquy and she wouldn't have noticed.

"'I had nothing else to do, because it was the vacation,'" I read. And to test my theory, I let a few pages turn by themselves, and I jumped in without worrying whether it would fit together. "'I have the right to get pleasure out of life, and I will get it, cost what it may.' 'Then you will degenerate still more, sir.' 'Possibly, yet why should I, if I can get sweet fresh pleasure? And I may get it as sweet and fresh as the wild honey the bee gathers on the moor.'" Now Cathy stopped in midstitch, listening without turning to me. "'It will sting, it will taste bitter, sir.' 'How do you know? You never tried it.'"

At this, Cathy looked at me, so I ceased my reading and looked back at her, peering out from under my bowed head.

I tried a few more words. "'How very serious, how very solemn you look,'" I read. "'And you are as ignorant of the matter as this cameo head—'"

"I think that's enough reading for tonight," Cathy smiled politely. "I have a little headache." Primly she snipped her thread, packed her mending, and stood. "I'll come tuck you in later."

I watched her walk out, I listened to the soft hiss of her shifting clothes as she moved down the hall, I waited for the click of her bedroom door as it closed, and then I shut my book and crept like a thief to the phone beside the couch. I was so relieved when James answered himself.

"Are you alone?" I asked.

"Not quite," he said. There was a clack and rustle as he moved the phone into another spot. "Now I am," he told me. "Have any adventures?"

I was about to tell him of the hidden pictures, but I froze at the sound of Cathy's shower switching on.

"I'm in trouble again," he laughed. "Mitch gave me a talking-to."

"Did he hurt you?"

"No, he just told me that I might have walked in on him with Libby, but *I'm* not allowed to have sex in his house until I'm eighteen."

My heart started drumming in double time. "Why?"

James laughed again. "Because Billy is an irresponsible, immature, insensitive—" James paused, "boy."

"What are we going to do?" I asked.

"It's all right," he soothed me. "He won't be home when we're together."

This, foolishly, placated me immediately. I told myself that tomorrow, again, I would be in his bed. A chain of days reaching into forever but starting with tomorrow and the next kiss.

A voice in the distance on James's end of the line made him stop and call, "What?" Then to me he whispered, "I have to go."

"Goodnight," I said, and he was gone.

When Cathy came tapping at my bedroom door, a piece of thick yarn held back her hair, the edges wet from her shower. Without makeup, she looked younger. She was wearing a flannel bathrobe and slippers and brought me a book.

She put *Why Christians Should Only Date Christians* on my bedside table and gave me a kiss on the cheek.

I looked at the book, repelled. Cathy probably meant it as the treasured wisdom passed down from mother to daughter. Perhaps she had also shown Jenny the ritual of ironing a man's shirt and defrosting a freezer. I wondered what Mitch had taught Billy about becoming a man. Had he taken his brother to work with him or taught him to shave? Or perhaps rites of passage had become extinct. I tried to remember my own lessons—did I struggle with the washboard or feel victorious after plucking a dead chicken bald? I could not recall.

Cathy paused in the doorway. "Do you understand why we don't want you talking to strange boys at school?"

"You're protecting me."

"We want you to choose right and have a good Christian marriage."

"Of course."

"Your father and I have words sometimes." She tightened the belt on her robe. "But it's nothing to worry about." Something she wasn't saying aloud made her eyes tear up. "I have so much. There are women in this world whose husbands beat them, who have no homes, who can't feed their children." She nodded in agreement with herself. "I'm blessed."

I felt I should say something. "That's true."

She sighed. "Say your prayers." Then the door closed.

I couldn't sleep. I read *Jane Eyre* until the clock said 1:37. That's when I heard the garage door grinding. I turned off my lamp and put my book on the floor. I heard the floorboards in the hall creak and my door handle turn. I closed my eyes and lay very still. After a moment, I heard my door latch gently click shut, and I smelled it again. The very faint scent that I thought I'd imagined on his white shirt.

Thirteen

When Cathy summoned me to Prayer Corner, Dan was already keeping shepherd over the trio of chairs. We sat holding our Scriptures. I flipped through Jenny's transcriptions, and phrases flew by—*abomination to God*—*rejected the word of the Lord*—*punish all disobedience.* I remembered then why July 6, the date in Jenny's progress folder, was familiar. The diary in my hands began July 7, one day after Jenny brought home a less than perfect report card. Someone had ripped out whatever was written in her journal, and the next morning she had sat in the Prayer Corner and neatly printed the words *Honor thy father and mother.* I fingered the edges of Jenny's lost memoirs.

"Is there anything you wish to tell us?" said Dan.

"About what?" I asked.

"Give the whole truth to God in prayer," he warned me. "He'll tell you what to do."

During silent prayer, Dan loomed over me, placing a leaden hand on my head. I fought the urge to jerk away. More chilling still was the hot dampness of Cathy's hand on my back.

"Lord, we call on you." Dan's voice was a death bell through my bones. "Come into Jennifer Ann's heart and purify her. Give her divine endurance in the face of temptation. Turn her thoughts from sin. Purge her of all unclean ambitions, Lord. You blessed us with this child, but she is yours."

An image of Abraham raising a sword over his child's head made me shudder. I was sweating under Dan's fingers. He entreated God to enter me, but I was sure that God had no interest whatever in comforting me, a stowaway in this girl's temple. Perhaps I'd be chased out like a demon, the legion banished into the herd of swine. No hope of heaven.

"Heal her of all deceit and willfulness. Show her the path of the holy."

When I spoke, my words overlapped with Dan's "Amen."

"I'm not your child." I regretted it even before I saw Dan's face.

"Jennifer—" Cathy was so shocked, she couldn't form words. She jerked her hand off me.

Dan pulled back a step. Cathy looked from one of us to the other. The journal stuck to my hands, I was gripping it with such fervor.

"I'm afraid you won't believe me," I said.

Dan spoke as if countering a blasphemy. "Whether you are five years old or a hundred and five, we are your parents."

"I mean that I'm not who you believe me to be."

"Don't talk to your father like that."

"Cathleen," said Dan. "I'll handle this."

"I just can't pretend to be Jenny anymore," I said.

"We know you're trying." Cathy was almost in tears.

"Your daughter—" I couldn't think how to explain Jenny's departure.

"Stop this nonsense right now." Dan placed his hand back on my head, heavier now. This wasn't going well. I had promised myself to be kind to Cathy, and now I was frightening her.

"Apologize to your mother." His grip tightened on my skull until my eyes ached and my scalp was sweating.

"I'm sorry."

"Your will is God's will," said Dan. "Say it."

"My will is God's will," I said. His grip loosened slightly. My head itched under his palm. "It's probably just part of growing up." I retreated as best I could. "I feel changed."

Cathy seemed relieved, but Dan still held me, so I added, "Closer to God."

"Explain," said Dan.

"I almost feel like another person. As if I should have a new name. I feel so different. I was scared you wouldn't believe me."

Finally Dan gave my head a little jerk and released me. He took up the Bible and paced as he read aloud. "'And just as they did not see fit to acknowledge God any longer, God gave them over to a depraved mind, to do those things which are not proper, being filled with all unrighteousness, wickedness, greed, evil.'"

I was so glad he wasn't touching me anymore I almost laughed, but instead I swallowed back the skittish instinct.

"'Full of envy,'" Dan read. "'Murder, strife, deceit, malice, they are gossips, slanderers, haters of God.'" He rattled off the rest of the list and was flushed by the time he shoved the Bible at Cathy.

She'd been nodding in sheeplike agreement, but her hand gripped the edge of her chair. The verse Dan gave her to dictate to me was from Ephesians. "'Put on the full armor of God that you may be able to stand firm against the schemes of the devil.'" I was halfway through the passage before I realized that I was writing in a curved hand nothing like Jenny's printing.

In the kitchen Cathy handed me a can of breakfast. "Don't forget your Bible." When I just stared at her, she said, "Bible study on Wednesdays, right?"

God bless her, she had forgotten, or never knew, about the half day of school. I went to the bedroom and found Jenny's Bible on the dressing table. Maybe I would read Song of Solomon to James in bed. Then I had another thought and opened the bottom drawer of the dresser. I tucked the Polaroid camera into my bag, hidden under the Bible.

As I passed the study, I caught a glimpse of Dan through the open door as he took two books off the shelf and put them in his briefcase. Something about the way he adjusted the books he'd left behind seemed peculiar to me, a man covering his tracks. He had an open accordion file on his desk chair. He packed his briefcase with an odd assortment—I glimpsed a jackknife, a few music disks, a stack of letters, a framed picture, a little wooden plaque that read: CHAMBER OF COMMERCE EXCELLENCE IN SMALL BUSINESS. This was curious, but thoughts of seeing James pushed the puzzle of Dan's habits out of my mind.

"Where did you get that button?" Cathy asked me as we drove to school.

"They handed them out in English class."

"You don't have English class," Cathy said.

"A friend gave it to me," I told her. As if she would try to pull it from my bag to examine it for fingerprints, I rested my arm over the button.

"Why don't you wear the button Grandma sent you?" said Cathy. "What would Jesus do?"

WWJD. *That*'s what it meant. "This is Dickens," I reassured her. "It's academic."

"Not everything academic is moral," said Cathy.

This struck me as a very disturbing way to live life. I felt annoyed with her suspicion of literature but kept my mouth shut.

Once at school, I unbuckled my seat belt as fast as I could.

"Behave yourself," she warned as I stepped out.

"God bless us every one!" I said, and waved her off, feeling not a bit guilty that I would be lying to her when I saw her next.

On my way to class I bent to pick up a penny from the ground and then stood up too quickly; I don't know which it was, that I hadn't eaten anything since the night before, or that I remembered what I saw in Dan's briefcase. But everything went gray for a moment, and I heard a warping echo sound like being under water. Next a janitor and a teacher I didn't know were helping me up. After assuring them that I didn't need to go to the nurse's office, I put my bag back over my shoulder and slipped away into the crowd. I left the penny unclaimed and missed making a wish.

The jackknife Dan put in his briefcase wasn't a new one. It was worn, the ivory sides scratched and brown with age. And the stack of letters was tied with a ribbon. The framed picture wasn't a recent portrait of his family but an old black-and-white print of himself holding up a fish he'd caught. It wasn't what you gather before you go on a business trip.

It was what you take when you know the house is going to burn down.

Like other half days I'd spent with Mr. Brown, each class was only thirty minutes long. Still, first period seemed like hours. I was too restless to sit at a desk. I didn't go to the rest of my classes but instead meandered the paths during passing periods. When I saw something I thought Jenny would like, I opened the camera, the way I'd seen Mr. Brown do with his, and took a picture of it. The photographs sprang out all gray and turned into images like ghosts materializing. A dead leaf caught on a window, a squirrel sitting on the grass beside a sign that said, KEEP OFF THE GRASS.

And even Mr. Brown. I saw him stop and talk to a boy on his way across the quad. His briefcase was fat with his novel inside. After the night I'd flown from him to James, he seemed anxious around the eyes. Today he looked like himself. I watched from a distance and waited until he was moving toward a farewell with the student; then I caught him on film. I watched the image darken on the slick little square of paper—a stolen moment of Mr. Brown's life. He was smiling, giving a wave over his shoulder, the white wall of the administration building behind him like a primed canvas. I put the picture into my bag, keeping it safe from bending by slipping it between two of my books.

While classes were in session, I hid in the girls' restroom. During passing periods, I collected several black-and-white pictures, filing them away with the portrait of Mr. Brown. By 11:30 the day was nearly done, and the students were to gather in the auditorium for an assembly. I shuffled through the crowded halls with my classmates, who celebrated their nearing freedom by teasing one another, trying to trip one another, boys bumping into girls on purpose and bearing the reprimands cheerfully.

I had just entered the dim theater when a hand grabbed my wrist and James pulled me into the back row of seats.

"Does your mother know about the half day?" he whispered.

"No."

We sat quietly, merely holding hands hidden by the armrest until the aisle cleared and everyone was seated. James leaned over toward me but stopped when a security guard stepped into our row from the other side and stood there to watch the program. The principal tried to quiet the hall. James moved close to my ear.

"Mitch is right. I am irresponsible."

"Why?"

"For not using protection."

The thought hadn't occurred to me until that moment. There would be no reason these two bodies couldn't create life. I instantly felt afraid, as frightened as I had been when Mr. Brown was naming his unborn child.

But James was not thinking of babies. "Before I came along," he whispered, "Billy could've been with a girl who had a disease that could kill you."

My pulse calmed. This seemed a trifle. The rules of this world were a wisp of smoke, easily waved away. "We're all right," I told him.

The principal made an announcement, and then the cheerleaders danced to taped music. We had to speak into each other's ears.

"When we're married," I said, "we should travel."

I wasn't sure he had heard, but after a pause he said, "By train."

"And ship," I said. "To England."

"And China."

"And Africa."

James brushed the hair away from my ear. "We can read to each other every night."

I rested my hand on his throat and could feel his heart beating. I tried to bring my pulse in stride with his, but mine had a faster gait. "What will we do for money?" I asked.

"I'd do anything," he said. "I'd dig ditches for you."

"I'd scrub floors for you," I told him.

As the applause for the dance faded, James jumped at the roll of a drum. He looked to the stage where the band was marching in from the wings. His attention had been stolen, a suitor called from my porch by a bugle's call. He watched the band and not me. I held the collar of his shirt, my hand hanging over his heart like a medal.

Finally the student body was dismissed, and James pulled me out the door, taking my book bag as we broke into daylight. I could feel that he wanted to run, and I did too, but we walked, hoping to avoid attention. When we got to the parking lot, he didn't move to the bike rack but led me toward the sidewalk.

"Are we walking?" I asked.

"My chain broke."

Half a block down at the city bus stop, we stood holding hands with our book bags at our feet. Students passed on bikes and on foot, a few laughing and yelling out the windows of passing cars, but none waited with us for the bus. One old man reading the paper sat on the bench. A car honked at a gray-and-white dog that trotted along the gutter across the street. As the animal turned suddenly into traffic, my heart jumped for the poor thing.

"Diggs!" James leaped into the traffic. A car screeched to a stop inches from his outthrust hands. "Look out!" His eyes were wild, and he was shaking as the dog shot guiltily between his legs out of the street and into an alley. Two other cars honked as well. James breathed deeply and blinked back tears as the driver of the stopped car rolled down his window and yelled, "Moron!"

James stepped back up on the curb as the traffic resumed.

"Was that your dog?" I asked him.

James took my hand. "I don't have a dog."

"Then who's Diggs?"

"Diggs?" He looked puzzled for a moment but shrugged it off with a smile. "I don't know."

A woman pushing a stroller passed us. The baby's hoarse cry sent a shiver through my heart. But then James put a protective arm around my waist, and I felt something relax inside me, like a braid unbound. I felt completely at home, as if we could go anywhere together with luggage no bigger than the two bags we had with us, and be perfectly happy until mortal age crumbled us to dust.

Even then, watching the hands of the elderly gentleman seated near us rub together like grooming birds, I wondered why old age should stop us. Could we not find two young abandoned bodies again when these bodies died?

When the bus arrived, James dropped several coins into the slot beside the driver. Up the narrow aisle we marched, making sure our book bags didn't bump into the passengers. As we took an empty row near the back, it felt as if we were on our honeymoon, eloping, escaping by stagecoach. I wanted to kiss him, but two nuns sat directly behind us. James pressed so close to me, one of the sisters could have fit on the seat with us.

I kept my voice low. "Are you sure the house will be empty?"

James smiled but took a moment to speak. "Mitch's last girlfriend didn't leave him."

This change of subject was so sudden I didn't answer.

"He broke off their relationship because he caught her giving Billy drugs. His friend Benny told me."

"Mitch loves you," I said. The shadows, as the bus rattled under poles and wires, flashed across his face like a silent movie.

"Last night he was reminding me about once when Billy was thirteen and they were trying to chase a mouse out of the garage. Billy put on this monster mask to scare it. Mitch was laughing so much when he told me, he could hardly breathe," said James. "He told me a dozen things I'd done that I couldn't remember, of course. Silly things."

I felt happy, imagining James and Mitch having fun together, but when he looked back into my eyes, the light still flicked over his features like the twin sides in a stereoscopic picture, one image slightly different from the other. My James and the James who came before, both hiding behind Billy's eyes.

"He misses his brother," said James.

My skin turned cold, for some reason. "He loves you, anyone can tell."

"He loves Billy."

I wondered if anyone truly missed Jenny.

"You didn't drive Billy out." I could hear the fear in my voice. "He ran away before you ever touched his body."

The nuns were staring now. The way James lifted his hand to his brow, smiling at them but forgetting he had no hat to tip, warmed me again and made me want to kiss him.

Although Mitch and Libby's cars were not in sight, James opened the door very slowly. "Hello?" We were alone, it seemed.

With a backward kick of his foot, James slammed his bedroom door behind us.

"We have hours," I laughed between kisses. But I was actually thinking, *We have forever*.

"I'm sorry." He stopped and looked at me. He was breathtaking, his cheeks flushed and his shirt half open. "No, I'm not," he said and he was kissing me again. It was no use. I imagined having eons together ahead of us, but we still made love as if we had only a stolen hour.

We were laced in each other, clinging and damp. James was gazing at the wall where a column of type showed through a magazine picture of a sports car. The window light reflected in his eyes like the moon.

"I think I used to write for a newspaper."

"I don't want to wait for thirteen months," I told him.

At this he looked at me, pulling my leg around him. "Billy might know someone who can sell us fake licenses."

I brightened at the idea but saw a shadow cross James's smile for a moment. I knew what it was, though he covered it. He imagined us running away together, but he also imagined Mitch finding that Billy had left him. I was stricken with envy. If only I felt that sort of love for Cathy and Dan.

He recovered his smile and rocked on top of me, slipping his hands beneath my hips.

Then I remembered what I'd brought. "Can you reach my bag?"

He shifted me under him, as ready to fill me as when he'd kicked the door shut. "Why?"

I laughed and climbed out of his arms, pulling the camera from my bag where it had been shamelessly dumped among our discarded clothes. I snapped the latch open and pointed the lens at him.

Quickly he pulled the sheet over his lap. "Miss Helen, I'm shocked."

"Smile."

"No. Come here." He waved me back into the bed. As delighted as a child on Christmas morning, I jumped into the sheets, and he put his arm under my head as we lay down. "We can both be in the picture," he said.

I tried to hold the camera far enough away from us and still manage to push the button. James, who had a longer arm, took the camera from me. We nestled our faces close together and just as the flash of light hit us, I pulled the sheet off him. He laughed and the camera spit the blank photo out at us like a metal frog showing its tongue. He gave me the camera but kept the picture away from my hands, flapping it above me as I fought to snatch it away.

"That's mine," I told him.

"We can both see," he said finally, lying back down, holding the picture up as it faded in. I lay with my head on his shoulder, watching the faces appear—two laughing, slightly out-of-focus lovers, their expressions so the same, naked shoulders and wild hair against the white pillow.

We spent a long minute admiring it, then James said, "May I keep it?"

"Yes."

He lowered the picture to his chest and let it rest there. "You and I were left behind on earth for a reason."

My blood cooled so suddenly, I felt ill.

James drew me in close. "But we've found each other now. It's all right."

I knew he was trying to comfort me, and himself, but there was still something wrong.

"Why do you think that is?" he asked. "Why were we haunting this life?"

"I did something dreadful," I confessed.

"What was it?" he asked without a moment's apprehension.

"I can't remember." Why would you want to remember a horror? I didn't know whether God had stolen my memories as a punishment, but it felt like a blessing.

"Whatever it was," said James, "I forgive you."

The simplest of words, but they squeezed at my throat. A fever-hot tear escaped my lashes and mixed with the salt on his chest.

"God doesn't forgive me," I said.

James turned his lips to the curve of my ear, his breath trembling my hair. He said one word, one I hadn't expected.

"Stubborn."

James was in love with me, and that made him a gentle judge.

I couldn't remember my sin, but I knew it was deep. My banishment from heaven was proof of it. He stroked my hair, but I felt as if I were falling away from him, as if we were being uncoupled by gravity.

"Perhaps if we could discover why we were marooned here, we could be free to be together," he said.

"How do we do that?" I asked.

James raised himself up on one elbow and looked at me. "What do you remember? Before you were Light?"

I saw dark water rushing past a broken plank. "Only what I've told you," I lied.

I thought he would sense my dishonesty, but he didn't. "After I went into Billy, I remembered little glimpses of things, but from the moment I first spoke to you, I've remembered more. This morning I remembered reading at my mother's sickbed. I read her children's books. That was all she wanted."

"What's the last thing you remember?" I surprised myself by asking such a thing. He might loathe recalling his last hours as much as I dreaded mine. But he didn't flinch.

"My father remarried and my cousin and I went to New York." He frowned, as if bringing back the images gave him a headache. "I worked at a newspaper. And we lived over a bakery. Our rooms always smelled of bread. We joined the army on the same day." He stared into the air in front of me as if adjusting his telescope. "I remember a tree." He was staring through me, his vision resting on the hollow of my throat. As if hibernating, his breathing slowed. I felt his flesh cool. "It's cold," he said.

I tried to warm him with my leg over his, my hands on his arms.

"I made a mistake."

"What do you mean?" I asked.

He was bone white. I knew he was seeing more than he was saying. He rolled onto his back. I was terrified of the fear crystallizing in his eyes. I took his face in both my hands and turned it to mine, so he'd have to see me.

"They all died," he said.

With a jolt, he looked deeper into my eyes, as if I had become someone else. His hand shot to my ribs and he pressed my stomach with his palm as if he saw some phantom wound. "Oh, God," he whispered. Fear was shivering through his hand into my chest. I pressed his forehead to mine, praying that this illusion would stop.

A flash of white, so bright it stung, turned into winter sky. I found I was Light again. I was floating formless beside a man I knew was James, though he was not in Billy's body. His eyes were darker, his hair lighter, but his smile was James. He straddled a thick limb and clung to the black trunk of a huge leafless tree in a landscape as bare as the moon. I stayed close to his shoulder, watching him as if he were my host. He looked down twenty feet to a small face that peered out of the trench. Both the young man and the hole he crouched in were powdered with ash.

· "Diggs," James called to him. Diggs glanced down the trench, narrow as a grave, and then crept out, staying close to the tree trunk.

"Are they moving?" he called to James.

James's uniform was as dirty and frayed as his friend's, but his helmet was hung on his back like a metal saucer instead of safely on his head. "We've been here for weeks and they haven't advanced a foot," James laughed. "We'll be here until the Second Coming."

"James?" I whispered in his ear, but he couldn't hear me. It was as if I had slipped into a memory of his—a story I could not affect but only observe.

Diggs started climbing the metal spikes that made the tree into a watchtower. "So, what's the matter?"

James looked up into the top of the tree where a round, dark patch trembled on the highest branch. "It's a nest," James said.

Diggs stopped ten feet off the ground and squinted at James. "A nest." He shook his head. "The Germans bombed every stick and stone into dust and that's a nest up there, that's what you're telling me?"

"Bet me," James smiled.

"No."

The day was nearly silent. No bird, no mouse, not even a beetle. The rumbling sounds were thunder, not shells. There was an audible wheeze as Diggs breathed. A soldier coughed half a mile down the trench.

"Let's play the game," said Diggs. "First day back, I'm taking a hot bath while I drink a cold beer."

"Peach pie," James said, but he was looking up at the possible nest.

"Susan O'Reilly," said Diggs.

"I'm going up," James told him.

"You'll get shot," said Diggs. "Or Brodie will kill you."

"I could be up and down in one minute."

Diggs started climbing down again. "No bet."

James laughed and slipped out of the rope he'd been using as a sling chair. Staying hidden behind the trunk, he climbed higher, using only gashes in the bark and broken limbs to pull himself toward the top. I rose with him just behind his helmet. The enemy line, laced in barbed wire on the horizon, breathed gentle smoke from one spot but otherwise sat lifeless. The top of the tree had been blown off, but the highest branches forked into the air like a triton. James could wrap his arm all the way round the trunk now, and he gripped the blackened bark with his knees. He stretched up and with two fingers lifted the dark oval. As James blinked at it, I heard thunder again and the hiss of what I thought was distant rain.

I saw now that it wasn't a nest, it was a child's hat, small and brimless. It might have been blue once, a baby's hat, mysterious and final. It seemed to come to life for a moment, jerking almost free with a buzz like an insect. It wasn't until James saw a small hole in the crown that he looked out across the barrens. I realized then that the hiss had not been rain. Now James watched in disbelief a flood of muddy uniforms flowing away from the enemy's sandbags. He let the hat drop and fumbled for the whistle that hung round his neck on a chain. A bullet cracked through his hand, spitting blood on his face. His arm jerked and the chain snapped. I cried out but could not touch him. James watched the whistle fall impossibly slowly to bounce off Diggs's helmet. Diggs gazed up, the baby's hat in one hand.

James opened his mouth, but no words came. Gasping for breath, he watched the river of men sweep toward the frosted trench below.

"Diggs!" He screamed. His friend smiled up, waving the

little hat, then hopped back as if someone had kicked him in the belly. He dropped to one knee and then fell. Barely touching the spikes, James slid halfway down the tree, then dropped. I flew with him, wanting it to stop. If this was his death, I didn't want to see it.

The wall of uniforms had roared into the trenches now. James clutched at Diggs's face, but the eyes were set. The coat was torn open at the waist, black and wet. James pressed a hand to Digg's belly, blood flooding between his fingers.

"Oh, God." He was still trying to hold Diggs together when a bullet pinged off the helmet at his back and another kicked at his head behind one ear, sending him rolling into the dirt where he stopped on his back, staring up the tree trunk, unblinking. This was his last memory. He'd remembered it.

His eyes were still open when I realized that we were back in Billy's bed. James was in Billy's body again, lying flat on his back, but he wasn't seeing me or the room around him. He stared up at the ceiling and frantically felt around his neck and chest, as if looking for the chain and whistle he had worn as a soldier.

"James?" I touched his arm. He was so cold it scared me. He didn't answer but covered his face and began to weep. I kissed and rubbed his chest, trying to warm him.

"It's over," I said. "Don't look anymore. Come back to me."

He stopped crying, but he kept his eyes covered.

"It's time to be finished with it," I told him. "Diggs isn't there anymore. None of them are. They've all moved on." I watched him as he uncovered his face and stared into the ceiling. "You don't need to go back there anymore," I told him.

James gasped in a breath. "He was just here," he said.

"No," I said. "We're back in Billy's house."

"Diggs was just here in the room." James searched the whole ceiling and looked around me into the corners. "He said he's been trying to tell me for years."

I felt frightened that a spirit had been in the room with us and I hadn't realized it. "What did he tell you?"

"That I was a jackass." James startled me by laughing. He held his ribs as if it were an ancient, unused laugh that might crack him in two. He pulled me close and hugged me. "It's all right," he told me.

He was back in the present, but he was changed; I could feel it, and it scared me. A weight had been lifted out of him, and he seemed untethered, as if he might float out of my arms.

James looked at me for a long while as if he wanted to tell me what heaven was like but couldn't choose the words. Finally he said, "Just walk up to your hell and give it a push. Run through it, and I'll be waiting on the other side."

But I had no idea how to start and was sure it was not as easy as he made it sound.

"Don't be afraid to remember." He smiled at me. "What do you say, Miss Helen?"

We hadn't heard the door open. But the voice shot at us like a crossbow.

"*Get out.*"

James sat up and held me behind his body as if he thought Mitch might throw something.

"Put your fucking clothes on and get out!" He turned his back on us as we scrambled for dress and pants. For one odd moment, I was crouched behind Mitch, reaching between his feet to pull my book bag into my arms. I felt like an elf about to be crushed by a giant.

"I'm sorry," said James.

"Shut up," said Mitch. I jumped up and backed away. James was trying to pull on his pants but was losing his balance.

"It was a half day—" he tried to say.

"Out!" Mitch interrupted.

"It's my fault—" I started to explain, but James put a finger to my lips and handed me the camera.

Mitch turned back around and stood aside, fuming, every muscle tight, as we hurried past him out of the bedroom, me clutching bag and shoes to my open dress and James, half naked, his shirt and sneakers under one arm.

Mitch followed us to the front door and flung it open so hard it banged against the wall. "Not another girl sets foot in this house with you," he told James. "Get her home, and if you're not back in thirty minutes, I'm calling the cops."

We stood speechless on the welcome mat as the door slammed shut.

I tried, but I couldn't stop shaking. We finished dressing on the porch, a man and woman from across the street watching us from their driveway. We walked back toward the bus stop, James with my bag over his shoulder. A silent police car rolled past us. We held hands and didn't speak. There's still the loft in the theater, I told myself, but the idea that we couldn't go to his house, and we couldn't go to mine, filled me with dread. As we passed the park, James was rubbing my hand with his thumb hard, as if he was trying to revive me from our shipwreck, but his mind had latched onto something else.

"You shouldn't come all the way home with me," I said, as we came to the bus bench. "You won't make it back in half an hour."

He put his arm around me and pulled me in so my face was hidden in his neck. But he wasn't listening. I could feel his heart drumming hard. I could feel his throat tighten. I knew there was something he wasn't telling me. I pulled back and looked at him, to see what it might be. Now my heart started drumming, too. He wasn't saying it out loud because he didn't want it to be true.

"We have to give the bodies back," I said. "Don't we?" He gave one shudder and looked me in the eyes. Please say no, I prayed, but he nodded. Something in me knew that having James was a dream, and now I was waking up.

"We can't," I said. "We don't even know how." But he just cupped my head in his hands and kissed me. The way he was studying my face was too terrible, as if he was going to fly up to heaven without me and wanted to remember the exact color of my eyes.

"Not yet," I said.

"Not yet," he agreed.

Over James's shoulder, I saw Mitch's car pull up to the corner half a block down, but he turned away from us and drove south. "There goes Mitch," I said. James turned, but the rusty car had already changed lanes and disappeared.

The bus filled the street with a diesel hiss. James stepped in with me long enough to drop in two coins but then lowered himself to the curb and handed me the book bag.

"I'll see you in the morning," I said.

"See you in the morning." He smiled as the door closed. We watched each other as I moved to a seat by an open window. Several passengers were climbing out the back door, so I had time to lean out and reach down to touch his outstretched hand. James turned as if he heard someone calling. The police car that had passed us earlier pulled up to the curb.

James let go of my fingers. "Go home now."

Two police officers approached James as the back door of the bus flapped shut.

"William Blake?"

James gave me one last reassuring wave and told them, "Yes."

I was still leaning out the window when I heard one officer say, "You're under arrest for accessory to rape." I called to them, but my cries were covered by the roar of the bus as it pulled away from the curb. The officers turned James's hands behind him and chained his wrists. The bus driver warned me to sit down. Mitch's car thumped up on the curb and he jumped out. I rushed to the back doors, but they wouldn't open. The wail of an infant in the back of the bus made my fists fly to the glass. I pleaded for the bus to stop, pulled on the cord until the bell quit. I struggled to the front door and stood crazed on the step, though the driver told me that she could open the door only at a designated bus stop.

"It's an emergency!" said the elderly man in the front row. I tried to look back to see what was happening to James, but my tears made the view through the windowed door a blur of silver.

Finally, two blocks north, the doors opened and I ran, my bag dragging at me so hard I dropped it on the sidewalk. By the time I staggered to the bus bench, there was no trace of James, Mitch, or the police.

Fourteen

I WAS STARING, seeing nothing out the bus window, riding north again. And I felt nothing until I spotted the maroon car sitting alone in the school parking lot. I got off the bus and walked across the street, scared but still too stunned to guess what she might do or say.

"Mom?" I leaned in the passenger window and saw that Cathy had been crying.

She jerked at the sound of my voice and looked over as if I were an apparition. "Where were you?"

I opened the door and sat with my book bag in my lap. "I went to the park to study."

"Why didn't you tell me about the half day?" She still seemed frightened rather than angry.

"I forgot." I put on my seat belt, but Cathy didn't start the engine.

Her hands were shaking as she put her cell phone back into her purse. "Why didn't you call me?"

"I did," I lied. "I couldn't get through."

She sniffed and looked at herself in the rearview mirror as she put on her own seat belt.

"I'm sorry I upset you," I said. I was so weary I didn't think I could say another word. I wanted to fall asleep and wake up with James free, as if it were this morning again.

"It's all right," said Cathy, and I could tell I wasn't the sole reason for her red eyes. I just didn't have the energy to care what was wrong.

Cathy reached to turn the key in the ignition and stopped, staring at my knees. "Where are your pantyhose?"

I moved my bag to cover my legs and lied again, feeling that it would be too conspicuous to say that I had decided to stop wearing them. "They tore," I told her. "I had to throw them away."

She frowned but said no more about it. I was already knotted with worry for James, and now Cathy's abnormal lack of interest in my bad behavior was making it worse.

I felt sick when we walked into the house, teetering in the kitchen doorway. I swallowed the acid back and Cathy caught my elbow hard, like a hunter's trap. I told her I just needed to rest, but she ran me a bath and I didn't protest. She left me alone and went to cook dinner. I sat naked and shivering, though the room was clouded in warmth. I imagined James at home with Mitch, watching television, eating pizza, being all right. I tried to convince myself that Mitch had called the police just to scare Billy and teach him a lesson. But I knew that something else was wrong. The phone rang while I was still sitting in the tub, and my heart skipped a beat. Cathy didn't come to the bathroom door, though; it wasn't James. I pictured him as the soldier, high in a tree, and wondered what forgiveness felt like. James had looked into the face of his nightmare and God had pardoned him. I saw the peace on his face when he came back. But it wouldn't be so easy for me.

I jumped as a sponge floating on the surface of the water bobbed against my arm. I finally dressed myself and came out into the dining room, where the table was set for two. Cathy brought us a dinner of chicken soup, toasted cheese sandwiches, and chopped apple salad. Her face looked pinched and ashen. I sat beside her and put my napkin in my lap, but the smell of food made me feel ill again. When she bowed her head in prayer, I closed my eyes and breathed like a seasick hostage.

"God, please bless this meal. Amen." Cathy opened her eyes and dutifully served the soup.

"Where's Dad?" The silence would have been a blessing normally, but tonight it seemed dangerous.

"Working," was all she'd say.

I sipped my water and tried to eat a bite of apple salad, but it made my stomach roll in on itself.

Cathy gave a sigh and put down her spoon. "Is there anything you want to tell me?" she asked.

My pulse skipped again—a missing beat, like a hole in my heart. "What do you mean?"

"When you were little, you used to tell me everything." She sounded betrayed.

"Not everything," I said.

"Everything important."

"What shall I tell you about?" I asked. The last thing I wanted was to be forced to speak, but it was the only thing Cathy wanted, and her will yanked at me like a leash. I slumped forward on my elbows.

"Are you involved with someone at school?" she asked me.

The question stung me like a slap. "Involved in what way?"

"Intimately," said Cathy, too embarrassed to look me in the eye.

"I've never even been out on a date," I said. "You know that."

"Do not get smart with me."

I waited until she spoke again.

"There's somebody at school you're interested in, who's interested in you. Someone you spend time with, isn't that true?"

"Since he doesn't go to our church, you can understand why I didn't tell you about him."

Now she looked at me, her face a white shale that flooded pink. She slapped her napkin into the table. "Who is it?" She seemed on the verge of calling the police.

"I didn't mean that," I said.

"Don't you dare go back to acting like you did before."

"Before what?"

"Before Daddy took away your camera."

Dan had gotten rid of his daughter's camera—the one that she had used to take the large, crisp pictures I had found. But Jenny had managed to hide the other camera, the one that took instant pictures. The one that did not require a laboratory to develop her images.

Cathy's fists were shaking. "You were always questioning everything, keeping secrets." She stopped to take an unsteady sip of water, but it didn't help. "I thought we were past that."

I didn't want to cause more trouble than I already had and

have her shorten my chain. "I apologize for being smart with you," I said. "I don't feel well."

She composed herself, folding her napkin and putting it back in her lap before looking into my eyes.

"So, what do you have to tell me?"

"There is someone I'm interested in at school," I said. "And he's interested in me, but it's still new and it's private."

"Private." She repeated the word as if she was about to go look it up in the dictionary and challenge my Scrabble play. "What's his name?"

I didn't want to bring James into this peculiar madness. "I'd rather not say."

Her lips went tight as she pushed her chair back and stood up. "Get out."

I was so surprised I just stared.

"Go to your room!"

I hovered in my bedroom doorway, my heart still pounding, until I heard the kitchen sink water running, then I tiptoed to the study and called James. His line was busy. I stood there, listening to the pulsing buzz, staring at the bookshelves and remembering, without meaning to, that Dan had been squirreling away special things into his briefcase. I saw a place where a little plaque had balanced on a tiny stand that was now empty.

I crept back to my room and changed for bed. As I buttoned my pajamas, I glanced across the room and felt a chill. My book bag was standing open and the contents were neatly stacked inside. Cathy had found the camera. On top of having a heathen boyfriend, I had committed the strange sin of taking pictures. I was so startled when she opened the door, I shrieked.

Cathy looked at me coldly as if I had called her a name. I tried to smile. I climbed under the covers and she came to my side, putting a thermometer under my tongue. I sat with her in silence for a full minute, her arms folded stiffly, her foot tapping, her eyes red.

"No fever," she told me, reading the glass stick at last. "Do you need an ibuprofen?" She shook the thermometer as if punishing it.

"No," I said. Then I added, "I'm sorry for making you angry."

"We'll talk about it later," she said. "With your father."

That sounded ominous. "Tonight?"

"He may be late." Her mind drifted. She stared at the floor, holding the thermometer now like a candle. "You say your prayers," she said without turning to me.

"I will," I told her. I prayed constantly—a flutter of pleading.

"And you ask God for forgiveness when you confess your sins," said Cathy, and left me alone.

I looked through my book bag, but my camera and all my books were still there. I considered calling the police station and asking about James, but I wanted to wait until Cathy had gone to bed. I sat in bed with the light on, too anxious to read, listening to the sounds of Cathy walking in the hall, clinking around in the bathroom, crossing through the hall again. I didn't remember falling asleep—only the vague impression of someone turning off my lamp.

I turned the radio in the car on myself, the atmosphere was so oppressive. Dan and Cathy had been arguing about something when I came into the kitchen that morning, and although I suspected it was at least partly about me, they didn't ask me any questions or give me any orders. Prayer Corner was brief, a long silent prayer with only a few words of Scripture wisdom. Again, the absence of reprimand was foreboding. Now Cathy was sitting forward as she drove, looking as if she hadn't slept, her grip so tight I could see the taut muscles on her thin arms stand out through her sweater. She didn't kiss me. She barely remembered to say goodbye. I watched her pull away and was surprised she didn't run into the students crossing in front of her fender.

I stood in the middle of the courtyard, searching every face that passed, but James was not one of them. I went to my first class but immediately asked to use the restroom. Wanting to hide in a hole somewhere, I climbed into the empty theater loft. The black cloth was still there. I smelled it, hoping to find a trace of James, but it smelled only like paint. I cried into my sweater so no one would hear me.

A sandpaper whisper stopped me. I lifted my head, wiping my tears with my sleeves. It came again, like a snake's belly on stone. Leaning over the edge of the loft, I saw a woman, as delicate and yellow as onion paper, ebbing back and forth in the darkness, her long dress floating behind her and her ringleted head bent over a small book. A faint and lovely scent of candle wax floated up to me. She read in a smoke-thin voice, too soft to understand, paused, held the book to her fragile heart, and closed her eyes. Her paper lantern face glowing up at me, she moved her lips as she committed her lines to eternal memory.

The bell was so loud it growled through my ribs like a passing train. The vibration seemed to consume the apparition with an invisible flame. The empty stage seemed impossibly dark until a band of day stretched in like a searchlight. I could hear the second-period drama class talking, singing, banging noisily as they dumped their belongings into the front row of seats.

The firm voice of their teacher interrupted, ordering two pupils on stage. Words filtered up to me. The two voices were awkward ducklings, but they were so free from shame, it was as if they were inventing the poetry for the first time. I recognized the verse, even though they had barely begun. It was Shakespeare. Romeo was luring Juliet into a first kiss. I felt foolish, suddenly. Why was I hiding? Juliet wouldn't sit on her bed and weep until they married her off to Paris. Go find him, I told myself.

I climbed down, not caring whether the drama students saw me. James might have been late to school, I told myself. I went to the office and looked at the clipboard that hung on the wall near the mail slots. This was where absent students are listed so the office could contact parents. The names were crossed off as the students arrived late, but Billy's name was not crossed through. Olivia turned from her phone call. She was unnerved by the sight of me, for some reason. I hurried out, pretending I didn't hear her call Jenny's name.

In the phone booth where James and I had spoken, I dialed his home, and Libby answered.

"Is Billy there?"

"No," she said. Someone in the background was talking to her. "Who's this?" she asked me.

"I'm a friend from school," I said. "I was worried about him."

"He's out on bail," she said, then I hung up. Mr. Olsen, the school psychologist, was standing outside the booth, waiting for me. I came out, feeling as if I'd been caught stealing.

"Jennifer, we need to speak to you in the principal's office." He was smiling, but his eyes, dark and tense, betrayed a trap. "Would you come with me, please?"

I walked beside him, silent as a prisoner of war, feeling he and I didn't have a common language. He was a mild man I had never taken much notice of before. The passion with which he dialed and redialed his cell phone was the most animated thing I had ever seen him do when I had been with Mr. Brown. He never spoke as he listened to the phone. Finally frustrated, he put the phone away and as we entered the administration building, I held my bag to my chest and kept my head down. When we walked into the principal's office, I stopped breathing. Dan and Cathy rose from two chairs against the far wall. Cathy looked as if she might cry at any moment. Dan was so tense his neck was twitching.

"What're you doing here?" I asked.

Cathy opened her mouth, but Dan cut her off. "Jennifer Ann, please wait until you are spoken to."

The principal wasn't there, but behind her desk was vice principal Flint. Mr. Brown had been polite to him, but neither of us liked him. His compliments were hollow and his smiles forced. He half rose and motioned me to a chair beside the desk. No one sat in the chair that faced the desk, isolated and waiting.

"We need to ask you a few questions," said Mr. Flint.

Don't say anything, I told myself. They don't know about James. I never used Billy's name.

Mr. Olsen crossed behind the desk and whispered something to the vice principal that irritated him.

"I'm in charge when she's away," Mr. Flint answered him. "Let me do my job."

Dismissed, Mr. Olsen stood beside Cathy's chair, holding his cell phone as if expecting a death-row pardon from the governor.

"Jenny, your parents have become aware of the fact that you've gotten involved with someone recently," said Mr. Flint. Like a proud usurper, he seemed pleased with his seat behind the large desk.

"Where's the principal?" I asked, not meaning to open my mouth.

"She's out of town today." Mr. Flint smoothed his tie and adjusted his smile. "Your mother found this." He handed me a piece of paper in a clear protective sleeve like exhibit A in a trial.

I took it and recognized it with a rush of blood to my cheeks. It started with the words: "Dear sir: twelve hours is as twelve years to me." And ended with the words: "I reread you, memorize you, every waking moment we're apart."

"Who did you write that to?"

I knew I was blushing, but I couldn't help it. "No one," I lied.

"Jennifer!" Cathy hissed. Dan cleared his throat, a warning growl that shut her up.

I handed the letter back and glanced up, noticing that Mr. Olsen was looking very distressed by the interrogation.

"Didn't you tell your mother you had someone special at school?" said Mr. Flint.

I knew I had to say something. "Just a boy," I mumbled.

"Even if that were true," said Cathy, and I was surprised to find that she was talking to the vice principal and not to me, "it's still rape. She's only fifteen."

"Cathleen," Dan said.

Fifteen. That couldn't be right. Then I remembered what had bothered me about Jenny's little paper license. The birth year. She was more than a year younger than Billy.

Mr. Flint held up a hand to Jenny's parents to be patient.

Cathy turned to me, teary. "I found the underwear you tried to wash. I read the letter. I saw the photograph. Tell us what happened."

What photograph?

Dan clamped a hand on her arm, but she rushed on. "The books you're reading now. They're not like you. I know what *Jane Eyre* and *Wuthering Heights* are about. They're about girls who are in love with married men."

"Enough," Dan snapped at her. "Let him handle the questions."

Mr. Flint faced me again. "Even the school secretary said she's noticed your feelings," he said.

I just stared at him.

"You confessed to Miss Lopez that you were in love, didn't you?" He tapped a pen on the desk and swiveled back and forth in his boss's chair as if he were screwing it into the floor. "We're not blaming you," he said. "But you need to tell us what happened so we can take care of it. This is very serious. We need to know the truth."

No, not the truth, I thought. I'm possessing your daughter's body, but everything's all right.

"Who gave you that button?" Cathy asked me.

I flinched, wanting to cover it instinctively where I had it pinned to my bag. Cathy jumped too, as if expecting Dan to strike her.

"I told you," I said. "A friend gave it to me."

"Did you take this picture?" Mr. Flint handed me another sheet protector, this one with a single black-and-white photo inside. I stared at Mr. Brown's face in the small square—he was looking back over his shoulder, the white wall of the administration building behind him. It was the picture I had taken of him with Jenny's camera. The picture Cathy must have stolen from my school bag.

"Yes," I said. I was confused now. Were they going to trace James through the button from Mr. Brown's class?

"Don't cover up for him," Cathy pleaded.

"Be quiet," Dan ordered. And she obeyed by pressing a finger over her own lips.

I had an odd urge to laugh. "You think the boy is Mr. Brown?"

Finally Dan spoke up. "Tim Redman, a member of our church, is a police officer," he told Mr. Flint. "He did us a favor." Now Dan looked at me. "We found out this morning that you called this teacher's home on Monday night."

A coldness started creeping into my heart and up my throat. I had the peculiar feeling that Dan enjoyed telling me about the phone call more than he disliked the idea of me making it. So a policeman from Jenny's church had helped Dan and Cathy spy on their daughter. Officer Redman. He must've been the man I'd seen at the picnic with a baby sleeping on the shoulder of his uniform.

"No," I said. "Well, yes, I called his house, but no, it's not Mr. Brown."

But then Mr. Brown walked in, as if summoned. Obviously he hadn't been told why. He looked blankly at Dan and Cathy, then his eyes rested on me. I was horrified that he would think I had accused him of something. I met his eyes with panic. "Run!" I urged him with my mind. "It's a trap!"

"You wanted to see me?" He glanced at Mr. Flint, then at the counselor, growing visibly more anxious.

"Have a seat." The vice principal motioned him to the chair in front of the desk, the chair in the center of the room, removed from all other furniture, like an electric chair. Mr. Brown sat. He looked at me again and asked, "Are you all right?"

I nodded and noticing I still held the photograph of him, turned it over on my lap to hide it. I felt as if the air were swallowing me, slowly digesting me with acid. I felt Mr. Brown wanting to read my expression, but I couldn't bear to look him in the face. I knew that Cathy was watching me, reading my distress as passion. And I knew that she was looking at Mr. Brown, imagining how I might have become infatuated with his face and form and how he might have realized this and cornered me in a dim classroom. With sweating hands, I pressed the picture of him to my legs as I heard Mr. Flint introducing him to Jenny's parents.

"Michael," said Mr. Flint. "You know this student, Jennifer Thompson?"

"Yes."

"Have you ever met with her outside of class?"

"In my classroom during my free period," he said, not seeing the ambush.

"Were you alone with her?" asked Mr. Flint.

"Well, yes." In the pause between those two words, I could hear him realize what was happening.

"Was the door opened or closed?"

"Open," he said, going pale. "I think."

"Have you ever had physical contact with this student?" Mr. Flint sounded as though he had watched too many courtroom dramas.

"No," said Mr. Brown. "Yes." He sighed. "I touched her arm, or her hand." He rubbed his palms on his knees. "Her head, maybe. I can't remember. She was upset."

"Was she crying?"

"Yes."

"Why was she crying?"

"I don't know."

"Have you ever had sexual contact with this student?"

"No," said Mr. Brown. A weight settled in him, a horror that pressed on his heart so heavily he had to take a deep breath to continue. He turned to Cathy and Dan to reassure them. "I would never do that."

"Has she ever called you at your home?" asked Mr. Flint.

"No." Mr. Brown turned to me now for support, but I couldn't speak.

"Never?"

"No."

"She didn't call you Monday night?" Mr. Flint cocked his head as if he had tricked him.

Mr. Brown looked Mr. Flint straight in the eye. "No." But now he didn't seem as sure.

———

"But she is special to you," said the vice principal, tapping the desk again, swiveling his chair.

Mr. Brown looked at me and didn't seem to know how to answer. I saw in his eyes that he felt something powerful between us. He sensed me, his lost companion, hiding inside Jenny. Once I would have done anything to hear him say that he knew me and loved me, but now I was terrified at the idea. Please don't try and explain it, I prayed.

"Michael, didn't you ask for her file just this morning?"

He looked away from me at last and blinked at Mr. Flint. "I was worried about her because she was upset on Tuesday, and this morning she looked as if she'd been crying—"

I looked up at Dan and Cathy. She was staring at Mr. Brown as if he were a monster she was afraid to confront. Dan held her wrist hard like a manacle. His expression was icy, but there was something missing in his eyes.

"She gave you this." Mr. Flint was holding up a clear page protector with a piece of notebook paper inside. Mr. Brown got up to take it and sat back down, reading it over. I saw only the back of the paper, but I recognized it at once. An itchy feeling of frustration started making my fists clench.

"You dropped it in the office yesterday," Mr. Flint explained.

"Oh," said Mr. Brown. He gave the page a shake to make it stand straight in its plastic sleeve. His jaw tensed the way it did when he was trying to avoid tears.

"This is from Jennifer, isn't it?"

"Yes." He cleared his throat.

"But you're saying you're not involved with her," said Mr. Flint.

"She didn't write it about me," Mr. Brown explained. "She just read it to me."

The harder he tried to be calm, the more I felt the urge to touch him, to rest my head on the back of his neck as I had so often before.

"Where did she read this to you?" the vice principal wanted to know.

My frustration jumped up my legs and made me stand. "Stop it!"

Mr. Flint gaped at me.

"Jennifer?" I ignored Dan's voice.

"Mr. Brown has never treated me with anything less than respect and kindness. He did not take advantage of me."

Mr. Flint took a moment and then said, "But you do love him."

My legs went weak and I sat down again, the plastic-wrapped photo in my fists. I looked at Mr. Brown and couldn't find the strength to lie. I knew the silence that came before my answer was condemning.

"Not in the way you mean," I said.

The room was perfectly quiet for a long moment.

"Might I make a suggestion?" Mr. Olsen still held his cell phone at the ready.

"Later," was all Mr. Flint said to him. He swiveled toward Mr. Brown. "Thank you, Michael. We'll let you know if we have any more questions."

Mr. Brown stood up slowly, and I know he was watching me as he left the room, but I felt too wretched to raise my head. I sat, rolling up the plastic sleeve that held my only picture of him, though I'd known him since he was Billy's age.

"Jennifer, I can tell you're a very caring person." Mr. Flint's voice was like a poison now, burning in my ears. "You would do whatever you could to keep Mr. Brown out of trouble, wouldn't you?"

"Yes," I said, hoping he would offer some escape.

"Even lie?"

I put the picture of Mr. Brown back on his desk. "I don't need to lie about his being innocent."

"Did he ask you to keep a secret for him?" Mr. Flint's poison was burning my eyes now too. "Some secrets aren't meant to be kept."

"Bring me a Bible," I said, and I heard Cathy gasp. "I swear Mr. Brown is not my lover." I looked the man straight in the eyes, ignoring the venom. "He would never do that to his wife. He's completely devoted to her. He lights up when she just smiles at him—" I stopped when I realized that Mr. Flint was frowning at me.

"Jennifer," he asked. "How do you know that?"

The room went still as a stopped clock. My defenses were gone. I retreated into mute surrender.

Mr. Olsen's voice was tense, his face red. "Both parties say nothing happened."

Mr. Flint bristled. "I promise we'll investigate the situation thoroughly," he told Dan and Cathy.

"Mr. Flint?" Dan's voice had a prosecutor's edge. "You've had your turn. Now I'm going to speak." He moved into the center of the room. "Tomorrow we will be transferring our daughter out of your school." He paused for effect, having chosen his words long before. "We will be pressing criminal charges. And we will be filing a suit against the department of education." Apparently Mr. Flint was speechless. Dan snapped his fingers, and Cathy rushed forward, lifting me from my chair by one arm.

All the way home, I sat like a doll, buckled in the back seat behind Cathy. Dan drove, neither of them speaking to me. Cathy said something to him quietly and he turned on the radio to cover their words. It was nothing like the music in Cathy's car. A symphony, heavy with violins. When we got home, I just sat in the car. Cathy had to open my door.

"Let's go." She undid my seat belt and started to pick up my bag. I felt a wave of panic that seared through me like a lightning bolt.

"I need to use the phone," I said. "I have to be somewhere." I didn't even know what I was going to say. I was vibrating with a desperate energy. "I need some time."

Cathy's face covered a flash of fear with a determined strictness. "Young lady," she said, her jaw taut. "Get out of the car and inside *now*."

I climbed out of the back seat and looked around the garage as I jabbered on like a lunatic. "It's hard to explain," I said. "I have to take care of some things."

Dan took my elbow and led me into the house. Next moment, Cathy had an arm around my waist and was leading me to Jenny's bedroom.

"I left things in my locker," I babbled. "I have to go back."

"Jennifer Ann, be still," Cathy snapped at me as if I were three years old.

I sat on my bed and, through the open door, watched Jenny's parents in the hall whispering in hot little bursts. I couldn't understand their words, but next moment, Cathy disappeared, and Dan was left in my doorway, gazing at me with an odd expression. What was it? He believed his fifteen-year-old daughter was having an affair with her high school English teacher, and although he had been angry in the principal's office, there had been something missing in his eyes, and the same dark hole was staring back at me now.

What was it I wasn't seeing? He believed his little girl had been defiled, yet he could feel only fury. This look that he gave me now, after the anger had ebbed, was not the pain of a man who had failed at protecting his daughter, it was a look of fascination. He was simply curious about me, imagining me with a grown man, having sex in an empty classroom. What was missing was sorrow. I felt a chill run through every rib. When Cathy came back into the hall, I saw his expression shift into disapproval again. Cathy came at me with a glass of water and a pill in her outstretched palm.

"Take it," she said, firmly. "And get in bed."

Dan slipped out of view and I picked up the pill, holding it between thumb and finger.

"What is it?" I asked.

"Valium," she said tightly. "I'm going to make you a doctor's appointment."

When she looked away to see whether Dan was still in the doorway, I pretended to put the pill on my tongue but kept it in my closed hand. I took the water and jerked my head back a little as I swallowed.

"I'll wake you for dinner," she said, "and you will tell us the truth. Have no doubt about that."

Cathy closed the door behind her, and I rolled the pill in a tissue before tossing it in the white wicker wastebasket. I didn't have a real plan. I just needed to be with James. I bunched up clothes and placed them down the middle of my bed, draping my blanket over the mound. I turned off the light and gently opened my bedroom window, climbing out right foot first. I wondered whether this was how Jenny left her body behind—one day she had to escape so she threw a blanket over her flesh and gently climbed out.

I hadn't even thought to bring my purse. I hopped into the eerie perfection of Cathy and Dan's backyard. No pet, no bird, not even a weed contaminated the silence there.

I crept out of the side yard and walked down the street, wanting to run but not wanting to attract interest. I didn't even have enough money in my pocket for the bus, but an old woman in the front seat, with a tiny dog peering out of her purse, gave me a quarter. I thanked her but was so embarrassed, I walked to the back where she couldn't see me. I had taken the city bus enough times now to know which stop was near Amelia, but I was too anxious to sit. I waited at the back door, standing on the step.

I tried to picture James explaining that the charges against him had been dropped. They couldn't jail him for loving me. He was still under age himself. Even if Cathy and Dan sent me to another school, we would find each other—in the library, at the park, in the shopping mall.

As I walked up to the Amelia house, I saw in the driveway two cars, Mitch's and Libby's. I knew I shouldn't knock on the door—

I had been banished, but I couldn't help it. Mitch answered. He was frowning, shirtless, his eyes darkly shadowed.

"May I talk to Billy?"

"No," said Mitch. "He can't see anyone."

"Just for a minute—"

"Go back to school," he told me, and let the door slam.

I just stood there on the front walk for a few moments, my mind running in little rat circles. I saw that Billy's bedroom window was curtained. Finally I decided to creep down the graveled side yard of the next door neighbor's house. Their driveway was empty and their windows dark. I stared in at Billy's backyard with my fingers through the chain link, straddling a concrete grave marker in the grass that read: OUR MITZY. We had decided we should return the bodies we'd stolen, but we had no plan about how to go about it. I didn't know what to do. I couldn't leave without at least a glimpse of James.

And then he was there. He came out on the porch beside the washer and dryer, scanning the yard secretively as if having heard someone was calling for him.

"Here!" I said. He ran up and put his fingers through the fence to touch mine.

"Are you all right?" I asked. "What did they do to you?

"I'm fine."

"I'll go to the police and explain," I said.

"It's not because of you." He glanced behind him to make sure we weren't being observed. "A girl from another school says Billy stood by and watched two of his friends rape her."

The thought seized at my heart. I remembered the girl, her

cheerleader uniform, the way she stared at James until her friend had led her away. "Will you go to jail?"

"They want me to testify against them." His hands were icy. "But I don't remember what happened. I wasn't Billy then."

Tell them whatever they want to hear, I felt like shouting at him. But I knew he wouldn't lie.

"I have to get him back in his body," James said. He looked me in the eyes for a moment and then let go of my hands. "Wait for me at the park, the one with the deer statue."

"Will Mitch let you come?"

"No."

I sat down on the base of the statue, but a voice sent me to my feet at once.

"Mommy!"

The park was deserted except for a small boy sitting in an empty swing, glowing like a full moon. Smiling, he kicked his feet, but the swing hung perfectly still. He was looking in my direction, but it wasn't to me he spoke. He ignored me completely and leaned back, tilting up out of the swing, then forward into the air. He jumped with a laugh and disappeared like a firefly blinking out. Feeling queasy, I sat holding on to the iron ankle of the deer and waited perhaps ten minutes before I saw James.

He held out a hand and I ran to him. We didn't speak until we were at the bus bench. I huddled against him, praying that the bus would come soon, not looking up at the cars, afraid of seeing a rusty one. James kept an arm tight around me. It wasn't cold, but my teeth rattled.

"My parents think I'm having an affair with Mr. Brown," I told him.

"What?" His whole frame jumped.

"I've made a mess of everything."

"Tell them it's me," said James.

I considered telling him that I was only fifteen but instead hid my face in his neck and breathed in the scent of him—sweet salt, laundry soap, something indescribable that was just James.

We managed to get on the bus without being caught, and James read the map on the wall above the seats, almost as if searching for the secret instructions on how to lure Billy Blake back into his flesh.

Fifteen

THIS TIME WHEN JAMES signed in at the hospital, I signed in after him, forgetting to write Jenny's name until I had already written the word *Helen*. After it, I found that I had written the word *Lamb*. My father's name or my husband's, from a life I could not recall. I dropped the pen and followed James.

The halls smelled like strong soap and coffee. When we came into her room, Billy's mother sat in a wheelchair. Verna held the silent woman's bare foot in her lap, carefully painting her toenails pale pink. We stood in the doorway, and Verna smiled.

"I guess the cat's out of the bag," she said.

James came closer, watching Billy's mother. She wore a yellow bathrobe with tiny roses on it.

"If I didn't pretend to need you boys to bring me," said Verna, "how would we ever get Mitch to come visit?"

James wasn't listening.

"Who's your friend?" Verna asked him.

"I'm Jenny," I said.

"Verna, you know how drugs can affect your brain?" James asked.

The woman stared at him, open as a sunflower. "Sure, hon."

He was in a rush, but he stopped and took a breath, smiling at Verna. "Are you my mother's best friend?"

"Since we were eighteen."

"Would you tell me what happened to my mom?" he asked. "I don't remember."

She thought about this for only a heartbeat. "Your father was drinking, Mitch was at work, you and your mother were home. He used a bookend instead of his hand, and he didn't stop."

"Why didn't I stop him?"

"Honey," she said, almost as if scolding him. "You were twelve. And he threw you through a window."

"And I think Mitch blames me," said James. "Right?"

The question threw her off for a moment, but she capped the nail polish and looked at him sternly. "Billy, Mitch thinks if he'd been there, he could've saved you both."

"What's her first name?" James asked. We had both heard it before, but I couldn't recall it either.

Now Verna looked a little unnerved. "Sarah." She lowered Sarah's freshly painted left foot and backed out of the way when James knelt in front of the wheelchair.

"Sarah," he whispered to her. "Billy isn't dead. I'm holding his place. But I don't know how to call him back." James took her right hand and tried to look her in the eyes, but her head was tilted forward and her mouth hung slack. "Help me," said James.

I was praying for James to get some kind of message. Verna looked very confused.

"Please," said James. "What should I do?"

Verna looked at me now, but I couldn't answer the question in her eyes.

"Please." James put Sarah's right hand to his face. "Show me what to do." Her whole body was as still as wax, except for a tiny twitch that started now in her left hand.

"What's going on?" Fear had crept into Verna's voice.

The overhead light flashed off the wedding band as the ring finger on Sarah's hand trembled.

"Look," I said. James followed my gaze and saw the twitching now. He touched the ring with one finger and it stopped shaking.

"Thank you," he said, and kissed the hand he held.

"Where are they holding my father?" he asked Verna.

"Glisan." Her eyes filled with tears. "Mitch never took you?"

"Where is it?" he asked.

"Straight out MLK." Verna reached for her purse. "I'll drive you."

"No." James took my hand. "Please stay here with Sarah."

Verna watched anxiously as we hurried out.

When we were halfway across the parking lot, I looked back and through the glass doors saw Verna borrow the receptionist's telephone.

James had to stand beside the bus driver for the first couple of blocks to get advice about where to transfer. A toddler in a man's arms three rows back cried a tired stream of tears that made my bones ache. When I was Light, I hardly heard the weeping of infants, but now every sob pulsed in my head.

When James came to sit beside me, he held my hand to his

chest. Like a knight before battle, he was gathering strength, watching the horizon, rubbing my fingers so hard they tingled. Please, I thought, please don't leave me.

I looked to the window across from us and saw what looked like a double image. There were two of him reflected, but only one of me. James squeezed my hand tighter.

"It's him," he whispered.

The double image was gone.

"Who?" I asked.

"Billy."

I felt a sudden joy; something that was happening here had called him back. I scanned every windowpane, wanting to see Billy Blake's spirit, if I could. But I felt anxious about his presence, too; I was afraid it signaled the end of my time with James.

When we transferred to a second bus and sat in the front row, James finally looked at me and kissed me as if savoring a dip at the well before crossing a desert. I felt an urgency fill him and his face warmed with color.

"What are you going to say to his father?" I asked.

"I don't know."

"What's going to happen to us?" I sat with my arms around him and my legs over his.

"I don't know." We were both trembling but not in the same way. Not like when we were making love. Now I was trembling with fear, and James was vibrating with excitement—a hunter tracking a bear; a child stepping out into the night on Halloween.

The Glisan County Prison was a slate-colored grid. A huge lawn stretched out in front of the office that sat outside the enormous fences. It reminded me of a mausoleum where they don't want the corpses to escape. Once inside the lobby, I waited near the glass doors while James talked with the uniformed man behind the front desk. Half a dozen people waited in plastic chairs surrounding a low table covered with wrinkled magazines: a few middle-aged black men in bowling shirts, a large woman with a gigantic purse, a pale girl with a patch over one eye.

A guard came and led one of the men down the hall and around a corner. The man behind the desk was shaking his head at James, but James didn't give up. I was standing so near the door that Mitch almost ran into me when he stormed in.

He was wearing jeans and boots but only an undershirt, as if he'd rushed out in such a fury that he didn't notice. He pulled James around by the arm, but James didn't flinch. I could hear Mitch's acidic whisper, but I couldn't understand the words until they moved away from the desk, back closer to the entrance.

"Are you fucking nuts?"

"I need to see him," said James.

Now I could see Mitch's face as he stepped around James, positioning himself between his brother and the hallway. "You don't talk to me? You just run?" Mitch had his hands on his hips as if angry, but I saw his wrist shaking, and it wasn't rage.

James whispered something I couldn't hear.

"If you're looking for goddamn answers, I got one," said Mitch. "Tell them what those two little fuckers did. I can't believe you're protecting them."

Again James spoke too low for me to hear.

Mitch put his face in his hands. "Shit!"

Now the other visitors were watching the two brothers. Mitch returned to the desk, slapped open his wallet to show his driver's license to the man behind the counter. He signed the clipboard, still seething. James moved close to Mitch, seeming to have forgotten me. I wished I had Jenny's camera with me. I wanted to photograph the back of James's head—the way his hair made dark arrows on his damp neck.

"Maybe it'll do you good," Mitch grumbled. "See what it's like in there."

A guard approached them, and Mitch clutched a fistful of James's shirt as if he were planning on dragging him into the meeting room by force to face his father. James put his arm around Mitch's waist and, as he spread his hand on his brother's back, Mitch relaxed. The guard led them down the corridor, and I saw Mitch cup his brother's head in his big hand as they turned the corner of the hall and disappeared.

I was about to quietly take a seat and pretend to read a magazine, when someone spoke to me.

"Jenny?"

I looked over to find a tall policeman with a gold mustache standing in the lobby, holding a folder. He looked familiar. He frowned at me, but the next moment he was grinning, sliding the folder under one arm.

"What're you doing here?" he asked, looming over me.

"My friend's father—" I started, but I didn't know how much to say.

"Where are your parents?"

"I came with my friend," I told him.

"Why aren't you in school?"

I opened my mouth, to say, what? That I'd been taken out of school because I'd been having sex with the English teacher?

His expression cooled. His name tag said Redman—the policeman from the church picnic, the one who had done Dan a favor—he'd gone through channels, copied phone records, proved that I had called Mr. Brown at home. "Wait here," he ordered.

I might've run, but I was waiting for James. I watched Officer Redman lean in toward the man at the front desk, exchange a few words with him, borrow his phone. I didn't hear all that was said, but he did laugh out loud when he said into the receiver, "Better look again. I think she woke up."

I felt my mouth go dry when he hung up and strolled over to me, as kind as the doctor who is about to tell you how long you have to live.

"I'll drive you home."

The shoulder strap of Officer Redman's patrol car smelled like tobacco and peppermint. He let me sit in the front seat, but I still felt like a criminal. I sat holding the strap with both hands. He was calm and never asked me whom I had been visiting at the prison. In Jenny's driveway, he opened my door for me like a suitor. Cathy was standing in the doorway, Dan on the porch. Officer Redman gently cupped my elbow as we walked up the steps. I couldn't look in their eyes, so I kept my gaze on my feet. Cathy held my arm hard as she brought me into the living room. She didn't offer to run me a bath or give me a pill. I sat and she paced until Dan finished a quiet conversation with the officer outside.

"I don't know what you're thinking," Cathy said aloud, though she didn't actually seem to be talking to me. Dan stood still as a pulpit, but Cathy moved like a caged thing.

"It's like I don't know you," she said.

"Who were you with?" Dan asked.

"A friend from school," I told him, my voice sounding paper-thin. "A friend whose father is in jail."

"You are not going back to that school," said Cathy. "And I'm not sending her to that private school." Cathy said this to Dan rather than me. "The drugs are even worse there." He gave her a scowl, and she was pacing again, holding herself around the middle as if keeping her insides from spilling. "I'm keeping her home."

This turned my blood cold. "No school?" My voice buzzed, ready to tear.

"I'll homeschool you," said Cathy. "Dwayne and Dotty did that for their son."

"Cathleen." Again it was not just her name, but a warning.

She shot him a hard look. "Do you even care what that man did to her?"

Dan's jaw stiffened. Cathy looked sorry, shook out her hands, and then folded her arms so hard you could almost hear it.

"I just can't stand you lying to me," she said, and although she looked at me now, I saw Dan shift as if ready to answer her.

"I'm sorry," I said.

"Are you?" She stared me down, and I wished there were another way of keeping Mr. Brown out of the struggle, but I couldn't think of one.

"I'll tell you the truth now," I said. "I'm ready."

Cathy looked ill, as if afraid of what she might hear.

"The boy I was with today is the boy I've been seeing. His name's Billy Blake."

Dan's expression was sage, but Cathy only frowned.

"You can pull me out of that school if you want to," I said, "but it would be wrong to accuse Mr. Brown. Please don't hurt him."

As soon as the words were out, I felt that the last phrase was a mistake. They narrowed their gaze on me.

"We'll look into it," said Dan.

Cathy straightened her hair and wiped her palms on her skirt. "I'm not letting you out of my sight. You're coming with me to women's group."

For two hours Cathy had me cut melon, peel peaches, wash dishes. She chose me a white knit sweater and skirt, which I put on without a word.

We drove to a house that looked almost exactly like Dan and Cathy's, me holding a bowl of fruit salad on my lap. Jenny's face was reflected in the plastic wrap, pale and warped in a way I thought Jenny would've liked to photograph. A flock of women, all about Cathy's age, wearing neat slacks, sweaters with tiny pearl buttons, large wedding rings, small flat shoes, and all talking and shuffling dishes, told me I was welcome and they wished more of the youth group girls would attend. The house was as tidy as Cathy's but had the constant hum of an aquarium pump. I was given the seat across the room from the tank. It was as big as a bathtub, lit from within, and held a dozen fish that circled the blue endlessly. I was given a plate of food, a tiny lace napkin for my knee, and a glass of lemonade.

A thin woman with short black hair who reminded me of a ballerina said grace and started to lead a discussion. Time management was the topic, but they digressed. My stomach was empty, but the smell of food made me feel sick. Even sipping the lemonade made me queasy. I stared straight ahead at the fish tank and let the sleek, leaf-shaped creatures hypnotize me. It looked nice and peaceful in there. But maybe it would seem different from the inside.

"I'm so sorry," a voice was cooing. "How's your mom?"

"She'll get through it," a redheaded woman answered.

There was something else in the air, another scent that wasn't food. It was flowers. Then I noticed a bowl of white blossoms on the coffee table.

"We're going out for the funeral on Saturday."

I watched the fish go round and round.

"Who's this they're talking about?" someone asked.

"Elaine's father went home to heaven," Cathy told her.

"No, he went to the great void," the ballerina corrected. "He wasn't a Christian."

Cathy looked sympathetic, and the redhead looked uncomfortable. I watched her as she almost spilled her plate of melon balls and tuna hot dish.

"Well," said someone, "that's a shame. Didn't they have a chaplain at the hospital?"

"He couldn't have declared," said the ballerina. "He was in a coma."

I turned to Cathy. "What are they saying, that her father went to hell?"

Obviously shocked, Cathy whispered, "He didn't accept the Lord into his heart before he died." It was as if she would be embarrassed for anyone to hear me having to ask such basic questions. What kind of mother would they think she was?

"How do you know?" I asked Cathy. She just stared at me. The ballerina was watching us now from across the room. "How do you know he didn't have God in his heart before he died?" Now every eye was on me, and there was only the sound of the aquarium bubbling. "Why does he have to say anything out loud?" I wanted to know. "Someone has to hear it?"

"I don't think you understand," said the ballerina.

"I don't think so either," I said. "Why does anyone other than God have to hear him say it?"

"It's a moot point," said the ballerina. "He was brain dead."

My heart was pumping at a gallop. I dropped my plate of food so abruptly on the coffee table, two melon balls popped up and rolled around the centerpiece like lolling eyeballs. A roomful of forks stopped in midair. Cathy grabbed my arm.

"Are you saying that God can't speak to someone who's unconscious?" I asked.

This sent a wave of disturbed whispers through the room. I shook Cathy's grip from me and glanced around at them, disgusted. As my eyes scanned over the coffee table, I noticed that the flowers were fake—formed from silk and plastic.

"It doesn't say anything about that in the Bible," said the ballerina, as if this would end the discussion.

"Are you saying that God can do only things printed in the Bible?" I asked. I felt an unexplained wave of strength straighten my spine. "I thought God had no limits."

I heard Cathy gasp.

———

"God *can* do anything," said the redhead. "He knows everything and he sees everything."

I felt a fever scorch up to my temples. I stood up, which caused Cathy to make a sound almost like a sob. "You have no idea what it's like to die or go to heaven or not go to heaven," I told them. "Who do you think you are?" Every mouth hung open. I noticed I was still holding a glass of lemonade. For half a moment, I thought of throwing it. And the redhead could tell I was capable of it—she lifted a protective hand to her face. Instead I set the glass down beside the melon eyes so hard half the contents splatted out. "How can you be so arrogant?" I asked. "You don't know where her father went."

Then I smelled that sweet flower scent again, and I knew what it was. Gardenias. And it wasn't coming from the fake-flower arrangement. And it wasn't a scent Cathy wore, but I had smelled it on Dan's shirt and in his car. Now one of the women in this room was wearing that scent. Someone in this room had rubbed against Dan's clothes, ridden beside him in the passenger seat with his safety belt pressing on the skin of her throat.

"God speaks to us through his word," the ballerina managed to tell me, so shaken her voice cracked.

"God speaks to me, too," I said. My muscles were burning. I could do anything. "He's telling me right now that someone in this room has been committing adultery." I studied the crowd, hoping to figure out who had been with Dan by the shocked expression on the guilty woman's face, but unfortunately, they all looked shocked. "One of you is having sex with someone else's husband. How about that for a discussion topic?" I pried Cathy's fist off my skirt and walked straight out of the house.

At first I paced the sidewalk, elated. Then I remembered my vow to commit kindnesses and felt confused. I waited, leaning against the car in the dark until Cathy hurried out to me.

"I'm taking you to therapy tomorrow," she said, hyperventilating, her hands shaking so badly she dropped the keys twice before she could start the car. I sat in the passenger seat three feet from her side, but Cathy seemed very far away.

What had those women said that had angered me so? That this man who hadn't called to God with his last breath was now in hell? None of my hosts had spoken aloud to God in their last moments, yet I felt sure they had slipped painlessly into heaven. I myself had cried to God countless times, but, like a magic spell that requires precision, perhaps I had to use the right words.

"God," I whispered. I closed my eyes, holding my hands tight. "*Come into my heart.*"

The voice I heard wasn't God. It was a baby crying, but not the hoarse high pitch of a newborn. It was the true tears of a frightened two-year-old. I knew her sound. I think I said something out loud, though I don't know what. Then I saw water running down dark steps in front of me. Mud and water. And there was a terrible grinding and crashing sound from above. Something howling. My mouth tasted like metal, and I could feel the weight of the little girl on my hip, clutching at my apron with tiny fists.

What I thought was a dog's bark turned into a car honking. Water was hitting the car window on my side, running down in a curtain. I found that I was clawing at the glass, weeping and coughing. The car was stopped in the middle of the street, and Cathy was shouting at me, holding the seat belt tight across me. I stopped and felt a tingling in my hands where I'd been hitting the window. Now several cars were honking. I looked over and saw that Cathy was trying to dial her phone, but I put a hand over the tiny machine.

"I'm all right," I said.

She gaped at me, horrified.

I hugged myself, cold to the bone. "I want to walk."

"What?" She snatched at me as I let myself out of the car. A sprinkler from the yard beside us rained down on me as I slammed the door.

I started walking down the sidewalk, shaking and wet now, not caring what direction I took. I heard her car chime as the driver door opened.

"Jennifer Ann, you come back here." She was following me at a distance.

I turned to her, suddenly angry again. "You have no idea what you did."

She waved in apology to a honking truck, having parked her car in the right lane of traffic.

"Stop this right now and get back in the car." She tried to look angry, but fear swirled through her. The hand that held her phone was shaking. She didn't try to touch me. She'd stopped a coffin length away.

"You crushed the life out of your own daughter," I told her. "She ran away because she'd rather wander in limbo than live with you."

"What are you saying? You sound crazy."

"She just wanted to write down what she was feeling and take pictures—"

"Is this about the camera?"

"Listen!" I charged forward, wanting to slap her, and she felt it. Panicking, she tried to dial her phone and dropped it on the pavement, where it broke in pieces.

I was right in front of her now, but still she made no move to reach for me. "Jenny tried to obey you. She said her prayers and fasted and copied down Scriptures for you until she couldn't stand it anymore, and then she left."

Cathy was kneeling on the sidewalk clutching the pieces of her cell phone. "Who left?"

"And I tried, too. I tried to fit into your house." I knelt beside her and took her arm in my hand. It seemed so alien to feel her flesh so hot under my grip. I remembered weeping at the feet of my first host, wanting to grip her hand, but it was Cathy who was weeping now.

"I tried, but I can't anymore, and I don't know how to get out of her body."

"Jenny." Tears were running off her chin. "You're hurting me."

"Jenny's dead!"

I released her arm. I'd said it out loud, and as soon as I heard the words, I believed it. Jenny would never come back. I was trapped in her body and in her life forever. I waited for Cathy to put her arms around me in comfort, but there was no embrace. Cars honked and Cathy dragged herself to her feet, but I stayed on my knees and wept into my hands until I heard Cathy talking to someone. I looked up. A blue van had pulled over, and Cathy was asking to borrow the driver's phone. For one peculiar moment, I imagined the police arriving and taking me to the same cell as James. But a mental ward was more likely my fate.

"No," I said, rising. "I'll get in the car now."

Cathy turned to me, white and stained with eye makeup. She returned the phone and the van pulled away. The porch light of the house across the street came on. Two other cars had also stopped, their passengers watching this strange drama—a frightened mother and her distraught child weeping on the pavement in a strange neighborhood. A dog barked at us from the yard next door.

The lawn sprinkler stopped just as I approached the car. Cathy kept her distance until I was buckled into my seat again. She said not a word the rest of the trip but muttered to herself, sitting far forward against the steering wheel.

As we rolled up the driveway, Dan was putting something into the back of his car. He slammed the door and waited, arms crossed, as we got out.

"Go to your room," said Cathy. Her knees were still shaking.

I went into Jenny's room and sat on her bed. Strangely, the clothes I had used as a fake body under the covers were neatly stacked by the pillow. If Mitch had found Billy missing, the clothes would've been thrown about in a rage. But Cathy had carefully folded sweaters and buttoned blouses closed up to the collars.

Through the wall I could hear the rise and fall of anxious voices though not the actual words. When Cathy opened my door at last, her face was stiff. She looked at the floor when she told me to come to Prayer Corner. Dan was standing by the chairs. Cathy asked me to sit, so I sat where I always did. They both stayed standing. The Bible and the journal were gone.

"We're afraid for you," Dan told me. "You lie to us and humiliate your mother in front of her friends, cause a scene on a public street."

"She had some kind of episode," Cathy said. I regretted scaring her so badly. There were scrapes on her knees from the pavement. "I think we should take her to the emergency room," she whispered.

"Don't get hysterical." Dan's voice was low, but she succumbed instantly.

"We made you an appointment for a counseling session with the pastor in the morning," said Dan. "And your mother will be getting home-schooling materials from the district office tomorrow."

Cathy hovered behind her chair, a marginal player, craving power.

"Mr. Brown never touched me," I told them. "Why don't you call my friend?"

"I did." Dan sighed, pretending it pained him to have to tell me. "Billy Blake says he doesn't have a girlfriend."

I couldn't quite believe what I was hearing. "Maybe he was afraid to admit it."

"I talked to his older brother," Dan said. "He told me the only girl he's seen Billy with lately is named something like Helen."

"That's me," I said, as if this would explain everything.

Cathy made a sound as if she were frustrated to the point of emitting steam. "Why would he call you Helen?"

I knew that if I tried to tell them the real reason again, they'd have me committed to a sanitarium. I felt the defeat tighten around my ribs.

"Kneel," said Dan.

It was so unexpected, the syllable didn't even seem like a word.

"On your knees, young lady," Dan commanded.

I obeyed, kneeling in the small circle of chairs.

"Pray for forgiveness and guidance," he ordered.

Now Cathy sat in her chair and folded her hands.

"Leave her," Dan snapped. Then to me he added, "I'll come to release you."

I watched Cathy slowly stand back up. She looked at me for one tortured moment. I had asked her for help, and she had sent me to the lions. I knew that she was trying to save her little girl, but sometimes mothers with the best intentions kill their daughters all the same.

She covered her mouth as she followed Dan out of the room, and I was left kneeling in the harsh light.

The room was so still, like a museum housed with the dead — boxes of puzzles unsolved and games that brought no joy, a stereo no one danced to, windows that looked out onto a garden in which no one had ever written a poem. But there was one beautiful thing in the room. The phone. The one that had interrupted the Scrabble game — the one Cathy had used to call Dan back and confront him. He had lied about why he was late to the church picnic, and Cathy had held this phone in one hand and the gasoline receipt in the other. The same phone I had used once to talk to James. I didn't know what would happen if they came back in and caught me, but I took the chance. I lifted the receiver silently and dialed, but the line was busy at the Amelia Street house.

I went back to the Prayer Corner and knelt, closing my eyes and pressing my hands together with a passion. "Please, God," I prayed. "Keep James safe and let us be together."

I wanted to imagine James in every detail, remember every second from the theater loft. I wanted to go back over everything he had ever said to me, one sentence at a time, but my mind would not help me. I kept seeing strange images appear and disappear like clouds passing over a field and revealing one place and then another in the wandering light. I saw a patchwork quilt as I shook it on a bare wooden porch. A line blowing with shirts and trousers as if they were coming alive. A one-legged sparrow flitting from the water pump as I approached. I opened my eyes, sure that this would stop the images, but now I could hear things that were not in Jenny's house. The soft bump of my rocking chair as it rolled on and off the edge of the hearth rug. The high whine of sap in a log on the fire. Crickets through the open bedroom window. The creak of a man's step on the wooden staircase.

These things unnerved me, but it was the smells that truly frightened me. As I looked around this dim and lifeless room in Dan and Cathy's house, I could smell the familiar mix of wet hay and warm milk, the lavender sachet pillow tucked into the linen cupboard, and the painfully sweet breath of an infant, like vanilla cream. I would not close my eyes but prayed over the sound of a rising wind with my eyes wide open. I didn't even want to blink. I prayed for help—I couldn't think past this simple need. I didn't remember collapsing, but I was on the floor, lying on my side when I heard the door. It might've been an hour or several. I was dizzy and my legs were numb when he came in. I sat up and looked at him, not knowing whether to expect sympathy or anger. His expression was unreadable.

"Go to bed now," said Dan. "The motion sensors are on out back," he added, as if to save me the embarrassment of being caught halfway across the yard.

No one came in to kiss me goodnight. I waited until the house was dark before I sneaked out into the hall. I tiptoed to the kitchen, wanting some distance between myself and the master bedroom.

Benny, Mitch's friend, answered the phone. It sounded as if there were several people over, laughing and talking, music in the background. When Benny called for Billy and he answered, I said only one word.

"James?"

"Who?" The voice was unfamiliar and sounded confused. There was a heartbeat pause and then Billy Blake told me, "Sorry. There's no James here." The line went dead.

Sixteen

"YOU'LL HAVE TO GO BACK," said Cathy. She thought I was trembling because I was cold. "Get your black sweater."

I didn't even remember putting on clothes that morning, but I was wearing a sleeveless dress. I got out and left Cathy in the driveway, the car idling. When I came into the house, I suppose that Dan didn't hear me. He spoke on the phone without his usual hush.

"What kind of emergency?" he was saying. He was in the study with the door open, looking through his desk drawer, with the receiver tucked into his neck. "How long?" He listened, lifting a key and inspecting it. "I'll meet you there." He dropped the key into his pocket. This was the first I'd seen of him that morning. There had been no Prayer Corner.

"I will as soon as she gets back," he said. Then he gave a little laugh. "She's a big girl." I thought he was talking about me until he added, "And Jenny, too. They'll be fine." I was standing in the hall staring in at him. "I have it under control," he sighed. "I know what I'm doing." He swung toward me with an ease that let me know he thought he was alone. "There's no reason to feel—"

Dan stopped and blinked at me. "Hey, Puppy," he said. "Forget something?"

I knew I had disconcerted him—he forgot to be cross with me. I remembered with revulsion the oppressive weight of his hands on me while he asked God to make me obedient.

"Don't ever touch me again," I heard myself say.

"What?"

I turned my back on him and walked into my room without a word.

"What took you so long?" Cathy asked as I slammed the door.

I buckled my seat belt and thought of saying, "I couldn't get the bedroom window open," but I didn't.

When we arrived in the church office, the secretary offered me a mint from her heart-shaped jar as if I were five years old.

"Pastor Bob had an emergency," she said. "But one of the lay counselors is taking his sessions this morning, if that's all right. Judy Morgan."

"Of course," said Cathy. "Judy's wonderful."

The room hung stiff with the smell of dead lilies and candle wax.

"You can come back for her in an hour," said the secretary.

"No." Cathy sat down on the couch against the wall with her purse in her lap. "I'll wait."

Before I even had the chance to take a seat beside her, an elderly woman came down the hall toward us. She dabbed her eyes with a tissue and looked embarrassed to have Cathy and me witness her tears.

"Go right in," the secretary said to me.

Apparently I was going in for counseling alone, for Cathy didn't move. I walked down the corridor and pushed open the door marked PASTOR. Just as I stepped in, the scent hit me. The woman behind the desk spoke to a red button on the phone. "Did you say Jenny *Thompson*?" She looked up at me as if I had caught her taking money from the collection plate. She pressed the red light and it went off.

"Hi, Jenny." She smiled, but her face was white. I took the chair across from the desk, breathing in the scent of gardenias. By the time my back hit the chair, she had regained her composure. She eyed me with cool wisdom.

"Pastor Bob had to go on a hospital call," she explained, smoothing down her short black hair.

What did the secretary say her name was? Jenny would've known. And Cathy must know her very well. She was the ballerina woman from the night before.

"Are you feeling better?" she asked. "Last night you seemed upset."

"Better."

"What's troubling you?"

I thought of several other answers, but said, "My parents think a teacher at my school took advantage of me, but it's not true."

"Why do they think that?"

Last night she'd been wearing a blue sweater with daisies on it and her favorite perfume. I tried to remember the look on her face when she'd heard the word *adultery*. And I wondered how much Dan had told her about the Mr. Brown affair.

"That's not important," I told her. "But he's not my lover."

"He's not," she repeated. "Is there someone else?"

The words were poison coming from her lips, and her perfume was making my eyes sting. "Yes," I admitted.

"Who?" Her sweater today was black with pink roses on it. I wondered whether she had a different flower for each day of the week.

"A boy from school."

"Jennifer, did you let this boy touch you?" The judgment in her expression made my cheeks burn. She folded her ballerina arms.

"Well," I said. "You know how it is. You fall in love and you want to do more than just hold his hand."

"But you knew it wasn't right," she reminded me.

"I'm sure you must've felt the same way," I said. "You know it's a sin, but you just want to be with him, as much as you can, no matter what. You'd do anything to have just one more minute with him. You can almost feel his body in your arms when you lie in bed alone."

Miss Ballerina had gone white again. She fumbled for a pad and pen.

"Haven't you ever felt like that?" I asked.

She didn't answer but frowned as if taking notes. The pen tapped spastically on the pad.

"Tell me about how you fought off that kind of temptation in your life," I said. "I need to learn."

She put down her pen.

"Of course, it's not like he had a girlfriend and we were sneaking around," I said. "That would be different."

"I think perhaps Pastor should meet with you," she said.

I stood up.

Now she looked at me. "Mrs. Leighton can make the appointment."

"Whatever you say," I shrugged. "No need to come out. I'll tell my mother."

She looked relieved. I stepped out the door and instead of going to the right, back toward the secretary's desk, I turned left and pushed open a door to the back parking lot.

I didn't know how much time I had before they'd send the police after me. I took the back streets because I didn't have bus fare, and I didn't want Cathy or Dan to hunt me down too quickly. When I'd found my way onto Amelia, I started remembering what I'd heard on the phone the night before. Ever since then, I'd tried to convince myself that James was still here—that he'd hung up on me only because there were others too near—he was trying to protect me. But now the truth was growing heavy in my limbs, like liquid metal filling my legs. I recalled the wretched emptiness of being left on earth as each of my hosts had died— wondering why God wouldn't let me follow. Now I dragged my feet along until I saw them, Billy and Mitch, standing in the driveway. As soon as Billy's eyes met mine, I knew.

"Gimme a wrench," said Mitch as he crouched down beside the rusty frame. Billy saw me standing two doors down on the sidewalk, staring, and he stared back.

"Wake up," said Mitch as he slid under the car on his back.

Billy pulled a tool from the apple crate at his feet and put it in the hand that reached out from between the tires.

I looked at the face of a stranger, a beautiful boy, but no one I knew. He frowned at me and flicked the hair out of his eyes with a jerk of his head, not with his hand the way James would've.

"Hey," he called. I was startled. I moved closer, just to make sure.

Billy wiped his hands on his smudged Skull T-shirt and came to meet me halfway.

"Do you remember me?" I asked, trying to keep a quaver out of my voice.

"Sure," he said. "You go to my school."

"You don't remember anything else?"

He squinted in the sun and shrugged. "Your name's Jenny something." Then fear gripped him. "Is this about the trial?"

"No."

He relaxed, but still it was so lonely being with him, my heart was twisting.

"Did you want something?" he asked.

"I needed to see whether you were okay," I told him.

He looked perplexed. I took a step backward, away from him.

"We used to be close," I said.

"We did?" He shook his head. "I got pretty messed up," he said. "I don't remember everything." He wasn't ringing hollow. He was Billy on the inside.

"It's all right." I turned to go.

"Sorry for whatever I did," he called.

I ran even though I could hardly see.

The cool wind made my eyes water down my face, but I felt dry, too empty to make real tears. Mitch probably should have been at work and Billy at school, but Mitch must have kept him home as if it were a holiday, and whether they knew it or not, it was a homecoming. But it was a celebration I could not share with them.

Something had happened at the prison that had sent Billy flying back into his flesh. I tried to imagine what magic words had called him home. When Mitch looked into their father's eyes, did all his rage finally explode, sending an alarm bell tolling into the void where Billy wandered? Had the boy rushed back into his body in time to catch his brother when the anger cracked into sorrow, the desire to hold him and to be held too great to resist?

If passion was the magic formula, why hadn't Jenny heard me raging at Cathy the night before and come flying back? Hadn't she heard her mother weeping?

All my mistakes were looming hard in front of me like iron bars. I shouldn't have written to or called Mr. Brown. I should never have taken his picture or gone to see him in his office. I should have made James take me back to the theater loft instead of to his bed where Mitch could catch us. I should've walked past Jenny's body. I should've stayed with Mr. Brown and let James fall in love with a human girl. I was so weary. I started to dream, though my eyes were open and I must've been walking over pavement and through streets. I dreamed I saw James, not with Billy's face, but with the face of the soldier he'd been. He seemed to be climbing down a huge tree toward me, smiling at me, though rain dripped from his hair.

"You're in uniform," I said to him, as if he had asked me

what he was wearing. Next moment, I was standing in Jenny's driveway alone. The garage was open, but only the maroon car was parked there. I could hear a strange sound from the house as if a wolf were tearing up the furniture inside. I was too tired to feel afraid. I walked in to face whatever was waiting.

I found Cathy taking framed pictures off the front room walls and opening them frantically, throwing down the frame and glass with angry growls and tearing the photographs, or twisting them if they were too tough to rip up. She didn't seem to see me. She had tears and makeup running rivers down her cheeks. She looked at the mess but stepped right on a pane of glass with her small shoes, breaking it and grinding it into the carpet as she hurried down the hall. I followed, feeling ill. I wanted to speak to her, but I felt so exhausted I just watched. She stormed into the den and pulled the Monopoly game off the shelf, bringing Scrabble down with it, plastic houses and wooden letters mixing around her feet as she crouched down and fumbled through the chaos.

She got something small in her hand and shot up, throwing it with all her might as a yell ripped out of her. The object hit the window with a crack and bounced to the floor not far from me. It was a tiny metal top hat.

Now she saw me. She gulped back a sob and stared at me, stunned. She wiped her face with both hands and smoothed her clothes.

"Where did you go?" she asked in nothing more than a whisper.

"I had to see my friend who was in trouble," I told her. "He's all right now."

"Well, that's good." Then she held her stomach as if she might be sick.

"What happened?" I asked her.

"We'll talk about it later. Go to your room, please." She wanted to sound stern, but then she looked at the mess she had made and started to shake.

I took a step toward her, but she put out a hand to stop me. "I'll clean it up after —"

"Where's Dad?" I asked.

Again she seemed to forget me. I followed as she marched into the study and started pulling books off the shelves, dumping them in a pile on the floor. She was jerking open desk drawers and rifling through them, throwing pens and, I suppose, other things of his onto the pile of books on the rug. She took one of the time management books and opened it in the middle, putting her weight into it but not able to tear it in two.

I had been feeling weak and numb, but now, watching Cathy's pain, I felt a surge of power the way I had when I'd shocked the church ladies. It felt as if the joy of loving James followed by the pain of losing him had galvanized something in me. "What did Dad do?" I asked.

"Didn't I tell you to go to your room?" She struggled with the book, twisting it at the spine. "Why do you have to fight me? Why can't you help me?"

I stepped closer, standing eye to eye with her, and took the book from her hands. Taking a firm grip, I wrenched it savagely down the middle and tore it in two, putting the pieces back into her limp hands.

She was so surprised, she just stared at me and let the pieces fall at her feet. Now I moved back out of the way and waited to see what else she wanted to destroy. In her eyes I saw a flicker of realization—we were allies now—I would never side with Dan against her.

"Thank you," she said softly, then walked past me into the hall.

I followed her back to the den. She stopped in the middle of the room, staring at the Prayer Corner where the Bible and diary sat each on its chair. I stood beside her and she looked at me for a peculiar moment. Then we rushed as one at the trio of chairs. Cathy managed to tear the leg off one and the cushion off another, the stuffing flying in every direction. I ripped the pages of the diary into little paper petals and tossed them over our heads. Cathy was still shaking, but now she was laughing. She flew at the cupboard on the wall and came back with a crystal decanter. I shrieked and jumped out of the way as she tossed what might have been brandy over the toppled chairs and shredded paper. I started laughing as well but picked up the Bible that lay half buried in cotton batting, saving it from the dousing.

Next Cathy grabbed the box of matches from beside the fireplace and struck a light, tossing it at the chairs. The flames undulated faster and higher than either of us expected. After a few seconds of delight, Cathy ran for the extinguisher from behind the door and spat white foam over the fire. I was still stamping out bits of handwritten Scripture that had levitated into the room and threatened to melt the carpet when Cathy dropped the red canister at her feet and swayed. She wasn't laughing anymore.

The deafening buzz of the smoke detector made us both cry

out. We jumped at the plastic shell, where it clung to the ceiling just inside the door, but missed it by inches. I ducked as Cathy smashed it to bits by throwing the empty decanter at its blinking eye. It hung in two mute pieces. The smoke smelled like caramel.

Cathy clutched at her mouth and ran for the master bedroom. I followed. She lunged for the toilet and vomited, then collapsed on the bathroom floor, crying with her face on her knees. I had never been in the master bedroom. The bathroom carpet was as soft as a bed. I crept up to her, almost afraid she'd bolt away like an animal. Sitting down beside her, I put my hand on her head. She rattled and her voice was a hoarse, tortured wail. I stroked her hair and remembered wanting to touch my hosts when they wept, but when I was Light, I had never been able to feel their hair or wipe their eyes. Her hair was as soft as a baby girl's.

"He left," she cried. "He's divorcing me and marrying Judy Morgan. They're moving to San Diego."

"I'm sorry," I told her.

"She sat there at women's group as if nothing was wrong." Cathy looked at me in amazement. "She sits in the pew behind us every week." Then she looked startled. "What did she say to you this morning in the pastor's office?"

"Nothing."

Her tears overcame her again. "He doesn't want me." She looked at me as if I wouldn't believe it if she didn't say it right to my face. "He says I'm too rigid," she told me, her eyes strangely glowing from the pain. "*I'm* too rigid."

I pulled a towel from the rack over my head and handed it to her.

"I wasn't even saved when I met him," she said, wiping her

face. "He said he couldn't date outside the church. He was the one who taught me." She looked at the makeup on the towel and started crying again, holding the cloth to her eyes. I got up and wetted a washrag, touching it to her hand. She gasped back a sob and looked up. "He said I'm stifling him—" She broke off as I wiped her face with the cold cloth. "He's not comfortable living with me anymore."

"Could it be," I said, "that he's a hypocrite?"

For one half second she looked at me, astonished, as if she might laugh again, but then I saw the reality crash in, the idea of being alone, of everyone in her life finding out.

A sudden sorrow filled my chest. I imagined James slowly walking the bases on the empty baseball field at night and the ghost of his friend Diggs trying to talk to him all those years, wanting to free him—the regret of all those desolate nights clutched at me so tightly I couldn't breathe.

I knew I wouldn't hear James call to me that night or the next. I would never be able to hear his voice again.

"I'm sorry I was rigid to you," Cathy sobbed.

The childlike wording brought me out of my thoughts. "What do you mean?"

"You're rebelling," she said. "I was too strict. Now you'll hate me, too."

"I don't hate you."

"You don't have to be like me," she wept. "I don't know what I'm doing."

"Nobody does," I told her.

"I don't even know what to think about God." She stopped, staring at nothing, looking terrified. "Did he lie about God?"

"Don't worry." I tried to sound comforting. "God loves you." But all the while I got her to her feet and helped her wash her face, all the while I got her a sedative and sat her down on her bed, all the while I made her tea, I wondered, *But what about God? Does He love me? If He does, why did He leave me trapped here? Why did He give me James and then take him away?*

When I walked in with the mug of tea, Cathy was weeping again.

"It's my fault," she sobbed as I put an arm around her shoulder.

"No," I told her.

"What happened to you at school," she said. "I wouldn't let you have friends. I burned your pictures."

"My pictures?"

"I drove you away from God," she confessed, and then her weeping made her cough so hard she had to fight for air.

"You burned my photographs?" I asked, rubbing her back.

Cathy nodded.

"Not all of them," I told her. I gave her the tea and put the blankets over her legs, then went to my room. When I came back with the envelope, she stared at me with large pink eyes. I sat beside her on the bed and took out Jenny's art.

"It's all right," I said. "Look." I showed her a picture of a hand stretching to touch a leaf. "See? It's called 'Adam's Reach.'"

Cathy took the picture with trembling fingers and gazed at it.

"And this one," I handed her a picture of Jenny leaping with a burst of light instead of a face. "This one's called 'Spirit.'"

Her tears had eased into a slow, hot crawl. Cathy leaned close to me to see each image.

"And this one." I handed her the untitled photo of blurry bird wings and invented a name. "It's called 'Angels.'"

Cathy smoothed the surface of the picture to remove a fingerprint.

I handed her one of Jenny, nude, sitting with her head down on her raised knees, her face hidden. "'Gethsemane.'"

Cathy took my hand in hers and held the back of it to her chest, the way James used to. A sorrow I hadn't expected shook me. I let her rest on my shoulder and waited until I felt her breathing slow and her grip go slack before I slipped away. She lay with Jenny's images spread over her like petals on a wedding bed.

I stood in the hallway for a long time. I stared at the carpet, smelled the sweet, smoky scent of what had been the Prayer Corner. I stood there and could not move. If Jenny had been devastated by a boy at school who had left her brokenhearted, she could have wept with Cathy. They could have held each other all night, whispered in the dark like little girls in the attic, keeping each other brave through a night of strange sounds and shadows. But I couldn't tell Cathy about James. I would never be able to tell anyone about him. Never be able to tell anyone who I was.

As I went to Jenny's bathroom and began to fill the tub, I knew what I was doing wouldn't help Cathy. But there was nothing I could do for her. She needed her little girl, but that little girl was long gone. I undressed and opened the cupboard behind the mirror, lifting down the bottle of sleeping pills. I counted thirty-three. With the steam fogging the tiny room, I balanced the bottle of pills on the corner of the tub. I stepped in, slowly lowered myself into the hot water, and turned off the tap. I could hear the dripping of the faucet into the bath water and the small sounds of birds outside the window. Somewhere far away there was a siren.

Somewhere nearby, I thought, Cathy's husband was holding in his arms a woman who is not his wife and was feeling relieved that it was finally done. Not far away, Mr. Brown was standing in a room full of children, many of whom would have already heard rumors. And only a few miles away, Billy and Mitch were trying to revive a rusty engine.

But James was gone.

It was time to stop. I took one small white pill from the bottle and looked at it. Like the button from a baby's dress. I put it in my mouth and scooped a handful of warm bath water up. I swallowed and tried two the next time. I found that the pills were small enough so that taking a few at a time was not difficult. Cathy may not survive this, I thought, and Dan may think that Jenny did this because he left them. These thoughts should have stayed my hand, but my mind and heart were already going to sleep. Either God would take me in his arms, or he wouldn't. I tried to imagine heaven, but all I saw was dark water.

I felt my stomach tighten as I swallowed my fourth handful. I couldn't remember when I'd eaten last. I closed my eyes and took deep breaths as I felt the pills creep down my throat. Then the faintest of all possible flutters, like a tiny bee shaking its wings, tickled inside me. I put a hand to my belly, flat and soft in the warm water, and fear jolted me. This felt familiar. My pulse started racing, but the drug was already pulling down on my arms and head like heavy snow on tree limbs. I gripped the side of the tub with one hand as I slid back, water up to my shoulders.

Had James and I made a child together? Even that, being but a pinhole of hope to me now, couldn't move me. I knew it was wrong, what I was doing. Like murder, but I needed to be done with it all. I felt my lids begin to relax and my heart beat slowly.

And then I felt I was being watched. I opened my eyes and focused on the room. There was no one there, only tile and mirror and tub. But there *was* someone there, curious about the speck of life inside me. She'd come back. Something that was happening here had called Jenny back. I felt that she was just behind me, but when I grasped the side of the tub to turn and look, I sent the remaining pills flying out of the bottle to roll across the floor like a broken string of pearls. I closed my eyes and tried to see her. A small oval face with large eyes and golden hair.

She was there, shyly waiting for me to die, her eyes wide, her lips slightly parted as if she might speak. She stood at the far end of the tub and watched with empathy but made no move to save the body that had once been hers.

Please, I thought at her, *come in. I'm going.*

I could feel the water tickling at my neck now. The hand that held the side of the tub slipped and splashed into the bath. And now there was something else in the room. A presence dark and nauseating. The same blackness that had thrown me out of a ladies' room at the mall. The evil inched out of the base of the wall and across the tiles. Jenny's spirit did not seem to see it.

Hurry, I thought at her. *Hurry, sweetheart.*

Water black, muddy, and ice cold trickled down the cellar's walls and steps. The roaring outside shook my nerves, but I smiled and said, "It's all right, baby. It's just a storm." My daughter, not yet two years old, whined and clung to me with all her tiny might, her fists full of my blue dress and dirty apron and her legs around my waist. I held her on one hip as I put the lantern on the shelf and looked around for the wooden stool that I used to store down there. The distant sound of glass breaking made me sorry that I hadn't thrown a blanket over the bookcase with my favorite books. Although the cellar was no bigger than a wardrobe, I couldn't find the stool, only firewood, broken tools, my straw baskets on the lower shelves. A crack of thunder and a flash made the child scream and begin to cry. I myself jumped and held her to me hard, then thumped her back cheerfully.

"Hush, baby girl." I sat on a stack of wood and she hid against my chest, still wailing. We had fled to the safety of the cellar when a broken tree branch smashed through the bedroom window and a loose fence post shattered a kitchen window moments later. But the cellar, which had seemed so sound at first, was slowly filling with rain. Water, two inches deep on the cellar floor, reflected the lamplight in little gold worms that appeared and disappeared. When the next crack of thunder split my ears, I shrieked and was on my feet at once. Half a moment later there was a crash that shook the whole foundation of the house and rattled my bones and teeth. The baby stopped breathing for one moment, then cried even louder. At once dark water was gushing into our hiding place through the seams in the slanted wood doors.

In disbelief, I watched for ten full heartbeats as a lake began to rise up my legs. Then I rushed to the doors and pushed on them, but they wouldn't move. Something was blocking them, holding them down. I couldn't put the baby on the floor, so I sat her on the woodpile and attacked the doors with all my power. Time slowed to an agonizing crawl as I searched for tools, then started hacking at the planks of the cellar doors with a broken garden hoe. I was slowed, but the water kept coming. Maybe the river, more likely the water tank. I tore at the wood with my bloody fingers and called for my husband, though I knew he was miles away.

The baby was crying so hard that I looked back and saw that even on the woodpile, she was chest deep in water. I snatched her up and sat her on the shelf. I went back to the doors and clawed and screamed at the stubborn wood until a plank finally tore free and I could see out. The enormous trunk of our oak was now pinning the cellar doors shut. It didn't move an inch no matter how I raged at it. The opening through which I could see the outside world was only about as large as a cat. The water was up to my shoulders now. My teeth were chattering when I took my baby daughter in my arms and said, "Sweetheart, you run to Fanny's house."

The storm that howled outside the mouth of the cellar looked terrifying, but now the water was to my neck. The baby held me around the head, clutching my hair and crying. "It's all right," I told her, moving to the gap in the jagged planks. "I'll come later. You go to Fanny. You run to Fanny's house."

She protested in wild yelps, but I pulled her off my neck and pointed her out the hole. "Not to Grandpa's," I said. That was downhill and too near the river. "Fanny's house. Run!" A bobbing basket tapped against my shoulder.

I held her waist as she crawled through the tiny space, sputtering as water hit her face. The lantern hissed and the small gold light behind me was gone. Once free, the baby turned around and peered back into the gap. The water was up to my chin. I coughed as a small wave surprised me. I spit the water out. It tasted like iron and soil.

"Mama?" she said.

"Don't wait for me, baby," I called. "Run!" She turned and disappeared into the storm. If I had been wiser, we would both be wrapped in a quilt under the bed upstairs. Another bone-tearing crash made me suck in water and gag. From above a high scream pierced me like a blade and was cut short as if the flood swallowed my child whole.

I felt water at my chin, still warm but not hot. I blinked and spoke out loud. "I killed my baby." Then I felt a hand on my belly, but it wasn't my own hand. I felt a falling sensation in my middle. My own hand drifted to the surface of the bath, and then my whole self drifted to the surface of my body. Not my body. Hers. I floated above and the body slipped below, gold hair spread on the surface of the water, darkening as it became wet. A hollow sound like an empty seashell began to softly ring from the tub.

The girl Jenny was watching this. "Go," I wanted to tell her, but I was as mute as when I was Light and hovering around Mr. Brown. Oozing like black mud, the evil was moving closer to the body than the girl was now, almost to the edge of the tub. *Take the body*, I thought at her. *I can't get through again. You have to.*

Jenny slid down into the water with her body, and the flesh trembled. Then the eyes opened at me. "Thank God," I thought, but next moment, a bubble rose from the face and the lids started to drift shut.

"No!" I tried to shout at her. "Wake up!" Her hair drifted down to her shoulders, too heavy to float now. Jenny wasn't breathing. I tried to touch her, but I was formless. Furious, I screamed at the bathtub with the naked girl sleeping below like a white doll.

If you exist, I told God, you help me.

I ducked into the water and brought my lips right to her ear. "Wake up!"

So many times I had moved a curtain or startled a bird into flight when I was trying to be silent and invisible, and now that I was frantic to slap her out of her apathy, I could not even ripple the surface of the water. She had gone back into her flesh, and yet the blackness that had crept into the room hadn't fled. Did it not realize that she was no longer empty? The blackness dripped up the side of the tub and relaxed into the water, coloring it a smoky gray.

Something about the arrogance of this infuriated me.

I came in as close to Jenny's face as I could in the darkening water and yelled, "Fight!"

Her body jerked, she opened her eyes again, and then she was sitting up, coughing and sputtering. The evil disappeared, leaving the tub clear. Jenny vomited and cried out in horror at the small white pills in the bath water with her. In confusion and repulsion, she let the water out of the tub and pushed the pills away from her as they went down the drain. She sat bewildered and shivering. She turned the hot water on and took a handful of it, drinking it down in a panic. She saw the pills on the tile floor. She sat in the tub, naked and wet, the tap flowing warm water over her feet.

I watched this from above her. I was like a kite caught in a tree at the corner of the ceiling. Then Jenny jumped at the sound of the doorbell. It rang over and over until the sound of Cathy's voice was heard, strained and rising. Now there was knocking at the bathroom door. "Jenny?" Cathy tried the handle, but the door was locked. "Are you feeling sick?" Jenny turned off the tap and listened, eyes wide with fear.

Then a boy's voice. "Jenny?" It said. "Can I talk to you?"

Then Cathy, "Honey, there's someone to see you."

Jenny didn't answer. She seemed paralyzed. It was as if she didn't know where she was, who she was, who were her enemies. The two voices argued in whispers.

"I'm serious." Cathy called through the door. She put on her calm but stern voice. "This is your mother speaking. You let me in this minute." The knocking grew to a loud thumping. The hinges rattled.

"Are you hurt?" The boy's voice again.

"No." Jenny's voice was so soft no one had heard.

"Open this door!" Cathy was getting shrill. "I'm going to call the police."

The door handle shook until the pills on the floor started vibrating. Then the sound of Cathy's voice as it moved down the hall. "I'm calling 911."

"I'm all right," Jenny called.

The door burst open with a crack of wood, and Billy Blake was standing on the tile floor, a sleeping pill crunched under his shoe.

Jenny hid her nakedness, holding her knees in front of her, shivering and staring at him in amazement.

"Are you okay?" he asked.

"I don't know," she said with a trembling jaw.

Billy took a towel and draped it over her shoulders as he kneeled down by the tub.

"I'm sorry I said I didn't remember you when you came to see me today," he said.

"I came to see you?" She stared at his face as if she were trying to recall a dream she'd had.

"After you left, I found this in my room." He took something from his back pocket and showed it to her. "This is us," he said.

With wet hands, she held the sides of the little black-and-white photograph, blurry and overexposed, two laughing faces close together, naked shoulders.

"I've been having some trouble remembering things," he told her.

She looked at Billy, still stunned. "Me too."

"You look happy with me," he said, as if this were unbelievable.

Jenny stared at the faces in the photograph with tears in her eyes, then took a breath. "Yeah, I do."

He sat down and, as she studied the picture, he gently rubbed the towel on her wet hair. She looked back at his face and asked, though it seemed to embarrass her, "Is your name Billy?"

He laughed. "Yeah."

All this I observed from the corner of the ceiling above them, but now I was passing out of the room, right through the roof. I felt my heart fold out like a blossom not only because Jenny had saved herself and Billy had found her but also because I was being drawn to heaven at last. I was sure I could see some light ahead and then James smiling at me as if through a hole in the sky no bigger than a cat.

But to my sharp sorrow, the hole was a hole in a cellar door, and there was icy cold all around me and only darkness except for that one patch where the storm jittered in lightning flashes above. I didn't struggle anymore.

"Helen?" His voice was right by my ear, and I felt James close his arms around me from behind. What a painful mix of desire and loss overwhelmed me. He was all that I wanted, but I knew I was only dreaming him. There was dark water all the way up to my chin. His arms weren't solid and his voice was inside my head. He pressed into me like heat. I wanted to weep, but I had plummeted past tears.

"You're not really here," I told him.

"I am," he said. He was melting into me.

A new chapter of my hell was beginning—my worst moment jailed around me for eternity and God dangling my unclaimable joy just outside the bars.

"Come with me," he said.

Mourning for the pleasure of our joined bodies, I wanted to weep, but I was dry as a skull. "I can't."

"You can break open these walls," he said. "You built them."

"Only God can tear down these walls," I told him.

He laughed, deep inside me, and whispered, "Stubborn."

"Mama?" I looked up into the hole in the cellar door and saw my baby girl's face staring in at me, frightened. A flicker of hope caught my heart. Maybe I could alter the nightmare.

"Hang on to the branches as you go," I called to her. She frowned at me, then the pale valentine of her face moved out of sight. I saw her tiny hand grasp the branch just outside the opening.

"Run!" You, my girl, can survive me, I thought. My beloved confidant. My savior from dark dreams—who rescued me with your sudden crying in the night, bringing me out of your father's cold bed and into your arms. You, my only child. You, my only friend. Don't wait. Run. *Live*.

To my horror, her small voice came again from just outside.

"Mama?"

Why didn't she go? I wanted to call to her, but water filled my mouth. I grabbed the edges of the torn wood and tried to rip them open. Small pieces of black kindling crumbled in my hands. If I could be certain she had survived, I thought, I could be at peace no matter how loud the storm raged, no matter how cold my body. Again I heard her voice in the darkness, above the face of the water.

"Mama, I've been waiting for you."

I dragged my head up closer to the hole and said, "No, baby. Don't wait for me."

Then I saw her. My baby girl's eyes were in the smooth, round face of a woman whose hair was streaked with gray. She peered down out of the light at me. When she smiled, I saw her dimples.

"No, Mama," she laughed, offering me her wrinkled hand. "I've been waiting for you."

I took hold of her and climbed half out of the cellar and into her arms. Not caring that I dripped mud, she stood on the wet steps and kissed the places where she had clung to me for life, my temple, my brow, my hair, and all I could think was, *She lived. My baby lived.* She cupped my face in the palms of her hands and patted my cheeks as she had when she was two.

Through those palms I felt the whole light-footed dance of her spirit. She had never been haunted by my death, never blamed either of us. In the clarity of her eyes I could see her long life—

her husband's wink as he pressed a fiddle under his red beard, her two freckled sons racing through the kitchen, her granddaughter pulling at her apron, grinning up with four tiny square teeth. Joy, like a warm wind, blew at my hair and skirts, rippling the water at my knees.

"Where have you been?" My daughter shook her head, but she was laughing. "Couldn't you hear me calling you?"

If at my last breath, when I'd swallowed down death, I had opened my eyes in the water, I would've seen that I had saved her by breaking a hole through the cellar door. Instead I'd closed my eyes and imagined hell. For year upon year I had hidden behind my hosts and stopped my ears. How long had she been calling me? Half a century? I was so sorry to have kept her waiting, I began to weep, but she lifted my chin, refusing to allow another moment of regret. She kissed me lightly on the lips and stepped out of the water.

A stone had been lifted from my chest, a fist of frozen tears. Light had never been this weightless.

And there was James.

I climbed the last step, reaching for him. He wore his uniform and put his arms around my wet body, lifting me like a bride over the threshold. It wasn't a dream. The breeze smelled of jasmine, the light dappled through moving leaves, mockingbirds called and answered each other. It was blazing with detail. And I was no shadow. I was just as real as the garden that folded out around me.

James set me on my feet but held me with one arm as if he couldn't bear to let me go. There was my oak tree, whole again and standing tall. And there was a cluster of smiling soldiers, drinking wine from the bottle and watching us with amusement.

At a table in the shade, four familiar gentlefolk sat having tea, turning to me from their conversation, as if I were the guest of honor—my Saint, my Knight, my Playwright, and my Poet.

This green place in which I stood with James turned slowly around us like a music box. All my memories returning, and all his. I could see and feel each of his days and he mine. Childhood songs, books read, hearts broken, arguments forgiven. The sweetness of these imperfections far outshining the regrets. Our lives overlapped as naturally as two blades of grass brushing together.

My pain forgotten, my clothes dry and clean, I pulled James close to me. As he lifted my chin, I felt no sensation of falling as when I had been Light touching one who is Quick. It wasn't the mere heat of a stolen moment in borrowed flesh. We touched now soul to soul, both of us Light. And when we kissed, the garden rocked, floating upstream.

———